Trophy
Wives
Club

By Kristin Billerbeck

THE TROPHY WIVES CLUB

The Trophy Wives Club

a novel of fakes, faith, and a love that lasts forever

Kristin Billerbeck

2.

AVON
INSPIRE
An Imprint of HarperCollins*Publishers*

HarperCollins books may be purchased for educational, business, or sales promotional use. For information please write: Special Markets Department, HarperCollins Publishers, 10 East 53rd Street, New York, NY 10022.

FIRST EDITION

Interior text designed by Diahann Sturge

Library of Congress Cataloging-in-Publication Data

Billerbeck, Kristin.
The trophy wives club / Kristin Billerbeck.
p. cm.
ISBN 978-0-06-137546-0
1. Women—California—Los Angeles—Fiction. 2. Married people—Fiction. 3. Rich people—Fiction. 4. Divorced people—Fiction. 5. Hollywood (Los Angeles, Calif.)—Fiction. 6. Domestic fiction. I. Title.

PS3602.I44T76 2007
813'.6—dc22 2007020310

08 09 10 11 OV/RRD 10 9 8 7 6 5 4 3 2

For Nancy

Prologue

I have a tendency to walk into walls. It's not a trait that I'm proud of, but I'm easily distracted. I get lost in my thoughts, turn, miscalculate doorways, and bam: I'm tasting drywall and plaster.

Once, I was walking alongside a friend on Rodeo Drive, she's relaying the most fascinating story about mineral makeup. Next thing I know, she's in the Marc Jacobs shop and I'm in their window. Complete face plant. They had to bring out Windex and wipe off my smeared lipstick, and I can tell you, they didn't do anything to help me! I threw the back of my hand against my forehead and swooned to the floor, hoping everyone would think I had some sort of fainting spells, bad batch of Botox . . . Something. Anything.

I went to the doctor to see what was physically wrong. Official diagnosis: klutzy and focused on the wrong priority for the moment. In fact, he said, "Haley, you need to get your head out of the clouds. You need to prioritize."

Well, there's an understatement. I need to keep my head out

of plate-glass windows, most definitely. (I actually paid money for that diagnosis.) I should have just gone for a pedicure. I can always focus better after a pedicure, and I don't feel dull-witted afterwards. There's nothing that says, *There, there, everything is going to be fine,* like a foot massage and fresh polish.

In retrospect, it probably shouldn't have surprised me when my marriage did its own face plant. But I was completely blindsided, my head in the wrong cloud once again. Jay had moved on, and I simply hadn't noticed. (Truth be told, there wasn't much difference between the marriage being intact, and its suddenly being over, except I had to collect my things and move out to make space for the new woman he'd selected to ignore.)

By now, I probably shouldn't admit that I'm blond because it has nothing to do with the fact that my head's in the clouds. Really, it doesn't. It's two separate facts: I'm blond. And I walk into walls.

Chapter 1

You'll keep the house?" Anna asks me. Anna is Anna Lynchow of Cutler & Lynchow, the producing partnership that garners tons of cash and few Hollywood accolades. Our husbands are the "lowbrow" entertainers of Middle America. If there is money to be made on bathroom humor, our husbands have found the key to its success.

I shake my head. "No, not keeping the house. Just the Porsche Cayenne." We both look at each other, understanding the comedy of a Porsche minivan. Or SAV, as they call it. *Sport activity vehicle.* Like that isn't a Carrera. "He bought the house through the business, and I only got a portion of it if we made it to ten years. I imagine your husband has more rights to it than I do."

Anna rolls her eyes, and in her New York drawl says, "Knowing Craig, he probably does. I don't think he drinks a latte without figuring out how he can make money on it. But God love him, I can spend it with the best of them, so I'm all for his making money."

Anna straightens out of her smile. "Not at your expense, of course."

"I'm entitled to $10,000 per year of marriage."

Anna stares blankly, unable to do the math.

"Which, being just short of eight years until the separation, if you call it that, puts me at about $70,000." *Less than my husband's annual golf fees,* I want to add. "But it's not the money, you know, Anna? He won't even discuss this. He claims that I know exactly why he left me." Two months of hotel living and still no answers.

"What's to discuss? He left you, Haley. It happens every day. It isn't right. It isn't fair, but men get bored. Jay got bored."

Even for Anna that's a heartless question. "What's to discuss? Our marriage. We made vows!"

"In Hollywood you made vows," she says in the same tone as *duh!* She leans back into her vibrating pedicure chair.

There are times when it's painfully obvious I didn't grow up here. I know I come from a boring, middle-class background, but I never will understand the lack of emotions here when it comes to marriage and their coming to an end. Whatever the statistics might be, I got married for the same reason she did. She was in love. She only gets credit because her husband was poor when they married, and mine wasn't.

I know in certain circles, it seems kind that Jay packed up my things neatly and arranged for me to stay at the Wilshire, but it's only kind to someone who has never seen their life belongings left on a front porch. To one who looks at a mansion and says, *This is it,* all I've earned for the last decade, it's devastating. A Porsche and a porch with three suitcases. And he left the Vuittons in the house.

I found myself paralyzed, unable to understand how my life had changed. I still had the credit cards, I was still officially married and driving the Porsche. What exactly was different?

"It's a good settlement, Haley. I mean, you did pretty well considering there's no kids." She turns her hand over and looks at her nails, "Can you make them more rounded?" Anna asks the manicurist before turning her attention back to me. "That money will help you get started again, buy the right clothes, get you to the right parties. You'll be back in no time."

"Back? I haven't even left yet, and I don't want to come back." I'm tired of playing house. I want to be loved, not worshipped like a forgotten treasure from the past. That's not true either. Right now I'm Garbo. I just want to be left alone.

"If the money runs out, you can sell the Cayenne and get a Prius, you know? This is L.A. Get something practical for crying out loud, now that you don't have to worry about Jay's colleagues thinking he's cheap. Or heaven forbid, a Republican who has money to burn. Not that round!" she snaps at a poor Vietnamese girl, who might not understand her words but recognizes the tone immediately. There's a rash of pressured conversation in Vietnamese.

"Anna, take it easy. You're scaring her."

"I'm not scaring her. She's screwing it up, and I'm asking her to correct it. I'm a paying customer! Look at them, they're plotting how to take revenge out on me this very minute. Listen." She narrows her eyes toward the poor girl. "Wicked manicurists. Someday I'm going to employ my own at the house and not bother with this. I'm probably getting some dangerous fungus as we speak."

Most days, I think Anna is a dangerous fungus. "Oh, I bet they'll jump at the chance to work for you," I say sarcastically. "Your picture is probably plastered as a warning at the beauty schools throughout L.A."

"Just because you let everyone walk all over you—I come in here for a manicure; they do it my way. It's that simple. That's something you never understood, Haley. This town will walk all over you. You're letting Jay walk all over you now."

One thing I've learned in my years as Jay Cutler's wife: There's no sympathy garnered for a trophy wife. We are, by our very nature, hated entities. We get what we deserve, or so they say. But I'm going to let you in on a little secret. I have yet to meet a trophy wife who married for money. Life as a trophy wife evolves. Any good woman in L.A. becomes what her husband desires—plays the part, if you will. Some men are just more shallow than others.

We married for the same reason most women marry; we were hopelessly, devotedly in love with Prince Charming, who swept us off our feet and made us feel cherished. He would provide the security we needed, the unconditional love we craved. What we failed to realize during our courtship was how calculated and well acted the role of Prince Charming was. How utterly naïve we were—putty in their aged and creased hands.

Is it any wonder I walk into walls as a hobby? Somewhere along the line, I stopped being able to be who I was. "Remember that time I wore the sequined gown to the SAG awards, Anna? Man, was I green."

"Do I? You looked like you were wearing one of Cher's old costumes, a cheap copy of a Bob Mackie creation." She laughs. "Oh, we got a good laugh that night. You were the talk of the town, and we all wondered how long it would be before Jay hired you a stylist."

"I think it was the next morning. I liked that dress," I admit. "I liked it a lot, in fact. I liked how it sparkled and how it was cut—I looked good in that dress."

"Haley, it was straight off the rack. It was polyester at best, probably made in some sweat shop on the south side."

"I liked it." I look her straight in the eye. "It made me happy to wear it until I incurred the wrath of all of you. That's something I'll never understand about this life. Everyone does exactly the same thing, or they're blasted. I'm different. I want to be different."

"Well, someone had to teach you. Being different will land you in divorce court."

"After all these years of learning the ropes, I'm still in divorce court, and I've forgotten what I liked because everyone told me what I liked was tacky and inappropriate."

"It was tacky and inappropriate. You have the worst natural taste of any woman in L.A."

"I think *I* am tacky and inappropriate. It's my natural state."

"If I remember correctly, that was a whopper of a fight you picked with Jay that night." Anna has a knack for remembering the negative of life. It's a gift.

"He thought I looked beautiful before everyone made fun of me. If I looked beautiful before we left for the party, why did he let everyone else influence his opinion?"

"You looked like an eighties' prom queen. You even wore frosted lipstick!" She laughs aloud again and normally, I'd giggle right along with her. But not today.

"I was a nineties prom queen, and all we had was grunge. Why wouldn't I long for what I missed? Besides, you were probably just jealous I looked good in 'off-the-rack.'" I want to add something about the amount of "work" she's had done, but my mama didn't raise me to be like that.

"No . . . we weren't. Haley, your husband is one of the foremost producers in Hollywood. You could have dressed in any designer you chose that night."

Foremost in money. Not respect. If he could make money at bodily functions, why couldn't I wear sequins? You see my dilemma. "But I couldn't really. Don't you see? I chose to buy off-the-rack. That was not acceptable. I was supposed to go to some uppity shop and be told what to wear and like a good robot I did just that after that night. Fell into line. Didn't you ever want to shake things up a bit, Anna?"

"You're telling me that you'd rather wear sequins than an elegant, well-cut Armani?"

I ponder this for a moment. I did wear Armani to a premiere once. It was a gorgeous gown of canary yellow and fit like a glove, but all I thought about that night was the dress and how I might spill caviar on it, or slip on the train. "Yes, I think I would rather wear sequins. You can't actually wear them and be sad. Sequins say here I am world, and I am ready to par-tay!"

"That's because you look like a disco ball."

"And what's more fun than dancing under a disco ball? They had one on this cruise Jay took me on one time and—"

Anna sighs. "You're hopeless, and if you want to shop off-the-rack, with your divorce, it looks like you just got your wish."

This was one thing I was actually looking forward to. I finally get to do what I want to do. Some days, life here feels like one big heaping pile of drama over nothing. We're getting manicures, and there's this silent catty struggle over how rounded a nail is. No one but me seems to get that this is a complete waste of time. Yet in everyone's mind, I'm the ignorant one. The poor fool girl who gets taken advantage of and dumped by her suave, successful husband because she can't play the game correctly.

A dying marriage is a sad and heartbreaking venture, and everyone else, including my husband, has just moved on as though nothing has happened. There's no service. No burial. No acknowledgment. It's just over, and my presence is no longer required.

Anna is currently yelling and using her sign language to get what she wants. I'll miss Anna. In her own way, she's a breath of fresh air. She says exactly what she means, unlike most people who just belittle you in their own subtle language. She just outright tells me I'm tacky. You can't beat that.

"Like I have a choice in the matter."

"You always have a choice. I don't care what that pre-nup says, lawyers' fees can add up quickly if you know what I'm saying. You have to wonder if Jay would have enough energy to fight it." She turns the massage chair on again and starts to vibrate while she speaks. "You know, I really thought you two would make it," Anna says, as pensive as she gets. "You did everything he asked. It's good to know rolling over and dying doesn't necessarily keep them around either. I guess it pays to be mouthy sometimes." Anna gazes at me. "Oh sorry, didn't mean anything, just taking mental notes for future reference. That's all."

I take it back. I won't miss friends like Anna. I'm tired of manners not being an issue. Friends who say whatever they please and expect you just to swallow any opinion of your own. No matter how subtle their comments are, they have the same stinging effect. I won't miss friends whose hearts are well encapsulated behind silicone and a suspicious view of everyone.

"Hopefully, Anna, you won't need any of that advice. May your marriage live long and prosper."

"He wouldn't dare leave me. It would cost him a fortune. You see, Haley, that's the beauty of marrying young, before they have anything. I have rights to half of everything. No starlet is worth giving that up for." She laughs and flips her hair. Anna is truly beautiful, mesmerizing to look at, and she doesn't look anywhere near her age, but I've seen Craig. He doesn't watch her with the same intensity he once did, and the truth is, she doesn't know that he'll be there forever. I suppose none of us know.

The fear of loneliness drives us to desperation. How could I have known *married loneliness* was worse? I've gone over the facts a million times, wondering if my fate could have been different, how I could have spared myself this overwhelming sense of failure. But the facts are that I was twenty years old, fresh out of Pasadena

City College, and Jay Cutler, Hollywood Producer, bought me, little Haley Adams, a tennis bracelet.

"It's for me?" I asked him, my mouth agape. I had never seen anything so beautiful in all my life.

Jay clasped it around my wrist without taking his eyes off me. "Who else would it be for, Haley? No one makes me feel like you. I'd buy you the world if I could package it with a bow."

"Jay"—I put my head on his chest, twisting my arm to allow the diamonds to sparkle and color under the sunlight—"you give me so much already. I don't need things."

"You'd love me if I had nothing," he states as fact, and I can hardly contain the warmth radiating in my chest. *He knows*, I thought. *He knows I'd do anything for him. That my love is infinite.* It wasn't long after that I had a pre-nup thrust in my lap.

In my defense, who knows anything at twenty? Add to that, the fact that I looked like Gwyneth Paltrow with breasts, and I was ripe for the taking. Fresh meat thrown into the lion cage that is Los Angeles. I gave my heart and soul for the price of a few longing glances and a tennis bracelet. I was a bargain.

I know what people think. Trust me; they're not usually shy with their opinions in this town. I know they think he threw diamonds at me, and I traded my innocence and youth for his riches. My eyes as wide as saucers, and my objective met, but that wasn't it at all. I wasn't a gold digger. Not for a moment. It wasn't the diamonds. It was Jay looking at me that way, like I was the only woman he'd ever laid eyes upon. He opened doors for me, made sure I had food in my fridge, a place to do laundry. His actions said, "I'll take care of you, Haley. You are so valuable, and you won't be alone. You'll never have to fear again. Trust me." But sign this first.

At twenty, nothing says *you can trust me*, like a diamond tennis bracelet. Nothing identifies Prince Charming quicker than a man ready to commit with jewelry.

Now it's so blatantly obvious to me, with hindsight being what it is, but to be the princess for the first time is magic. To be the one Jay Cutler wants to be with, while all the tittering starlets vie for his attention, it's magic. There's an aura of pixie dust lifting you into the night sky. It's living Cinderella.

But, of course, loving a narcissist is the first step into hell on earth. You'll be wearing Prada, naturally, but it won't prevent the singe of fire that is to come. When they start making Jimmy Choos in asbestos, I'll be the first in line.

There's a photograph of Jay and me smiling at one another at our wedding. I took it before he'd notice its absence. Jay's looking at me as if I'm the missing puzzle piece to his life. I'm gazing at him as though all my troubles have just evaporated into the night sky on a champagne bubble. That photograph is the last time I ever remember Jay looking me in the eyes.

From that moment on, I think the only time he ever noticed me is when I did something wrong, and I did most things wrong. I'm intimately acquainted with plate-glass windows. Does that sound like someone who doesn't need guidance? The first time I really remember him actually yelling though was when he came home to me in yoga pants. The horror!

"What's this?" he said as I scrambled upstairs like a child past bedtime. "What if I'd come home with someone, and you looked like that? Unacceptable, Haley. Unacceptable. I did not marry the type of woman who thinks it's all right to be walking around in sweatpants."

I looked down at my skintight yoga pants. "Sweats? These are yoga pants, and I think I look hot." I twisted my booty toward him.

It was a joke, but apparently my comic timing is not what you might think.

"Don't mince words with me, Haley. You look like you just came from the gym. And what's that, that stuff on your face?"

"I flush when I work out."

"You look like a little old lady in a rest home who got ahold of her blush. What if the head of a studio came by, and you're looking like that? Go change."

The smell of the top coat being applied to my fingernails brings me back to the present.

"I don't want a man to stay with me because he has no financial choice, Anna. That's no security."

Anna's face darkens. "Craig doesn't stay with me because he has to."

"No, of course not. I didn't mean . . . It was me who chose to leave my career for the marriage," I say out loud to Anna, as though typing college papers and working at the Gap was a career, but whatever. It's all I can salvage for dignity at the moment. If my one talent in life is folding the perfect shirt, I'm embracing it. I'm not proud.

"You did a lot, Haley. I know you worked hard. Supporting a successful man is probably the hardest job in the world, don't you think?"

I hate to admit that's what I did. It kills all my thoughts of being a strong, independent woman—the kind you read about in magazines—and makes me sort of weak and pathetic. It's bad enough I'm klutzy, do I really need to identify with weak, too? I'm thinking one major issue is enough for any woman. I let out a deep and haggard sigh. "Absolutely."

I look at Anna. In her eyes, I see the briefest flicker of understanding, but it evaporates before it has a chance to ferment. It's too deep a moment, and Anna immediately retreats to the shallow. "The money was a major coup. Girl, you got something in you that just makes men melt. If Jay Cutler is opening his wallet at all, the rest of us should bow at your feet, but I hope you thanked him. You must have had some spell over him early on." In her mind, this is a compliment. So why do I feel the distinct need to slap her?

I look into Anna's startling blue eyes for a sign. "Do you really believe that? That Jay did me a favor by changing the locks? Would you really feel that way if your husband suddenly told you it was over?"

"I told you. There's no way. It would cost him too much." She cackles like a witch in a children's play. "I still can't believe he really did that." She shakes her head. "He's got rocks!" Anna pops a piece of raw broccoli, from a Ziploc baggie she pulls from a two-thousand-dollar purse, into her mouth. "What do you want me to say? It's time to move on, sweetie."

"My goldfish didn't die. It's an eight-year marriage." I roll my eyes, knowing my pleas to make her understand are pointless. For once in my life, I'm incensed. "I'm definitely moving on." I stand up.

"Not ready!" my pedicurist shouts.

"I'm done. So sorry," I lean down and say. "Great job. Thank you so much, but I must run." I walk toward the machine to dry my toes so I can get out of this stifling air as soon as possible. I look back at the façade that was my life. Honestly, the pedicurist who speaks very little English gets it more than Anna. She at least understands I'm upset. Unfortunately, she thinks it's about the pedicure. She grabs Anna by the wrist and points at me.

Anna drops the broccoli, "Haley, don't be mad. I'm only saying it like it is. You have to move on, that's all. There's nothing left to hang on to. Would you want me to lie to you?" Anna is as cool as a cucumber and looks to the pedicurist to see if she's done the right thing by me. Maybe I do want her to lie.

"Hopefully, he's found someone more pliant than me," I say.

"How is that possible? Sometimes I think if Jay told you he was bringing home an extra wife or three, you'd ask if they were staying for dinner."

"I think I just forgot what my opinions were, you know?" I say to Anna. "It was easier. Besides, I was only a kid. I didn't really have any time to form opinions."

"You have to tell these men how to act, Haley. They don't know." She slips on her rhinestone-encrusted "pedicure" shoes, and the salon women wait with bated breath to see if she's leaving. "Are you up for dating yet? John Galvin's single again. He's a catch. And he does art movies, that would make Jay crazy! Oh what I wouldn't give to see that opening, with you on his arm!"

Ex-wives are not considered "used" here, they're considered "trained" like pedigree puppies. I now know to go on the paper and not don sequins.

"I don't ever want to date again," I say with conviction. "I'm thinking I'd like to have my own business. Maybe I could help other wives organize their homes so they have more time with their children."

Anna laughs. "If you're going to go entrepreneur on me, I think you should consider selling the eggs for your perfect genes. Of course, you have to get that fashion thing worked out. No one wants a baby who is happy in cotton onesies when it could be wearing Prada Baby."

"You don't think I could do it, do you?" I ask, willing her to tell me I can't. Maybe it will provide much needed motivation.

"You've got the advantage of time on your side. And only twenty-eight. Oy, we should all be so lucky." Anna pushes out her chest toward me. "I'm thinking of having them made smaller, what do you think? They look sort of eighties, don't you think?"

Considering they look like two Southwest airplane noses thrusting off the tarmac that is her chest, "I think that's—"

"You know, these big things are just out. Most women are getting them smaller, and teardrop-shaped, you know? Dainty is in. It's all that yoga and Pilates, bodies need to be more streamlined nowadays. *You* wouldn't know. Good ol' Mrs. Natural over there, but with yoga they get in the way, you know what I'm saying? Have you tried to do the Cobra position with these? I'm telling you!"

"You're beautiful, Anna. Quit messing with stuff. You don't want to look like one of those old ladies at the club with their windblown faces." I try to pay for my pedicure, but they keep trying to lure me back to the chair to finish.

"Upkeep just makes it easier down the line."

"Every time you go under that knife—" I start to tell her.

"I make Craig poorer, and much, much happier. The younger I stay, the more virile he looks." She makes the noise of a race car.

"Oversharing. Craig doesn't care a thing about teardrop-shaped implants, Anna." It sounds so odd to hear this out of my mouth. It's an actual opinion. "You know, the biggest mistake the women in this town make, is too many surgeries, too young, and then it's over before they're fifty. They've got no skin left to pull back, and the chemical peel is but a distant dream. It won't work on that taut of skin no matter what those surgeons on Bedford Drive say. Women in our neighborhood need to start planning ahead, and no surgeries whatsoever during menopause until their hormones aren't driving the decision."

"Haley, I didn't know you noticed things like that. You go, girl!"

Anna is red-haired, with a nose that sticks out nearly as far as her chest. If I were her, I'd tell her the obvious surgery she might have, but I'm not. And thank heavens for that! "Like who has done the chemical peel?"

"Mary Ellen Geyser, for one." I sit back down next to Anna but wave off the pedicurist. Maybe I would have had more friends if I'd had more opinions.

Recognition clouds Anna's eyes. "Yeah," she says slowly. "You know, you're right. When she talks, it's like a dummy moving its mouth. I can almost see the cracks."

"April Welling, for another."

Anna's still nodding. "Yeah, her, too! They need to go in and see if a thread lift can fix them up. Those old face-lifts are just scary. You see how much more fun you are when you gossip?"

Gossiping? I thought I was just stating an opinion. All these women are beautiful, don't get me wrong, but they cease looking like actual human beings. Expressions become lost in a sea of Botox, and smiles interrupted by overly indulgent collagen shots. Everyone here thinks they're so enlightened, that the "middle states" wait for word on what will happen next in this town, so they know which trend to follow, but the fact is, Joe Bob, sitting on his front porch after work, knows who he is. Anna, and even my Jay, never will. They'll just schedule another surgery/noninvasive treatment before they have to think about it again should insecurity rear its ugly head.

And I'll be wearing sequins. My cell phone chirps, and I carefully fumble with it, but I see that it's my soon-to-be ex. My heart jumps. "Hello."

"Haley, it's Jay."

"Hi," I say too enthusiastically.

"Listen, call Rosario and tell her to pick up my shirts. I've got to go to Switzerland unexpectedly tonight."

I look at the phone to connect with what I'm really hearing, and my stomach drops. "No," I say quietly.

"What?" he barks.

"I said no." My heart begins to pound, but I look to Anna and feel my confidence rise. "Call her yourself. We're divorcing. You do remember changing the locks," I remind him. I'm thinking my lackey duties are over, and I know full well he has no clue how to reach Rosario. In fact, I'm sort of shocked he even knows her name.

"What does that have to do with anything? Haley, you can't do your husband of ten years a favor? Did I mean nothing to you all those years? You got the car and a settlement and I was more than fair. All I'm asking for is a phone call so I can get on the plane without stress."

Systematic dismissal of all opinions. "And all I'm saying is no. What makes you think I want you to live stress-free? We weren't married for ten years, and don't act ignorant about that, you made sure to end it before the severance package was raised. My guess is you can tell me to the day how long we were married."

"I'm thinking the floors need to be reconditioned, as well. I noticed some of the shine of the travertine is wearing off. Don't you take pride in your home?"

"It's not my home. I said no, Jay. Call her yourself. Are you kidding me? You locked me out of my own house? And now you want me to maintain things?"

"I took care of things for you all those years, I just thought you could handle some of these details for me. And since you're taking the Porsche, you're aware it needs to be waxed monthly."

"I'm selling the Porsche, so it really doesn't matter."

"What do you mean, you're selling the car?" *Ah, he heard that.* "No one will give you a loan for another one." It's another of his scare tactics. Completely devoid of facts. I worked briefly for a loan broker part-time to earn extra money during school. That's where I met my fate and the charming Mr. Jay Cutler. Not only could I get a loan for another car, but I could pretty much show my divorce settlement and buy whatever I wanted with it. Keep in mind, Jay cares little about my selling the Porsche, only that he can't *control* my selling the Porsche.

"I won't need a loan, Jay. I'll buy something cheaper, and I'm moving home. I'll have plenty to live on until I start a job."

"You're moving? To your old apartment? Pasadena has gotten a lot more expensive since you lived there, Haley. You have to be realistic about the settlement."

"No, not Pasadena. Home to San Carlos. I never really cared all that much for Southern California. I miss San Francisco's fog, and people who don't look like Heather Locklear."

"You're moving to suburbia?" He finds a lot of humor in this statement, apparently. "Haley Cutler, you'll never survive. I've taught you to appreciate the finer things in life. What are you going to do when you see women wearing Old Navy?"

His laughter only steels my resolve. "If I can survive nearly eight years with you, I can survive anything. Besides, I happen to like Old Navy."

"Haley, you can't live like that. What are you going to do, marry some hometown hero? You spend more in a week than the guy next door makes in a month."

"*You* spend more in a week than that guy. I just run the errands for you. Besides, if you cared about my spending habits, perhaps you'd like to fund them." I let out a laugh. "And what makes you think I'd ever marry again?"

"You're not as strong as you think, Haley. You're a summer blossom who needs lots of care to avoid wilting in the sun."

"How utterly poetic. Are you through?"

"I've taken good care of you, Haley. L.A. is your home. You're destined for this."

I feel words, but they're stuck in my throat, and it's probably for the best. Jay could pass me off to another man without a look backwards. "Not anymore. I'm going home, and I'm going to be happy." I'm going to have opinions.

"Listen, don't do anything stupid because you're mad at me. Don't forget to call Rosario."

"Bob, tell her what she's won! As our parting gift, Haley Cutler has won the right to be a doormat for one more round."

"You've turned bitter, Haley. I don't know how that happened," he says before he hangs up.

Gee, I can't imagine. Twenty-eight, bitter, completely void of any real emotion and going home to live with Mom. It just doesn't get any better than this.

Anna snaps her cell phone shut as I hang up. "Was that Jay?" she says in her apologetic voice, like she hasn't just heard the whole conversation.

They say the truth shall set you free. Well before I go, I'm giving Anna a lesson in truth. "I wanted a child," I say to a horrified Anna. I slide the cell phone into my purse, lamenting what will never be. "I wanted a child and a family." If I'm going to have an opinion, I'm going to have one that matters. "I thought once Jay saw his child, things would be different. Don't you ever wonder about that?"

"Why should I? Who needs a cute young nanny running about while you're fighting to keep your figure?"

Obviously, Anna doesn't want to go there, but I can't stop. If she has any depth whatsoever, I want to feel it! I want to believe there is more than just a high-maintenance machine within. I scoot to the edge of my chair, as close as I can get without actually sitting in her lap. "I missed what it felt like to be someone's world. If Jay didn't love me, I thought his child would." No response. "You never wanted a baby, Anna? A little precious bundle to hold close to you at night and whisper into their ear? Someone who would look up at you and see your love?" I clasp my eyes shut. Why didn't I understand that I was only an infatuation for Jay? I thought he'd at least want to perpetuate his name for ego's sake.

Anna studies the back of her hand disapprovingly. "A child? Absolutely not. It's common knowledge Jay doesn't have time for a child, what did you think he's going to turn into Brad Pitt overnight?" Anna asks. "Things could have been worse. He could have left you in your forties, when your chances were nil for having a kid. That's all I'm saying. It's still not round enough," she barks at the young manicurist. "Do I need to call the Board of Health on you to get this done right?" The girls obviously understand that much English. There's more frantic speech in Vietnamese, then one of the girls stands up next to Anna.

"You no come back here no more."

"What did you say to me?" Anna shouts, to the annoyance of all the other patrons.

"You heard me, you no come back here. You go to fancy salon in Beverly Hills. You go to spa. You leave us alone. We no like you."

I have to bite back my smile. This is probably Anna's fiftieth nail salon, but she keeps plugging along, oblivious to the trail of destruction behind her, and I have yet to see her with naked nails, so something is working for her.

"Like me?" Anna screeches. "I don't care if you like me. I'm here to get my nails done. Well."

Two things I have learned. Jay doesn't love me, and Anna is incapable of deep conversation. It's time to cut my losses. I hand my credit card over and watch while Anna continues to steam at her manicurist. Val, the spa manager, hands the card back to me. "No good. Another one?"

I slide a second one out of my pocketbook wondering what extravagant gift Jay has purchased this time. A private plane membership? A different country club? I hand Val a second credit card and wait while she is punching numbers into the machine. The machine thinks, but makes no satisfying noise.

"No good," Val says, shaking her head.

"Jay probably canceled your card, Haley," Anna says coldly as she approaches the desk.

I dig through my wallet, messing up my nails, but I only have $8 to my name. "I don't have enough," I say, lifting the wallet to show Val. "I'm meeting with a lawyer about my settlement today. Can I come back after my meeting and pay you?"

"You pay right now." She bangs the desk for emphasis. "No free ride!"

"I can't pay right now." I look to Anna, who hands her credit card over to Val.

"This is the last time I'm coming here," Anna says, like it's taken as some sort of threat. "You all have an attitude, and you need to know who the customer is!" The machine spits out Anna's receipt, and she signs quickly, heading toward the door.

"Anna, wait. I don't have any money!"

She flips her red hair about as she faces me. "You have to stand on your own at some point." She zips up her purse. "I wish you the best, Haley, I really do. You'll be fine." With that comment, Anna rushes out of the salon and leaves me standing there with several messed-up fingernails and an inability to pay for them.

"I can't pay," I say again, thrusting my $8 toward her. "Please take it for now. I'll bring back the rest. I promise. Here, this is a Hogan bag," I put my purse on the desk. "A real one. I'll leave this here until I get your money."

Val puts her hand up. "No problem, you keep money. Keep purse."

"I will be back when I get some cash. I promise." I lay the cash on the table.

"No worries." Val pushes the money back toward me and touches my wallet. "You paid in full." She looks at me and grins.

"No, I'll be back, really."

Val smiles. "I charge your friend's card. You paid in full. I want to wait to see if she offer. When she no offer, I offer for her."

This makes me laugh out loud.

"Haley"—she grins—"you left a nice tip, too. Thank you." And with a wink, she opens the door wide for me to exit into my new life.

Chapter 2

My heels click resolutely along the tile. I sound most unfeminine, but standing up to Jay this morning gave me a new outlook on life. Besides, determined is the way to go. I'm too vain to be too bitter and too poor for Botox. I've got to find my inner-sequined Haley again, the inner disco ball, the one who dances like nobody's watching. I take a twirl in the hall just for effect, and more importantly, I stay upright. "I will survive!" I wail like a deeply moved Gloria Gaynor. A man comes out of an office and clears his throat. "Did you see that?" I ask him. "I didn't fall! I'm telling you, it's a new day!"

He nods, clearly afraid of me, and ducks back into his doorway.

The lawyer's office is what you'd expect, with its Disney architecture and shared space alongside real estate moguls and plastic surgeons. Jay is probably in first class right now, ordering another glass of wine, laughing about getting my credit cards canceled. He probably claimed they were stolen. I can't help but hope his own were canceled at the same time. Jay's not great at details. Meanwhile, I jump through hoops to get what little money is mine. Canceling my credit cards before I have a penny to my name is below the belt.

If someone in this town did that to their dog, it would be all over the tabloids, demonizing him or her as an animal terrorist. When Britney Spears got rid of her dogs after she had her children, she was voted "Worst Pet Owner." You'd think she skinned the animals alive rather than adopted them out. But a wife you're done with? Treat her as you please. You're entitled to be happy. Just hand her off to the lawyers and let them do the dirty work.

I open the door to the office. The secretary is dressed in pressed linen and a shantung silk shirt, which tells me she's overpaid as a secretary and most likely looking at clients such as my husband for her own turn as a trophy wife. She's the sort that plans, not the type who's blindsided. I envy her. I bet she never walked into a wall in her life.

"Did you have an appointment?" she asks in a soft, elegant voice.

"Yes, at twelve." *And I'm a little ticky at the moment, so don't make me wait,* I want to add.

She peruses her calendar. "Haley Cutler?"

"Yes."

"If you could just fill these forms out, so that we might update our files. I understand you won't be living in the Brentwood home, is that correct?"

"No, I won't be living there. My husband is, you see, and he apparently doesn't want to be my husband anymore, which makes it terribly awkward to go home again. He changed the locks, and climbing into the windows is hard, so no, I'm won't be living there."

She raises her brow but doesn't say what she's thinking.

What? she asked. I take the offered forms and fill them out with my mother's address in San Carlos and hand them back.

"Oh," she says, as though disappointed. "This isn't a local address." She hands the papers back, as if I'm going to move for her.

"That's because I won't be local." I try to say this with a sweet smile, one that I've practiced over the years.

"Does Hamilton know this?"

"Well, I don't know. I haven't seen Mr. Lowe in years, and I really didn't think I needed to run my living arrangements by him."

"I can't imagine why your husband tossed you out," Miss Linen mumbles under her breath, and my only wish for her is that she may find a husband just like him.

Was that rude? See, I can't even tell anymore.

I'm led into Hamilton's office and I walk by a Bible quote on the wall. "I can do all things through Christ who strengthens me." How appropriate that a man helping Jay steal my life has a Bible quote on a plaque. Maybe it helps him sleep at night.

Hamilton is sitting behind his massive lawyer desk in standard mahogany, and he stands up to greet me. He's tall. I'd forgotten that. Not too many tall men in Hollywood, so it catches me off guard, as do his eyes, which are greenish hazel and intelligent. A smart man stands out here in Hollywood. He's unmoved by my appearance. Disdain might best describe his view of me. He's not gay. I have great gaydar, and he's not dressed well enough, so he has to think he's too good for me. Which makes me wish I wore my sequins.

"You can wipe that smirk off your face," I tell him. "I'm not afraid of you, either. Let's just get this over with. Tell me where to sign, and I'll be on my way."

"Well, now that the niceties are over, why don't you sit down, Haley." He holds out a hand to the chair. He pulls out a legal-size file and starts reading over it, like he doesn't know the details by heart. "This is a copy of your prenuptial agreement, which you'll remember signing eight years ago."

"Hamilton, we both know what's in there. Just tell me how to get my money, so I can get started on the life that doesn't include Jay Cutler or Hamilton Lowe. Then, we'll all be happy. You can go back to proselytizing and ripping women off, and I can find myself another job at the Gap."

"It's not quite that easy, Haley."

"Of course, it's not. You're a lawyer. You live to make people miserable and find all new forms of torture."

Despite himself, he smiles. "I need to make sure you understand everything. That's part of my job."

"If I understood everything, I would never have signed that agreement. You seemed to be okay with my ignorance then. I don't seem to remember your describing in detail how my husband could legally lock me out of my house and cancel my credit cards."

"The way you looked at Jay all those years ago, I think you would have signed anything, and if you'll remember, I did try to go into deeper detail—"

"Yeah, yeah. You're safe. I don't have rightful cause to sue you. Your T's are crossed. Can we get on with it?

Our eyes meet and for the briefest blink of an eye, I feel like Hamilton understands. *It hurts. It really hurts.* I haven't allowed myself to feel the pain, but this is clearly not the place, so I go right back into resolute mode. I spent eight years suppressing my emotions, what's another few months?

"I don't want to be too quick in this meeting and miss something, Haley. I want to make sure everyone's satisfied that the contract was met."

"Contracts satisfied? I could have made more working at McDonald's over the years, so don't sit there smugly, acting like I'm waiting for what's Jay's. You're not doing me any favors. Either one of you." I cross my arms, and I let my face muscles go lax. *I can't afford Botox, remember?* No sense letting Jay's henchman tense my brow. "Jay never worried about the house staff, he never worried about the parties to promote his films, his reputation. All of the details fell to me, and you should know, it was no picnic. It's not easy to maintain the proper tone of elegance at a party for a movie where flatulence is the main punch line."

Despite his austere front, Hamilton chuckles under his breath. I don't get how no matther how old men get, they are always twelve again when it comes to a good bodily function joke. "Haley, I'm very familiar with the desire to get what's coming to you, but the facts state that you came into this marriage with nothing and—"

My pulse doubles, and I scoot to the edge of my chair. "Is that what you think, Hamilton? That I came into this marriage with nothing, and that's what I should leave with?" I move forward into my seat until I'm practically on his desk, willing him to look right at me. "I came into this marriage with hope and a deep love for the man I thought Jay was. I came into this marriage with a future before me, a desire for a family. I wanted to take care of my husband and make him the happiest man on the planet."

He pretends to write something down while I say my piece. I am sure he has this down to a science.

"I came into this marriage an innocent and I leave a bitter twenty-eight-year-old, who can't trust a Labrador retriever, so don't act like you know me, Hamilton Lowe. You don't know me at all."

He clears his throat, stacks the paperwork, his expression placid. "Very well then. Let's get started. According to Addendum C, section twelve—"

"No, you're not getting off that easily, Hamilton. I have a right to speak. You may think that I'm getting what I deserved, but I fail to see how falling in love allows me to deserve this. I've been treated like the weekly garbage, shoved out on the doorstep without keys, without my cat, and minus my self-esteem. I have nowhere to live, and you're actually sitting there defending what my husband has done. You're not an innocent in this, so quit with the act, as if this is all business. This is personal, whether you think so or not."

Hamilton's eyes flash, and I'm content I got at least some sort of reaction from him, but his voice goes on as drone as before. "You're entitled to $70,000, but the agreement has it doled out in ten-thousand-dollar increments each month for seven months. You'll come to the office, sign off that month, and the check will be cut for you."

I stand up. "I am not going to become your dog and pony show for my money. And incidentally, don't think I don't know how close I got to $80,000 when this marriage was ended. I'm moving to the San Francisco area, I can't be schlepping down here to your office every month to stand on my hind legs and beg. Remind me again the point of that clause? Besides Jay's desire to make interest off my money, of course."

"It's part of the agreement." He holds up an underlined section of the pre-nup.

Curse the naïve girl I was when I signed that piece of paper. "A pre-nup that you created. What's the point of it?"

"Money given in smaller increments allows the principal, that would be Jay, to ensure that all clauses of the prenuptial agreement are met during the course of the payouts."

Lawyer speak for *how should I know*?

"What are you giving me today? I have no money, and I just found out Jay canceled all my credit cards, which means I have no idea how I'll pay for the Wilshire for the next two nights. Even if I got a job today, they won't pay me for two weeks, Hamilton. A girl needs some warning, you know? Contrary to most of the women in this town, I do eat."

"If you sign the monthly settlement today, stating you will not drag Jay Cutler's name into the tabloids, you will be sent $10,000."

"Ah, there it is." I tilt my head back, and a bitter laugh escapes. "Jay cannot believe this town cares enough about him for the tabloids. Hamilton, he's not Spielberg, for crying out loud!"

"Jay just wants to know his reputation will remain intact, Mrs. Cutler."

"Reputation? Jay produces flatulence movies. What reputation does he have exactly? He makes money for the studios. That's it. That's where his reputation ends. "

"Mrs. Cutler—"

"Don't call me Mrs. Cutler. If Jay was concerned about dirty laundry, he might have considered his own actions first." I lean over the desk. "I need money to get to northern California, and I'm not leaving until I get it."

"Haley, I can't give you any money today. Maybe you can ask a relative to wire you the money."

I sit down and cross my arms. "No problem. No one is expecting me, I can wait. I take Sweet & Low in my coffee, which your linen-wearing secretary never offered me."

He eyes me, trying to see if I can follow through. After a pause, he says, "Amber!" Miss Shantung comes to the doorway. "Get Mrs. Cutler a check, payable today for $1,000 from accounts payable."

She huffs off.

I smile. "Are you certain she knows how many zeroes that is? And you forgot the coffee."

"Haley."

"Tell me where to sign."

He turns a paper around, and I sign it as large as I can, as though I'm Marilyn Monroe herself.

"I advise you to read it first," he says, shoving it back toward me.

"I believe it was your advice that got me into this mess eight years ago, Mr. Lowe." I slide it over to him. "Without my signature, there's no money?"

"Right."

I shrug, "So what's to read. More lawyer words for, take a long walk off a short pier?"

"Jay is trying to make this as painless as possible."

"Oh I could tell," I turn around. "And quick, too, so that must mean there is someone else already. Is that why he's headed to Switzerland? By the way, it was really painless to have my house off-limits to me and my credit cards canceled like I ceased to exist. It makes me all warm and tingly inside, it's so painless."

"You agreed to the deal." He slides the pen back into his chest pocket. "When I advised you—"

"You're no better than him, you know? You may think yourself above him because *you* wouldn't marry a woman based on looks and therefore, you're above this type of common household strife. I imagine that's how you can hang a Bible quote on the wall and avoid the fact that you destroy lives for a living."

He just stands there. His firm jaw clenched at my accusations.

"You hired your secretary that way, didn't you? A trophy secretary. You know what that tells me? You're not even man enough to commit in the first place. Jay has that much on you."

"You're angry. That's understandable."

"Don't placate me, Hamilton. I've known you long enough to know I have never seen you at any function with a woman, and you don't dress well enough to be gay. We were talking about you."

"You were talking about me. I was just waiting for your check to arrive so that you might take your leave."

"So are you married now?"

"No."

"Engaged?"

"Not at present, no."

"Dating anyone?"

"I don't see how any of this matters to your situation."

"Yes you do," I challenge him. "You think you have no guilt and aren't affected by what you do for a living. That I'm only a money-hungry blonde out to grab as much cash as I can get. I'm merely pointing out how much you *are* affected."

Amber comes back, and Hamilton signs a check, handing it to me.

I clasp the check in my hand, "Don't judge me, Hamilton Lowe. Clean your own house first."

Amber walks out of the room, and Hamilton keeps a firm grip on the check. "I might ask the same from you. Don't judge me."

I pull the check and put it in my bag. I look Hamilton straight in the eye, and he focuses on his laptop rather than meet my gaze. "Just what I thought."

Hamilton continues to stare at his computer. "I want a woman to look at me, like you looked at Jay that day so many years ago." His words stop me cold. I think it surprises him as well. He looks up finally. "But I know the ending," he says absently, as though he's only just voiced this emotion for himself for the first time.

"My mom still looks at my dad like that, Hamilton. I never truly understood that marriage could end when I was so in love, that's why I signed those papers, and it's why I'd sign them all over again. I may be naïve, but I'd rather be that than to have just shut down. Believe it or not, it would have been worse had I known what I was getting myself into because I still don't think I would have walked away. Sometimes, ignorance is bliss."

He stares at me, but his expression gives nothing away. "Wait a minute, Haley. Before you go." He opens a drawer and takes out a sheet of paper. "Someone at my church asked me to hand these out. I don't know if it would help you to talk about it, but—" He slides the sheet toward me.

I scan it quickly, my eyes widening in disbelief. "The Trophy Wives Club?"

"Forget the name, they mean it a different way. They're not trying to be offensive. It's a Bible study group in my church. A few women who have walked in your shoes, and I thought maybe you could use their support. They gave me that flyer in case they might be able to help someone else."

"How many people have you given this to?"

"You're the first one."

"I'm not a trophy wife." I feel the fight go out of me, and my shoulders sag. "Or at least, I wasn't a trophy wife." But yeah, I was. He was twenty years older, paid me to step in line, and trained me like a chorus girl. That's pretty much a trophy wife by most people's standards.

He shrugs. "I didn't mean to imply anything, just thought you might need the support. I know sometimes it can be hard after your friends . . ." He pauses. "After they move on."

"My friends aren't moving on just because I get divorced." Well, Anna seemed to move on today, but I don't think I ever really liked her anyway. Now that I'm allowing myself to have opinions again, there really wasn't much to like. Shallow and rude aren't exactly qualities one looks for in a friend.

"I'm sorry about this, Haley. If it means anything to you, I'm sorry."

I refuse to cry in front of Hamilton Lowe. I crumple the paper and stuff it in my purse. "Send the big check to my mother's. We'll worry about next month, next month." I stride toward the open door, past Miss Linen and to the elevator. It dawns on me that this is really happening. I have nowhere to go. No errand to run, no fund-raising fashion show to model for. My life is a blank slate, and I should be happy about that.

"Haley!"

I swing around to see Hamilton heading toward the elevator with a piece of paper in hand. A soft bing beckons me, and I step onto the elevator. Hamilton presses his hand against the elevator door. "There's one more document I need you to sign. Can you come back in my office?"

"Just give it to me, I'll sign it here."

"I think it's best if you come back, it's a private matter."

I step out of the elevator. "Just give it to me. It's not like I have any dignity left."

I swipe the piece of paper and my hand starts to tremble. "Further Claims. No further claims may be made against this estate. By signing here, Haley Adams Cutler agrees she holds no interest in or . . ."

"I'm not signing this."

"Are you saying there may be further claims?" Hamilton probes.

"I'm saying I won't sign this." I look up at him and shake my head. "I can't make things perfect for Jay. Let him have a little insecurity. They say it's good for building character." I step onto the elevator. As the doors shut, I feel my muscles collapse, and I lean heavily on the railings. Jay's rejection of me is now complete. Mine is just beginning, starting with dropping the car off and hoping for a decent payout.

Chapter 3

Arriving in San Francisco two days later doesn't exactly bring the hometown warmth I'd hoped. I look back at the plane, wondering what lies ahead. My mother couldn't pick me up at the airport, and, naturally, this brings up memories of standing alone in front of the school with the sinking feeling she'd forgotten me again. There's something terribly tragic about a mother who forgets her child. Well, perhaps tragic is too strong a word, but if you're below your mother's radar, it hardly helps issues. All I'm saying.

Bless my mother's heart, she is as sweet as pie, gentle as a kitten, but she's the sort, that if her head wasn't attached . . . let's just say she'd be only slightly handicapped that day.

I haven't been back home in two years, and I'm sort of thinking it's her *job* to pick me up at the airport, but one can't be disappointed if they have no expectations. She probably would have forgotten me anyway, so it's just as well. I sold the Porsche to a local dealer. He's going to find me a used Mini Cooper. I've decided

I'm not the Prius type. I saw one before I left that said, "Your SUV sucks, My hybrid sips." I thought, yeah, that's not me. I don't want to be identified with the obnoxious, save-the-earth types. Sad, but true. I'll stay off private jets and recycle instead.

I'm homeless. Carless. And I'm relationshipless. I'm alone. What an odd feeling. I want to ask Jay what he thinks, but that's the point, isn't it? I'm single now. I don't get—strike that—*have* to ask anyone.

Angry whispers smack my ears. *There's someone else*, I hear them taunt. Shame covers me like molasses when I think about my husband and another woman. Wasn't it bad enough he didn't love me? Why'd he have to wait until there was someone else?

And then after I relive the shame, it's as if I'm flying, free from that burden. The puddle of molasses left for someone else to clean up. *Someone else has to try to please him*, the happy voices say. Still, I'm left to wonder about my future. I thought I'd have children by now. Can I have children? Maybe I'm infertile. After all, I'm twenty-eight and in eight years of marriage. Nothing. Those were my prime years, and if nothing happened, well . . .

The fact is, I'd be attached to Jay forever if there were a child involved. There was no manner for this to end well. Jay didn't want what I wanted. He only wanted the illusion of marriage. My body soars a little higher, farther from the sticky mess behind me. Not really, but I feel better for the moment, and it takes my mind off the fact that no one picked me up at the airport.

After a harrowing taxi ride from SFO, I let myself into my childhood home. There should be some childhood memories stirring, but, really, I just feel bad my parents never water their lawn. Their poor neighbors. The house is mostly surrounded by juniper bushes, which are the nastiest smelling and most painful of foliage to get thrown into as a child. (I had a brother, did I mention that?)

As I push the door in with my suitcase, I hear the fridge close.

"What are you doing here?" My brother Mike, a live version of Shaggy, Scooby Doo's friend, comes out of the kitchen with a hot dog in his hand. No bun, no condiments, just the hot dog. He bites off the end and pushes it toward me. "Want some?"

"No." I grimace. "And eww."

He shrugs. "Too good for hot dogs now? Rich people don't eat hot dogs?"

"No, I just don't like to share meat, all right? Can't you get a napkin? A plate maybe?"

"No, Martha Stewart, I can't. Mom is at Grandma's. She know you're coming?"

"It's been two years since I've been here!"

"Yeah, so? You think we should all bow or throw out the red carpet or something."

"Mom knows," I say, walking toward my room and halt in the doorway. The room now boasts a couch and a giant-screen TV. It's way too big for the area, like being in the front row at a movie theater. "Where's my bed?"

"Isn't it at your house?" Mike asks.

"Not anymore. Didn't Mom tell you Jay left me? Or I guess I should say he left me at the doorstep because *he* didn't go anywhere."

"Harsh."

"Yeah."

"He was a wuss, anyhow. He probably fell in love, and now that you're gone, he'll see it was just his reflection in the mirror." Mike laughs and takes another bite of his hot dog. "What kind of guy carries a designer briefcase?" Mike shakes his head. "On his honeymoon!"

"It's an L.A. thing."

"You know who you should date?" he says, wagging the hot dog for emphasis.

"I'm not dating anyone, Mike. I'm going to get a job. I'm embarking on a new career."

"At the Gap?"

I sigh. "Maybe. What are you doing here anyway?"

"I live here."

I raise my brows. "At Mom's house? Since when?"

"Since I got laid off from Best Buy. You know, I help out and stuff."

"Doing what?"

"Taking the garbage out. I take Mom's car to get the oil changed, that kind of thing. Mom's not as young as she used to be."

I'll let that slide. The idea of my mother infirm is a bit ridiculous, since she'll have energy to control everyone's life from her deathbed. Perhaps, she's slightly codependent on her aging son needing her, but that's another issue altogether. "Are you working?" I ask him.

"What are you, the unemployment office? I just told you, I run errands for Mom."

"I'm just asking." I shrug.

"Well, don't. You don't come around here enough to ask questions, and if you're staying, it's not like you're any better than me, all right?"

He's got a point. "I was just asking."

"Get off your high horse, Haley, you're not perfect anymore. Mom's got your bed in her sewing room." He thrusts his chin toward the hallway. "She'll be home soon. Grandma's rest home was having a craft fair, so she had to stake out the competition. Other grannies with dueling needles, you know?"

I hesitate outside Mike's room, which hasn't changed a bit. He's got posters of bikini-clad Jessica Alba and old *Sports Illustrated* swimsuit calendars lining the walls, even a Denise Richards on his ceiling. I roll my eyes. Mike is the reason Jay Cutler will always have a job. If men with seventeen-year-old mentalities didn't exist, Hollywood would be out of business, and judging by my brother, they're not going anywhere. They're playing video games at their mamas' houses as we speak.

This is my older brother by the way. He's thirty, in fact. He just plays a seventeen-year-old in real life. He's home flailing a hot dog around and giving me life advice.

I toss my bag on the twin bed in my mother's sewing room. She has it all daintily set up in a peach polyester quilted bedspread with coordinating colored lace pillows. "It looks like Princess Belle threw up in here." *But I'm not exactly in a position to be selective, am I?*

I hear the garage door rumble up and ready myself to meet my mother. I sit on my bed and practice smiling. Too fake. I try it without teeth. "Hi, Mom!" I say aloud. *Too enthusiastic.* I'll wing it.

Mom has teddy bears all around the room, staring ominously straight ahead. It's like being in one of those rooms with the paintings, whose eyes follow you. People buy this stuff. Teddy bears made out of whatever sale fabric she could find at Wal Mart, quilts from old clothes at the Goodwill, stuffed monkeys from old gym socks. She was an environmentalist before it was cool. And say what you will about Hollywood and its recycled glass countertops, you still have to get rid of an old countertop. My mom's got them on landfill material because she has her original orange laminate countertop to prove it.

I open the dresser to unpack, but it's filled with quilts she's readying for the show, so I sit back down on the bed and wait.

"She here, already?" I hear my mom ask Mike.

"Your sewing room, already judging me," Mike shouts over a

video game where he's blowing up various tanks or learning to steal cars and shoot cops.

"Darn it, I thought I would be here! Now Michael, Haley's just been traumatized. Be kind to your sister. We're her source of strength right now."

God help me.

I stand up and brush my jeans, trying to slow my breathing. "Hi, Mom," I say as she enters the doorway. *Good. That was good*. But it's no use; at the sight of her I start crying. She bustles toward me and envelops me in a tight hug and I fall into it like a little girl socked on the playground.

"There. There. It's all right, Haley. It will be all right."

I nod against her shoulder.

She steps back and clasps my arms. "Have you two seen a counselor to work through this?"

"Mom, I'm pretty sure he's with someone else. I don't know how you counsel through that. I think it's pretty much a given that it's over." Call me naïve, but when a man is willing to hire lawyers to be away from you, I'm thinking that's more than a subtle hint.

"You never know, Selma Hampton and her husband were both about to marry other people, then"—she claps her hand—"God took over and repaired their hearts. Never underestimate what God can do."

"I don't underestimate God, Mom, but I think you're vastly overestimating Jay."

"Maybe he didn't sow enough wild oats before you got married, and he's going to have his midlife crisis. Did you –" She pauses. "Did you push him into marriage?

"He was almost forty when we got married, rich and living in Hollywood. If he sowed anything else . . . well never mind. He was

Prince Charles for the greater L.A. basin and"—I roll my eyes—"I thought he was a catch."

"Well, so did Princess Diana, dear. You're in good company. I have to admit, I'm glad you're telling me this, it makes me feel better about what I did today." She hops onto the bed and puts her hands in her lap. "I just had a feeling, and I acted on it."

Uh-oh. "What did you do today, Mom?"

"Of all things, I ran into Gavin at the gas station, and I told him you were back."

"Would that be the gas station by his shop? And by any chance did you happen to go into the shop?"

She looks down at her Lady Macbeth hands, then looks away from me. "And I relayed the unfortunate circumstances of your return."

"Of course you did. Nothing like letting my high school boyfriend know I'm still a loser."

"Now, Haley, don't say it like that. I thought he might cheer you up. He always was such a nice boy." Unspoken: You should have married him like I told you to.

"Cheer me up? What does that mean?" I ask fearfully.

"I invited him to join us for dinner. He's not married yet, you know. I know it's not appropriate for you to date yet, but I thought getting reacquainted wouldn't hurt."

"Peachy." I sigh.

"You're mad at me."

"No, Mom, it was sweet of you to think of me, thank you." I pat her hands. "But your hopes for me and happily-ever-after are not meant to be. The divorce isn't final. Whatever Jay has done to me, I respect those vows."

"Nonsense. You've been living in that fairy-tale land too long. I want to be a grandmother, and in case you haven't noticed, your brother Mike isn't exactly speeding toward the altar unless it's a computerized car that will take him. You're my best chance, Haley."

"Then I would go out and buy a lottery ticket, Mom, because you'll have better luck with that. The odds have got to be better."

She pats my leg, "I have to go get the roast in. Gavin always liked my roasts. The Golden Globes are on television tonight. I thought we might watch them together. Maybe you can tell us if you know anyone famous on TV."

I nod. "Sure, Mom. Can you call Gavin and cancel though? I don't feel right about that even if Jay is done with me."

"It's just dinner with the family, Haley. It will cheer you up and be like old times. When you used to smile. Why don't you change your clothes, darling?"

I glance down at my jeans and blazer. "What's wrong with me?"

"Well, you haven't seen Gavin in a long time." She shrugs and flashes her eyes. "Don't you make some sort of effort?"

Subtle as a linebacker. "No, Mom. I really don't—" I shake my head, not that it matters, she's already taken care of everything. I notice where my uncanny ability at not having an opinion started. Then I remember Jay's many tactics. I decide to take a page from his playbook. "Do you really think that's appropriate, Mom? For a married woman? Would the ladies at church approve?"

She has a momentary expression of terror. "I didn't think of it that way." My mom, God bless her, believes the key to happiness is marriage, and I'm so thrilled that for her, it has been. For me, it's been the doorway to a nightmare, and I don't ever want to see that threshold again. I tried. What I hate most is that I sound just like Hamilton Lowe. Maybe I should study law and become his female equivalent.

"We don't want to get the tongues wagging, do we? I've only been out of my house for two months. Let's finish it appropriately."

"All right, dear. I'll back off if it makes you uncomfortable, but you and Gavin have always been friends, since you were toddlers, in fact, so there's no reason he can't come and cheer you up and have dinner." She crosses her arms and her claws come out. "Besides, who says he's panting to be around you?"

"No one, Mom. Just so you know, I'm not one of those women who pines after the one who got away. Instead, I sort of wish more than one had got away."

"Don't talk like that. You sound like a bitter, old spinster."

"I am a bitter, old spinster. Okay, maybe I'm not that old. I just got married first, so I get off on a technicality, but I'm a spinster just the same."

"Did I say anything about marriage with Gavin? Get changed. I'm still going to have him over, and it just makes a man feel nice when you take time to look beautiful for him. It makes him feel virile."

"Ew, Mom. It's not my job to make a man feel virile, all right? I'm embarking on a divorce, that doesn't exactly make me desirable if you know what I'm saying."

"Making a man feel virile is important. Your father and I—"

"No!" I shout, as I stick my fingers in my ear and start singing until she leaves the room. I shudder as I close the door. "Ick. Will my mother ever get a filter?"

"I heard that!" she yells through the door. I let my forehead pound on the door.

I brush a little powder over my face and climb into sweats. Not yoga pants, but sloppy, holey UCLA sweats. Firstly, because I can and secondly, because I am not letting Gavin think I took any effort.

You never do forget your first love. Oh, you may try, but those first sloppy kisses, the rules your father sets for you, the outfits you wore, your hairstyle at the prom, they never fully evaporate because the emotions are so new, so full of hope. Somewhere inside of us all, there's that innocence that we wish we'd appreciated more when we had hold of its power. *Okay, a little lip gloss won't hurt.*

As I wander out to the kitchen, the doorbell rings, and my mother gets all aflutter. "That's him!" she bellows. "Now, Haley, don't talk about the divorce. He already knows it's final next month."

"Did you tell him my cup size, too?"

"Haley, don't talk that way. Trashy women talk that way. I didn't raise you like that." She checks the oven. "How incredibly vulgar you can be."

"I know. Hollywood taught me. You raised me to be perfectly normal. What a cruel twist of fate I am."

"I did raise you to be perfectly normal."

"You're off the hook, Mom." I kiss her on the cheek. "I'm weird all by myself. Bad DNA."

"Get the door, smart aleck."

I open the door and instead of an aged high-school boyfriend, there's a young Fed Ex driver with a package. Who, I must say, is an improvement if he weren't jailbait. "Haley Cutler?"

"That's me."

"Sign here."

I take the package, slam the door, and rip open the package. Inside, instead of a lipstick or a new pair of shoes is a copy of the divorce papers from the courts, with the luminous date: March 14, when it will be final. I even have to hate deliverymen now. They used to bring me nice things.

"Is it Gavin?" My mom comes out of the kitchen, wiping her hands on her apron. "Haley, what's the matter, you're white as a sheet."

"It's my divorce papers." I look up.

"You knew it was coming. What difference does it make?"

"I guess, as pathetic as it might be, there was a part of me that thought Jay would change his mind, Mom. That he'd change his mind, and this was all a rotten misunderstanding. I thought he'd realize—"

She presses her hand on my back and rubs my shoulders. "You signed the papers, Haley. Jay has never been one to mess around legally. Not if it cost him something."

"I know, but I thought my signing would scare him, that he'd chicken out and worry he couldn't run his life without me." Truthfully, I thought he'd fall on his knees and beg for forgiveness. I thought the Jay I fell in love with would return to me, and maybe we'd renew our vows in a romantic ceremony with rose petals up the aisle, perhaps our son as a ring bearer . . . gosh, I'm pathetic.

The doorbell rings again. I open the door to my prom date, ten years later, and it's not the "after" one hopes for. He's bald, has a beer belly and didn't bother to iron his button-up shirt. More ammunition for why Jay mystified me when I met him. But he has a twinkle in his gaze and he's still the same, warm boy from high school, with an offset grin and shining, blue eyes. He reminds me of the hope I once had for my future.

"Hi, Gavin." I try to muster a little enthusiasm, but it sounds just like I feel.

He holds out a bouquet of sunflowers. "I thought these might cheer you up. You're still as beautiful as ever. More so." The way Gavin says these things, it's not a pickup at all, and I can tell he feels exactly about this meeting as I do. We're friends, and that's all we're ever going to be, despite my mother's desperate and oh-so-transparent attempts.

I take the offered flowers and let him kiss my cheek. "Thanks,

Gavin, you always know how to cheer me up." I shut the door behind him. "Well, you always did anyway. Let me get these in some water." But before I can escape to the kitchen, my mother is there to take them from me.

"Go talk to him." She pushes me toward the foyer. "Good to see you, Gavin," Mom trills. "You look like you're eating well."

I'm sure that's a compliment in some third world country, but I'm humiliated to my core. Why didn't she just call him Porky?

Gavin pats his stomach. "I never miss a meal, Mrs. Adams." He kisses my mother's cheek. "Especially one of yours when it's offered. I saw the quilts for Africa. As usual, you had the most beautiful."

Now, you might think that Gavin is a bit of a brown-noser, but the truth is, he's one hundred percent authentic. He means what he says, and he rarely says anything unkind. He makes me feel unworthy standing next to him. I can't even keep my thoughts that nice. Is it any wonder our relationship didn't work out?

I find my bearings. "You look great, Gavin. Very happy."

He nods. "I am happy, Haley. The store's doing well. I added siding to the retail line. We have to compete with box hardware stores, but they can't compete on customer service. I get them there every time. People expect quality when they're buying new windows. They deserve to be treated well, it's a big expenditure."

"You were a born retailer, Gavin. Your dad would have been proud."

He stares right into my eyes and drops the small talk. "I would do anything to take this away from you, Haley. You didn't deserve this. You always were the prettiest girl in town, inside and out, and nothing has changed. I'm glad to see he didn't get that part of you."

"You're the first person to think I didn't deserve this, so thank you." I feel a lump rise in my throat as I realize Gavin has more empathy in his little finger than Jay ever possessed. *How did I get it so very wrong?*

"No, I'm not. Just the first person to say so, maybe." He pats his stomach again. "So you know how I'm staying so healthy?"

He makes me laugh. "No, how are you staying so healthy?"

"I'm a bachelor in your mother's church. The sewing group is determined to see me married off, and it involves a lot of pot roast. They bring their single daughters and beef. Sometimes pork."

We laugh together. "So the big question is, are you avoiding marriage for the pot roast?"

"The shoe just hasn't fit anyone yet," he jokes.

"I would have thought you would have married Susie Anderson in college. She was such a sweetheart."

"You didn't think so back then."

"Well, she wasn't me, and back then, I didn't think she was good enough for you."

"So what changed?"

"Marriage isn't what I thought at all. If you can find someone who loves you back, that's a gift you should grab and never relinquish."

"Apparently, Susie thought so too because she found someone who did."

"Oh." I start to walk toward the living room. "Come on and sit down." My brother is playing a loud video game when we enter. "Mike, go get a life." *See? I can't even be nice for five minutes in front of Gavin!*

Mike groans and shuts off the television, slinks down the hall, and slams the door to his room. "Nice to have you back!" he yells through the door.

Gavin clears his throat and sits back on the couch, "I always thought I'd be married, but it never happened. The truth is now

I don't know that I could be. The business takes so many hours. I don't really think of myself as the fatherly type, and I never met a woman who made me think about marriage." He looks at me, his brow furrowed. "Sorry."

"I'm not offended, Gavin, I admire your ability to know who you are, I suppose. What do you do with yourself to keep busy?"

"I have season tickets to the Giants and the 49ers. I organize trips for us older singles at church, and I work. It's a full life."

"Is it?"

"It is, Haley. You'll get used to it. What about you? What else have you been doing besides being a wife?

"Would you like something to drink?"

"Too personal?"

"No, I realized I hadn't offered, that's all."

"Nothing for me. I'm sure your mom will have a nice, cold glass of milk waiting at dinner."

I look into his steady eyes and despite how I've learned to keep everything inside, my truth comes bubbling out like a Napa geyser. "I don't ever want to feel this way again, Gavin. It's not worth the pain."

"I hate to hear that, Haley. You always had so much passion for life. I envied that about you. You can't let one mistake change who you are. You need to buy a really sparkly outfit and go for a night on the town. I'm game if you are."

"I've moved on from just sparkly," I say with my shoulders straight, but then I burst into giggles. "My last closet purchase that I never showed to Jay?"

"Yes?"

"Giraffe-print boots. And they're kind of furry."

Gavin starts to laugh out loud.

"And I love them."

"What are you two laughing about in there?" my mother asks.

"Well, a man who can't see the good humor in giraffe-skin boots isn't worth having."

"All I'm saying." It's amazing that I can pour my heart out to Gavin, but it's like I'm back in my graduating class. I trust Gavin. I always have, and I always will. He could never do to me what Jay did. Of course, he could never make me feel like Jay either, and that is why I'm steering clear of men. I have no common sense. The boots should tell me that much.

"The Golden Globes are starting, Haley. Turn them on. I'll bring dinner out on TV trays." My mom is giddy. Is it any wonder I have a thing for sparkles? I started young watching every awards show on television. The American Music Awards, the Grammy Awards, the People's Choice Awards, and of course, the granddaddy of them all: the Oscars.

"Mom, we can watch after dinner." I think this is where my love of tacky may have started.

"No, no dear. It will be fun. Gavin knows we watch all the shows."

The really sad thing is that Gavin gets up and goes to the hall closet and pulls out six aluminum TV trays circa 1963 and sets them up in front of the couch.

"Not much changes around here, huh?" I ask.

"The difference between you and me is I see that as a positive. If twenty years from now I'm still eating pot roast on a TV tray, I'm good with that."

My mother scuttles out of the kitchen with classic glasses with wheat designs (they go with the burnt orange appliances and Formica) and a gallon of milk. She places one on each TV tray and pours a tall glass of milk for each of us. "They say *Grey's Anatomy* is going to sweep this year."

"My vote is for *Ugly Betty*," I tell her.

"What would you know of *Ugly Betty*, princess?" my dad asks as he wanders into the room. My dad talks like the dad on any sitcom in America, but there's no actual emotional connection. He's old school. Notice he didn't say hello to me when he got home, even though I haven't seen him since Christmas when he and mom graciously visited me holed up in the Wilshire. He talks through my mother, if he talks to me at all. Unless someone is present to hear his *Leave It to Beaver* impression, he doesn't bother.

"Hi, Dad, when did you come in?"

He comes over and kisses me on the cheek. "Welcome home, Haley." He sits down. "Gavin, how's the window business treating you? You seeing things clearly?" My dad laughs at his own joke. Like Gavin has never heard that one before.

"Better than ever. The more freeways that get built, the more double- and even triple-paned windows necessary. I added siding to the business too. You might call me for a quote. I noticed you could use some upkeep."

"I might do that," my dad says.

Probably about the time he'll get around to mowing the lawn, which, by the way, "Why isn't Mike mowing the lawn?"

"What?" Gavin asks.

"If Mike is living here and doing errands, why does the lawn look like it does?"

"Mike's back is not good, honey." My mom sets my glass of milk in front of me. "He hurt it working at Best Buy. Those televisions just get bigger and bigger, don't you know?"

"Actually, they're getting thinner. Let me help you, Mom."

"No, no, you sit. Your friend is here, and you have a lot of catching up to do." She glimmers at Gavin.

I'm not divorced yet, Mom. Let's allow the body to cool, shall we?

The Pre-Awards walk on the red carpet starts, and we take our pick of obnoxious hosts, finally settling on Star Jones's version of dissing and kissing.

"Jay's movie is nominated this year," I announce, trying to keep the melancholy out of my voice. It's the first one I ever produced myself, is the truth of it. And Jay's first serious film. I talked him into the script. I found the star, Rachel, on television one night and deemed her perfect for the part. Naturally, he'd never remember it that way. But that is my movie, my actress, my nomination. "The one with Rachel Barlin in it."

"Rachel Barlin, I love her," Gavin says, and I can't help it, I shoot him a dirty look. Like I care that he loves her. Who doesn't? She's gorgeous, has a perfect, albeit-enhanced figure, and comes off as the girl next door in a vixen's costume. Men fall for that trap every time. Same old game. "What's not to love?" Gavin wiggles his eyebrows.

Gee, let me count the ways. Late-night phone calls to my husband, whining about how her trailer needed better water, a more comfortable bed, a better makeup artist, blah blah blah. She expected Jay to fix it all. When she argued with the director, she'd call Jay. When she didn't have Evian coming out of her tap in her trailer, she'd call Jay.

"I think she's pathetic," I hear myself say. "Too needy, don't you think?"

"She's so beautiful, and she seems like a really sweet girl."

"*Seems* being the operative word. Men see what they want to see. If someone's had a career in the porn industry, a guy can rationalize how she only did it to pay her way through college. It's a stereotype, you know. The hooker with a heart of gold thing. Some of them have hearts of stone and use that old stereotype to get whatever they want. You all want to believe she's Rahab, not Jezebel, and you never believe other women, even though we have radar for that kind of thing."

"Haley"—my mom smiles proudly—"you do remember your Sunday school lessons. Of course I'd rather have you remember something other than the prostitute stories, but one hopes they're in there too."

"When Mrs. Kensington talks about hookers, it's not something you forget," I explain.

"Well, I see a beautiful woman with a sweet spirit. She reminds me of you with brown hair, Haley," Gavin comments. "You know," he says, pointing a fork at the television, "I bet she's really small-town. She grew up in the Midwest with church potlucks and county fairs."

"My point exactly. If she's small-town, you think her small-town mama would have taught her calling another woman's husband in the middle of the night is what the girls-on-the-wrong-side-of-the-tracks did. I see a spoiled brat who uses her wiles to get whatever she wants."

"Haley!" Gavin raises his eyebrows. "Is this upsetting you?"

"She is an actress, Gavin. Maybe she's better than you give her credit for."

At that comment, Star Jones starts to interview Rachel Barlin. Even the sight of Rachel makes the hair on my arms rise and I want to fast-forward her, but my mom hasn't heard of TiVo. She's wearing a sparkly, gold gown, and while I'm sure it isn't sequins, it does sparkle. I have to wonder if now my fetish for glitter would be acceptable.

"Look, there she is!" Gavin says, sitting up on the sofa. "Speak of the devil."

"Exactly," I say.

"She is so hot." Then he corrects himself. "Really beautiful, you know? Like the girl next door," he says wistfully, as if he's heard nothing I've said.

My heart takes a dive as I see the man standing behind her is my Jay. The same Jay who said he was leaving for Switzerland. The same Jay who told me I didn't need a gown for the Golden Globes because "we" weren't attending. I look around to see if anyone has noticed yet, but everyone's eyes are fixed on the glittering Rachel. Jay's watching her too, in a way he looked at me, before we got married. Something inside of me falls dead to the ground.

Star fawns over her. "Rachel, you look beautiful. Your dress is . . ."

"Vintage Mackie," she coos.

"Vintage Mackie," I repeat. "In other words, no one would lend her a new one. She got Cher's castoffs from decades gone by."

"Who is this handsome man on your arm?" Star asks. "Is this the new love of your life?"

That would be my husband. My eyes are transfixed on her. *Say no, Rachel. Please.*

She giggles coquettishly, but she doesn't answer the question. "This is my producer, Jay Cutler." She takes a finger and smooths it along his jawline. "Isn't he wonderful? Everyone said I couldn't handle a serious role like this one, but Jay fought for me. He believed in me, and the rest is history."

It's here that I catch it; their eye contact. It's something any wife would understand, any woman would notice in her man, and I feel my strength leave me, but I push the TV tray in front of me as recognition pummels me. My eyes fill with tears.

My mom gets up and shuts off the television set, and we're all sitting around it with TV trays and no picture.

"How about them 49ers?" my dad asks, and though I'm no football fan, I know their season is well over.

"Haley, are you all right?" my mother asks.

"The settlement isn't enough," I say quietly. *I want revenge.*

"Haley, the fight isn't worth the money. You've wasted enough on him."

I stand up. "If Jay is dating one of Hollywood's rising stars, it increases his tabloid value," I explain.

"It's not worth it, Haley," Gavin says.

"Honey, you don't want to do this," my dad adds.

"Hamilton is about to find out just how ditsy this trophy wife is. I may be tacky and inappropriate, but I am not stupid." I take the papers and walk to the hallway.

"Haley," my mother cautions. "Where are you going?"

"I'm going home to claim what's mine."

"I thought her husband's name was Jay. Who's Hamilton?" Gavin asks.

A man who is about to regret the day he met me. That's who.

Chapter 4

The Trophy Wives Club meets Wednesday nights at a local church hall. The wrinkled flyer said so. I've driven by this church a million times, but never noticed it was here. Probably all those nightmare Sunday mornings I had under Mrs. Kensington's guidance. She was the kind of woman who had a shelf for a chest, and her body seemed to break off into oblivion under an oversized floral gown. That woman scared me. How come church people can be so scary? Come to think of it, I never did see Mr. Kensington. I wonder if the authorities ever looked into that?

I'd thought I'd thrown the flyer out. Let's face it, I meant to. The last thing I needed in my life was more advice from Hamilton Lowe, but I found it still crumpled in my handbag. An odd circumstance, but one I'm willing to concede to if I can unlock the secret to a great divorce settlement.

I imagine a bunch of dried-up old women, bitter and without

Botox, lamenting how their husbands got away, but if they're well dressed, and their foreheads are stagnant, I'll know right away their settlements were decent, and I made the right choice in coming.

The church is packed, like there's some kind of live concert going on. I'm flagged in by a clean-cut man in khakis and an orange vest carrying a flashlight. This is what the AV kids in school do when they grow up. As I look around, I see families getting out of the cars, their Bibles clutched to their chest. There's a tiny pang, I admit.

I don't have a Bible. I begin to feel like I did that night I found out Hollywood didn't wear sequins. I get out of the car, and a man says hello and stares too long. His wife gives him a dirty look, and he runs off chasing her. Okay. This is not going well so far.

I've decided tonight is the moment to embrace my tacky side and show how poverty-stricken I've been left. I'm wearing ratty Keds, from before my wedding, and Levi's from college. I refuse to dress the part of trophy wife. I am Skipper: her younger, shorter sister with ghastly clothes and pocketbook.

Like salmon swimming upstream, all the people go directly to their rooms, and I'm left in the hallway at the last door. The hand-written sign on the door reads TWC, as though it's an undercover group, like AA for the badly married set. I pause and take a deep breath.

I don't want to be here. I don't want to be a part of this group. Why didn't I marry a simple man? I could have thrown cocktail parties for people who need new windows and dine on BBQ-sauced weenies out of Crock Pots. I open the door and welcome their stares, as they assess their newest member. *That's it. Drink it in, there's not a designer label on me. Show me the money!*

There are five of them. An older lady, a striking blonde of about fifty (probably sixty-five, but with the work, she *looks* fifty), the matriarch of the group I'm assuming, stands up. She has a warm smile. She reaches her arms toward me like a long-lost friend.

"Welcome," she says, taking my hands and clutching them tightly. It's been so long since anyone truly touched me with that kind of warmth, it's disconcerting. I flinch and pull my hands away. "You're here for the"—she lowers her voice—"the trophy wife club?"

I nod. She notices my shoes and immediately averts her gaze. *That was nice.* Maybe I'm not as strong and self-reliant as I'd hoped because what I wouldn't give for a pair of Donald Pliners at the moment.

"I'm Elizabeth Taylor. Not *the* Elizabeth Taylor, obviously." She rubs my shoulder (she's really into the touchy-feely thing). "You can call me Bette. We are so glad to have—" She flashes her eyes, waiting for my name.

"Haley Cutler."

Bette exhales deeply. A few of the women nod, and I hear a few audible gasps.

"Yes, *that* Haley Cutler," I say.

"So . . . Jay Cutler?" A brunette asks.

I nod.

"I'm so sorry, sweetie." She stands up. "I'm Penny, it's a pleasure." I reach out for her hand and shake it. Penny is a petite brunette with huge, exotic brown eyes and thick, dark ringlets of hair cascading on her shapely shoulders. She must do Pilates. She's in that kind of shape. Strong and wholly female. I hate her already.

"He's not the first husband she's stolen," a redhead says.

"And most likely won't be the last," another blonde comments. "I think some women collect them like human charm bracelets."

"Ladies," Bette says in a tone not unlike Mrs. Kensington's from my childhood. "Let's try to remain Christian in our talk."

Like I said, I may not remember much about my Sunday school

days, but the Bible was full of loose women. Hollywood had nothing on the Hebrews.

The redhead reaches her hand out. I can't tell if she's natural or not, but her brilliant red hair is eye-catching and ominous. I don't even want to know who her husband left her for. She's not the kind of woman you want in the same room during a party, let's put it that way.

"Helena Brickman," she says. "My husband is not sure if marriage is for him. I think his girlfriend isn't sure either, and he tends to take her side in these matters." She rolls her dark green eyes. "And he wants alimony, if you can believe it." She shrugs. "*C'est la vie*. We know your story—at least part of it that we saw played out on the red carpet. Is there no decorum anymore? I ask you! Anyway, I figured you'd want to know ours so you'd know you're not alone."

"They're not all so dramatic, Haley. I promise," Bette says. "Let her sit down, ladies. Give her a chance to breathe before you pummel her with information and scare the life out of her."

I wish these women weren't nice. I'm not here for nice. I was hoping for younger, prettier versions of Mrs. Kensington. That woman could have entered the lions' den, and I don't think she would have needed God's help. She'd just take them down with that glare of hers! I'm here for information. How to get Jay where it hurts—in that leather heart he wears in his back pocket.

These women don't look like they could hurt an accountant, much less pinch the wallet out of his pocket. They're not remotely as threatening as Mrs. Kensington. I go over the questions in my mind so I don't miss my opportunity:

How much money exactly do tabloids pay for inside information?

How do I approach Jay and Hamilton, or do I make the first move and stealthily throw out the first number?

No, Jay says never throw out the first number. It's the first rule of negotiation.

"I'm Lily Tseng," an Asian woman pipes up. She looks like an international film star, and she's dressed to the nines. Her clothes are expensive; if I had to guess I'd say Michael Kors: structured and elegant, with the slightest bit of fabric to add feminism. I wonder what she'd think of my giraffe boots, or if she ever wore sequins in her life. Somehow, I doubt it.

I have to say if these are the wives, I'd love to see the room full of the other women because this seems like a support group of women who might say, "I'm too beautiful to be loved."

Blech.

"Well, please sit down. We'll finish the introductions and talk about our weeks and how we've done with our assignments. Can I get you some coffee, Haley?" Bette asks, and I shake my head. "We'll introduce ourselves and tell you a little about our individual situations, so you don't feel so out of the loop. Helena, you want to go first since you already started?"

They pull their chairs so there's a wider circle, and I sit, trying to ignore the fact that everyone is still staring at me like I'm a caged animal. Why is it that women can't resist sizing up other women? It doesn't matter whether the environment is a Hollywood after-party or a Bible study like this one; we have to size up the competition.

I resist the urge to make a mad dash for the exit and play lockdown with a tub of chocolate frosting. The church smells mightily of new carpet, but it's not in here. This is a science experiment. One of the walls is half–knocked down, with duct tape lining its edges. I almost expect them to pass the basket at the sight of it.

"Do we get to bash the walls?" I ask, sort of salivating at the idea of picturing Jay's head behind the drywall.

"I'm afraid we don't, dear. This is just the only room they have left," Bette says in that same voice, before people like her bring out the axe. No one is that peace-filled.

I want to leave, but something keeps me grounded here in the midst of these women who feel like my only hope at the moment. They're all beautiful. I guess I expected that much. No, that's not true. I didn't. I thought some would have had some heinous physical malady that forced them to become part of this group because they'd been relegated to the "outside" like the Flintstones' cat.

The majority are like me. Too young to be in this position. None of them seem exceptionally bitter, which disappoints me. I was hoping for a *Dynasty* rerun, with dripping jewels and catfights and delicious details on how to fight back. This place is innocuous, and they really have Bibles! How vixenlike can they be, with pink leather Bibles in their manicured hands?

Perhaps we young ones are the ultimate failures in trophy wives. We couldn't even hang on to our husbands long enough for our time to be up. No one looks exceptionally saggy or wrinkled.

An optimist would say we were the lucky ones, we got out young enough for a second chance. But please. Knowing what we do, I can't imagine any of us running to the altar at this point. Our days in Vera Wang are over.

Helena stands up. I get the impression Helena has no issues with being the center of attention. She's goddesslike, with flaming, red hair and green eyes. She has a tiny, teenagelike figure and flawless skin. I can't even tell if she's wearing foundation. *Oh, so hate her too.*

"I'm Helena Brickman, as I was saying. I have a Ph.D. in biochemistry and specialize in genetic engineering. I'm bright in all the right places except when it comes to men." She grins. "I have a bad habit of taking people at their word, and I'm learning to discern who I should give that trust to."

"Helena," Bette interrupts, "why don't you tell Haley what you're doing now?"

"Right. I married the CEO of my company and retired from the business. It wasn't good for stockholders to see the CEO marry an employee, so we agreed that I would get a golden parachute retirement package, and Robert would work."

"Helena, that's not what I meant," Bette says.

She interrupts to finish her story. "He went back to school to get his doctorate on the company dime and had an affair at the same time. If only he were that productive at work, I'd have stock value to show for my trouble. At some point, he dropped out of school and just used the time for her. He is currently in the process of divorcing me. I haven't worked in two years, and I'm pretty much a dinosaur in the business. No one will hire me, so I'm going back to school and changing my focus. Is that better?" she asks Bette. "Positive enough?"

"What a dog!" I say. Maybe I need to rethink college. I don't even have a clue what Helena does, but if she can't get a job, that was a heck of a waste of time. A Ph.D.? How many years is that flushed away? At least at the Gap, I was useful and I know how to fold a polo shirt correctly and I can size anyone in jeans by merely looking at her. That talent doesn't grow on trees.

Bette speaks up again, in her soft, cottony voice, "Haley, I should tell you, the point of this group is not to man-bash."

"Hence, the wall being safe."

"We're here to take responsibility for our part in failed marriages. Even if we were treated horribly, there's something within us that attracted us to such selfish or needy men, and we're here to explore that together, so we don't make the same mistakes and we become more useful in the Kingdom of God."

"Oh"—I raise a palm at her—"you don't have to worry about me. I'm never getting married again, and I was never really very useful to the Kingdom of God to begin with. No offense, you all do your thing, get to that healthy place, but I'm not into analyzing everything about how things could have been different. If I learned anything, it's never to trust my romantic instincts again. Even though I told Jay's lawyer, Hamilton, that he was afraid of commitment . . . I realize I'm really no different than him, which is, I suppose, why I saw fit to lecture him in the first place—" Everyone's mouth is open. "Sorry. I got carried away. There's no one to really get out my daily word count on, sorry." I scoot back in my chair.

"Hamilton Lowe?" a tall, willowy blonde asks.

"You know him?"

She tightens her mouth, and I watch Bette give everyone "the gaze."

Bette gives me that, *there, there dear* shake of the head like she is so in touch with her inner peace. My mother gives me that look, and I hate it! It means, ignore the truth and let's focus on how sweet and wonderful everything is, when in fact, everything isn't sweet and wonderful. The blonde knows what Hamilton Lowe is, she just can't say so.

It's time to make my move before I implode under all these manners. "I'm actually here to find out about settlements. See if anyone has had luck in selling information to the tabloids, negotiating a price, that sort of advice. I got your name from the lawyer—" I look back at the blonde. "The infamously smarmy Hamilton Lowe," I choke his name out. "Right now, my settlement is $70,000 for seven years of marriage. Even though it was devastatingly close to eight years." I clear my throat. "Since everything here is to be kept confidential, I thought you might be able to help me. You know, get more so that Jay feels my pain. I don't want to destroy him or anything, I just want him to sting a little."

Bette pats my knee, "Dear, we don't discuss those types of issues here. We're here to get healthy, not to exact revenge. *Revenge is Mine, Saith the Lord*."

I shake my head, "Okay, then color me red, I'm totally in the wrong place because I just think the Lord"—I make the sign of the cross from my childhood—"just isn't going to move quickly enough for me. I'm into handing out justice the old-fashioned way. Did you ever see *A Fistful of Dollars?*"

Bette is still gazing at me openmouthed. Apparently, she did see the movie. "We've all been there, Haley, we know what it feels like to hurt like this, but it won't do any good to get more money. It will only increase his hold on you."

"No, that's where I'm different from you. You're like my mother, you see the good in all situations, and wow, I totally admire people like that. In fact," I say, putting up my forefinger, "I think I used to be like that, but then I walked into one too many walls, and I realized no one is going to prevent you from the impact. You totally have to look out for yourself, you know what I'm saying?" By their expressions, I'd say no, they don't, so I continue. "Jay Cutler will never have to face what he's done without this situation hurting his bottom line. So in this particular case, I'm going to have to say revenge is mine, meaning Haley's, not God's. It's not that I don't trust that He could do a better job and all that, if He's around, I'm just certain He's really busy, and it's not high on his priority list. Whereas I can devote all my attention to the matter, as I have no job or life at the moment. Just this really strong desire to get Jay where it hurts. Understand?"

She pats my hand again. "So you're helping God out, is that what you're saying."

"Exactly!" I point at her. "You got it!"

"I understand that the pain is fresh—"

May I just say that the whole psychology tone is lost on me. I'm sure Bette is a very sweet woman with fabulous intentions, but is she really at peace? Or just denial?

"Holding on to these dark memories only makes your situation worse. We can all testify to that. Forgiving . . ." She pats her chest. "Forgiving is for us, not for them. Revenge is like giving ourselves poison and expecting the other person to die."

They all nod in agreement. Well, except for the one vivacious brunette, oddly enough the one with the Pilates body, and the only other blonde in the group. I could have sworn she rolled her eyes.

"I'm going to make sure Jay drinks the poison. You sure you saw *A Fistful of Dollars? Pale Rider?*"

"Haley, one of the things we focus on here is how to break the negative patterns in our lives and be free of the chains that bind us in miserable situations. You have to ask yourself if the fight is worth what you might be able to build on your own, without Jay's money."

"Think how much farther ahead I'll be with his money though." *Am I the only one with any practicality here?*

"What do you want to do with the money?" the blonde asks.

"I'm sorry?" I say to her.

"I'm just saying if you have no plans for the money, what do you need it for?"

"Have you seen the price of shoes lately?"

"Some women are left with nothing, and they have kids to support," the brunette pipes in.

"Two wrongs don't make a right," I say smugly.

"What you're really pissed about is that the other woman is getting your spoils. Admit it," the blonde says with a glimmer in her eye.

"Lindsay!" Bette chastises.

"No, it's okay. She's entitled to her opinion. Oh, and I can tell you, she's not getting my money. She makes her own. Well, her twenty-year-old body double makes it for her, but the public doesn't know that."

The brunette starts to giggle and soon, the other women join her, but straighten up immediately as Bette shoots them the look. *We can't be having a giggle melee.*

"Laugh. We can laugh, can't we?" *This is exactly what happened to me.* I slowly learned "the right way to act" until there was nothing left of me anymore;—only the girl who walked into walls because I second-guessed everything.

"Not at someone else's expense, dear."

"I'm sorry. I can't lie to myself anymore. I've spent nine years telling myself lies, and my body just won't allow it anymore. Excuse me, won't you?" I start to rise.

Bette snaps up from her chair, and I want to warn her if she pats me again, there's no telling what I'll do. "Haley, this is a long road. Please don't give up. I know we all sound fanatical to you, maybe even a little crazy—"

If I had a straitjacket . . .

"It's not just your marriage that goes in these situations; it's your lifestyle, your daily routine, your clothes, your makeup, your hangouts. Literally, everything in your life changes overnight, and we're here to tell you after the hard part, that's when life really starts."

"I'm ready for life to start now," I say absently as I sit back down.

"Fighting for money isn't worth your energy. You have to focus that energy into positive places. It's like purging your system. Have you ever been on a cleansing diet?"

"It was worth Clint Eastwood's energy, and don't you worry, it will be worth mine. I play to win." I clutch my purse to my chest. "I still have my friends, by the way. If anything, my friends are out looking for a new husband for me right now. Not that I would want one again."

The brunette holds up her cell phone. "Go ahead then, call one. We'll wait."

"I don't want to call one. I've just been out of town, and I'll call them when I've found a place to live. I thought I was going home to my parents, but that's not working, so I'm staying at the Wilshire until I rent an apartment."

The Wilshire. Unless, they've suddenly decided they don't need credit cards for ID, I won't even get a room in their Dumpster. Jay and the tricks up his sleeves! But appearances . . . appearances.

"If they're really your friends, they'll take your call. What are you afraid of?" the snippy brunette asks.

My stomach tenses at my last encounter with Anna Lynchow at the salon. If Anna is anything, she is industrious, and there is little doubt in my mind, everyone has been informed of my lack of conformity—and my outright refusal to date the latest castoff.

"I'm not afraid of anything; I just don't feel like calling."

"You haven't even begun this walk, Haley. You seem to think we're ignorant of your situation, like we don't know what it's like to be kicked to the curb like you never mattered, like you were something on the bottom of his shoe, not his wife. You think that's foreign to us?" the redhead pipes in.

"It's not as bad as you think." I take out my phone and flip it open, "Fine, I'll call." I dial Anna's home number and wait for David, her butler to answer. Sure, she ditched me at the nail salon, but Anna's moody that way. She's probably started working on finding me a new man as I speak. "Lynchow residence."

"Hi, David, It's Haley Cutler, can you put Anna on?"

There's a pause. I feel my heart jump. I am so not worthy of a pause. Pauses are for telemarketers and friends you're ticked at, or dumping . . ."Ms. Cutler, Mrs. Lynchow is currently indisposed—"

"Indisposed, are you kidding me? David, get her. How many Botox parties did I go to for her to get a free shot? I want to talk to her. I've got a bone to pick with her. She left me in the nail salon for one thing."

"I'm sorry, Ms. Cutler." He hangs up on me. The women are all staring at me, and I feel my self-respect dwindling, and I'm standing all alone in sequins once again.

I shrug. "I'll just call her on her cell, her butler is pulling a hissy fit. No biggie."

I dial Anna's cell and wait for it to ring, but the message machine picks up immediately. "Anna is unavailable. Please leave your message after the tone."

"She's not available right now."

"Call another friend," the blonde challenges.

"I don't want to call another friend." The fact is, if Anna's not speaking to me, the chances are good she's made certain no one else is speaking to me either.

"Don't push her, Lindsay. It's a traumatic time."

"It's supposed to be traumatic. She just lost her husband and her friends and probably her unlimited credit card. Isn't it better that she faces it now than live in denial and use her last dime to fight Hamilton Lowe in court?"

"I didn't lose my friends!" I stamp my foot like a preschooler.

"You did," the brunette challenges. "You just don't know it yet."

"Real friends don't dump you because you're getting a divorce," Lily, the beautiful Asian woman says.

"That's right, real friends don't. We wouldn't. But this is hard on friends, too. They don't know whose side to take, and they're waiting it out," Helena says.

"But you'll lose," Lindsay, the blonde adds. "The person with the least power in this town always seems to lose."

I remember when one-upmanship was all about the most exclusive shoes, preferably custom from a sought-after designer, and the biggest, clearest diamond. I actually remember sliding my hand up against another woman's ring, so we could casually check for the four C's. Only the rules have changed here. Now it's who has the most pathetic story and considering that mine played out on national television with a film star, I think I take top honors. It's nice to know I can win at something on this side of marriage.

I sweep my hair behind my ear. "Anna's just busy right now. I may have lost my husband, but as you probably saw on the Golden Globes, I didn't lose much. She's probably hosting a dinner party and can't get to the phone." Though in my heart, I know Anna has about as much chance of hosting a party as her husband does of working with Oscar material.

"What about the friends you had *before* you got married? You're going to need lots of support," Lily says.

Oh yeah, them. "I haven't seen them for nearly a decade. They were busy with college," I admit. I cringe at the thought of how I was busy with Jay and deserted them. I was in love. I didn't need to crowd my world with people who took me away from Jay and his needs. *Oh man, I could kick myself.* I remember telling myself they didn't understand. One by one, they just drifted away, tired of calling and hearing how busy I was with Jay's schedule. "I always had someplace to be, and they got tired of waiting for the scraps to fall from Jay's table."

Lily nods. "I understand."

"I should call them up."

"I'll bet they'd like to hear from you," Lily says gently.

"What if they tell me they saw it coming?" I shut my eyes. "What if they saw Jay on television?"

"What if they did?" Lindsay asks. "Maybe they're at home feeling for you right now. Not everyone thinks like that group you've been hanging around with."

"Maybe they're not. Maybe they think I got what I deserved."

"I don't think any woman watches a woman like Rachel Barlin snag someone else's husband and rejoices in the fact. It's a loss for all of us. She's a gorgeous reptile. They know. Trust me, they know," Lily explains. "You belittle your sex thinking otherwise."

I look to each of the beautiful faces surrounding me and think it's impossible for them to truly understand. "I should get home," I say, knowing it's impolite not to listen to everyone's tale, but in all honesty, I can't bear any more.

The blonde crosses her arms and looks directly into my eyes before casting a sideways glance at Bette. "I'll tell you how to take him down," she whispers out of the side of her mouth. She pulls away. "If you're sure that's what you want."

And just like that, the clouds begin to part.

"You'll help me?" I ask, without bothering to cloak my desperation.

"Lindsay," Bette chastises. "You know our rules."

At the censure, Lindsay calmly looks at Bette. "I'm sorry, Bette, but sometimes a girl has to do what a girl has to do." Lindsay stands up and heads for the door. She looks back at me. "You coming?"

I clamber behind her, grabbing up my purse, and look at all the astonished faces. "Thank you for welcoming me." I rush to the door, for fear someone, especially the hand-patting Bette, will try to stop me and pummel me with Bible verses. And no thank you. I am done being a human doormat.

If I wanted to embrace denial, I would have stayed home with my mother. She does it best. But that kind of living lasts only so long, because at some point, your whole being cries out for truth.

Bette's face morphs into a nervous expression with a profound crease in the center of her forehead. I think she'd hoped to convert me by now. "Haley, I need to give you the origin of our name and explain a few of our rules so you feel safe here. We want everyone to feel safe here. Don't run off just yet."

Bette speaks in her soothing voice. "Sit back down. Just for a moment. I don't feel we did us justice." Both Lindsay and I saunter back to the hard chairs and sit down like repentant children. "I feel I got off on the wrong foot trying to protect you at a time when you need to be heard. I'm sorry about that, dear." Again, with the hand pat. "We're a support system for one another, and that involves feeling free to share our experiences, good and bad. We know nothing leaves this room, and we want to focus on the positive. We don't want to start in the wrong place with you."

"My husband's a dog. That's where I am right now," I say honestly. "Even if he was ready to move on, didn't I deserve to be told? I mean, what did our marriage vows mean?" *I know what they meant, of course. They meant more write-off for Jay and that he could land a twenty-year-old blonde*. "All those years I tried to shut out the facts. He was busy I told myself. He was a workaholic and the biggie, he was doing it all for us. Someday, we'd have a family, and he'd be able to spend time with our child when the time came."

"I understand," Lindsay says.

"I do too," Helena says.

"Yeah," Lily adds.

Bette stands in front of the door and opens her Bible, so I can't escape. I mean, leave. *Here we go, let the pummeling begin. Let the guilt mount.*

"In First Corinthians 9:24, there's a verse about running our race, our life, toward the prize. It reads like this." She moves her finger along in her marked-up Bible. "Do you not know that in a race all the runners run, but only one gets the prize? Run in such a way as to get the prize. Everyone who competes in the games goes into strict training. They do it to get a crown that will not last; but we do it to get a crown that will last forever." She looks up at me. I think she's expecting an epiphany.

Okaaay.

"What does that verse say to you?"

"That's where the Trophy Wives name comes from. The prize?"

She nods excitedly as though I've just aced my LSAT. "We're running for the prize in here, Haley, and we already found the one that wouldn't last. We change our focus and He changes us. For His approval, all we need to do is believe. Nothing else! Isn't that exciting?"

Thrilling.

When did I become such a pessimist? I used to wear sequins and dance like no one was watching. Now I can't even sit in a Bible study without rolling my eyes. *I've turned into my father.*

I start to get up slowly, looking longingly at Lindsay. *Please come with me,* my eyes plead.

"We'll be here for you, Haley," Bette says. "When you're ready."

I nod.

"It's hard to fully grasp the pain you're feeling right now—"

I shake my head. "I'm not in pain. I'm just waking up, that's all. I've been in pain, I just didn't know it until Jay let go."

Bette sighs deeply. She doesn't believe my denial. But I really don't feel pain; I feel only numbness when it comes to Jay—and maybe a big desire for revenge. It's humiliating and shameful that I gave my heart to a man who cared so little for it. He thinks I don't matter, but I'll matter when he goes to his bank account, I can promise that.

"Have you ever read the Song of Solomon, Haley? It's a book in the Bible," Bette explains.

"I know what it is, and no, we weren't allowed back in the days I went to Sunday school. Mrs. Kensington said it was scandalous." Which, I want to add, only made us want to read it, but I never did. We didn't have Bibles back then; we used small books that had the stories within them.

"I suggest you read it because it's how a man should care for and love his wife. It's full of passion and desire, and it's an allegory for how God cares for His people."

"He doesn't care for me that way. No offense, but if something can go wrong, it will go wrong with me."

"What about your dad? Didn't he love you like that?"

"I don't think my dad ever noticed me, to tell you the truth." For some reason, my eyes well up saying this. I feel as though I've betrayed my own father. I want to give in to my sadistic self that says Bette's swigged too much happy punch today, and her sunshiny view of life has about as much basis in reality as fairies do, but there's a tug within me that I can't ignore, and it's that the blonde, Lindsay, has the information I need.

"Sweetheart, you can be loved like this. That might feel impossible never having experienced it, but I promise you this love is real. You probably feel as if you've been in a race that has no finish line."

I do feel like that. With Jay, it was simply a race I couldn't win. I feel my head bob up and down subconsciously, and tears prick my eyes. *Stop it.*

"Now—" She pats the back of my hand, and I note I still have my wedding ring on. I look around and see that about half the women do. "—is the time to relax and let God take over. Did you ever think you could just lie back, relax and let someone else do the driving? You need a soft place to fall, Haley. The world is not so harsh if you have a padded nest."

I stiffen at her words. "I'm not a passive person, Bette. I don't wait for things to happen to me. Not anymore."

"Does Lindsay seem passive?"

Um, Lindsay seems to be manic. "No, but—"

"I thought I'd be married forever, Haley," Lily says in a quiet voice. So quiet, I wonder if she's been tranquilized in the last second. Finally, I got a shot at something that matters, not a beauty contest or a mascara ad, but a real shot at being someone's other half—the perfect wife—He loved me." She looks me straight in the eye. "And I couldn't get it right. I wasn't good enough. There was always something wrong with me. My dress wasn't the sexiest, or it was too sexy, and I looked like a slut. Or someone else's wife looked better at the party, she must be doing more yoga, maybe I'd slacked off that week. Maybe they had a better caterer, and I should get their name for our next party. I could never succeed, which only made me try harder and virtually made me more pathetic in his eyes. By the end, he looked at me with complete contempt." She touches her stomach. "It still makes me ill to think about it, but there was nothing I could have done. He didn't really want a wife. He wanted someone to fix his insecurities. No one can do that for another. You both have to be complete. We're here to help you become complete."

"He said those things to you?" I've never heard anyone else admit to her daily failures like this, and my breathing becomes erratic.

"And worse. It took me years and lots of therapy to realize I never could have made him happy and that I wasn't responsible for his happiness. This group has helped me create my own place in the world. I'm the director of HR for a major agency now and live in one of the best neighborhoods in West L.A. in a town house that I own. I drive a Lexus. None of those material things matter, I had all those when I was married, but I love myself now, and I know I'm worthy."

I can't take anymore. It sounds like an AA meeting, and I made a mistake. I want to move on. I'm not stuck in addictive behavior! I stand up and move toward the door as casually as the new girl can. If I make believe I'm invisible, maybe they'll buy it too. As I push on the door, I use all my force, allowing the exit to spit me out like a projectile. I focus toward the end of the hallway and run as fast as my legs will carry me.

"Haley, wait!" Lindsay calls in the hallway. She is following me, and she has her purse and notebook with her. Unwittingly, I quicken my pace. I'm almost at the door to the parking lot.

I cover my ears as I glance over my shoulder. "I don't want to hear any more, Lindsay."

She beats me to the door and stands in front of it, wearing Hudson jeans with their telltale front pockets and a cropped, form-fitting jacket and stiletto heels, but she can still really move in them. I'm impressed. I'd have been in several walls by now.

Lindsay doesn't exactly look like my image of a church girl, but I imagine the Trophy Wives Club isn't your normal Bible study. "I don't know why that bothered me—"

"Just give me a minute, Haley. You have to face it at some point and look at the bright side, you can't be more pathetic than the rest of us. Your husband is gone. Your friends are gone. Those are facts."

I needed *that* brought up again.

"The good news is that the cavalry has arrived. Your real friends who will be with you while you detox from this relationship."

"Revenge is my last resort. Did you see how handsome Jay looked on television? Nothing has touched him. If you all could just let him get away with that and trust God to take care of it, wow, I totally admire that. But I can't do that. It's not right. It's just not. I've lived like a doormat too, you know. You all forget I did the doormat thing, and look where it got me."

"Don't mind Bette, Haley, it's been a long time since her husband left." She crosses her arms and leans in toward me. "But she means well, and she'll be there for you no matter what you need. Do you see that, at least?"

"I do, she's sweet, but I've been sweet too, Lindsay. I'm not that person anymore."

"So what kind of person are you? What do you want to do with your life now?"

I look at the tacky carpet while I ponder. "I know how to produce a movie, but of course, I don't really have the capital to start. I know how to call the caterer. I know how much shrimp cocktail is needed for a gathering of seventy-five and I know exactly how long I can go before my nails need to be filed, but other than that? I'm very good at doing what I'm told. I'd make a great Labrador. Do you know anyone who needs a well-trained dog?"

"See? You think you're all victim here, but that's exactly the reason you married that type of guy. You've got an excuse for everything."

"You don't even know me."

Lindsay smooths a lock of hair between two fingers. "Here's the one piece of advice I will give you."

"Am I asking for advice?" I look around me. "I don't think I asked for any advice other than how I can get more money."

She ignores me. "Whenever you feel tempted to blame Jay or say his name? You need to think of another route because that won't fix anything. It will make you feel better for a moment, but over time it will drain you and everyone who has happened to stick around this long. You become people poison."

I hold up my hands. "Whatever. " I turn toward the door.

"Stop! You want help with the settlement; that's the only reason you're here."

"Bingo." This feels like the times in grade school when I'd meet Joey Belingheri behind the bleachers and buy candy for class.

"You want my real story. The whole truth and nothing but the truth, not Bette's edited versions." Lindsay looks down at her feet and twists her foot to gaze upon her stiletto before she looks back. "If you'll commit to us, to this group"—she points back at the door—"for two more weeks so you can see how these women can help you, I will tell you everything. You think you're going to be fine on your own, but Haley, we know better. Even if you think we're beyond strange, give us a chance, won't you?"

"Why?" I narrow my eyes, trying to muster as much severity as I can. As I said, I look like Gwyneth Paltrow, so I'm not exactly frightening. "I've had my life ripped away from me and have no choice in the matter. My mother is trying to set me up with a window salesman, and the simple fact is, he's too good for me. Do you have anything that can make me feel happy about that? And is it legal?"

Lindsay looks back toward the room again and puts her arm on my shoulder for a moment. "Let's go get a coffee. I'll tell you what you need to know." She halts. "If you promise to come back next week. And the next."

"You're blackmailing me? With Bible study? Is that even allowed?"

She shrugs. "Take it up with God." She shimmies out the exit and turns around like a runway model. "You coming?"

I sigh. "I'm coming."

Just as I get to the doorway, the door swings open, and my worst fear comes to fruition. It's Hamilton Lowe, lawyer to the dogs. My dog, in particular. The one who knows that my husband hates me so much that he spent hard-earned cash to get away from me. I feel as though I'm standing here naked as he looks me up and down.

"Haley"—he shifts unnaturally—"what are you doing here?"

"Nothing," I whisper. "I'm at church. Is that against any stipulation in the contract?"

"Of course not," he says in far too cheery a voice. "I'm just happy to see you here, that's all. Maybe slightly surprised."

"The Trophy Wives Club. You invited me, remember?"

He looks to Lindsay, and his smile disappears. "Of course, I didn't think—"

"Come on, Haley. Hamilton is one of those never-been-married types who is too good for rabble like us." Lindsay clasps my wrist.

"Lindsay," Hamilton says smoothly, "I said I was sorry. Aren't you ever going to forgive me? It's your Christian duty."

Lindsay narrows her smoky blue eyes. "Probably not. If I were you, I wouldn't be preaching on duty, Hamilton. You don't want to pass by the hallway now." She leans in close. "You might get a little divorce on your sleeve. It's in the air, you know." Lindsay's eyes flash for a moment, and she takes her hand and brushes Hamilton's lapel. "A scarlet A would look mighty fine there."

"Ladies." He nods, his gaze landing squarely on me. "Haley. Always a pleasure."

"Pompous, arrogant—" Lindsay says under her breath as she exits, then rests her gaze on me. "Sorry about that. We have a personality clash. These things will happen, you know."

"What was that about?" I can see Hamilton's frame through the glass cutout in the door, and his straight, upright gait slows as he turns and looks back toward me, though I know he can't see anything out here in the dark. "I thought I was the only person who saw through Hamilton's charms."

"Hamilton has charms? They must be lost under his cloud of righteousness."

"You really don't like him." *Delicious.* Maybe I spoke out of turn when I said Lindsay had issues. I know, at the very least, she has good taste.

"Hamilton found out about our group. We're like AA. We don't publicize ourselves, and you have to be recommended to the group via a flyer to come. They're numbered."

See? I didn't just imagine the underground AA thing. "It's as secretive as all that? What are you afraid of?" Currently, I'm afraid of it too. Is some whacked-out husband going to come in shooting first and asking questions later?

"We're not afraid of anything. There's a divorce care group, and we started out there, but we found out we didn't really fit there. We would mention how the divorce came to be, and get these blank stares like we were from another planet. The age difference was one thing. The financial settlement another."

"What do you mean?"

"We were younger for the most part—than the other divorcees." She pauses. "Thinner."

"Ah, the other women didn't like you in the group." I roll my eyes.

"No, it was more that these men who were down on their luck and anxious to get back in a relationship were working it hard. Bette suggested a few of us start a new group. So we could get healthy without getting a spouse." She giggles.

"Underground church. Very cool."

"Not really. Nothing we do is all that cool. Hamilton had tried to stop our group, which of course made us women bond. It's not like we had a great love for men at the time anyway. But Hamilton said the church shouldn't support women who have left their covenant of marriage. And he was totally serious! The unforgivable sin, you know. He, who makes men rich when they abandon *their* covenants. It's disgusting. The pastor made him repent and pass out numbered flyers at his work. Since then, he acts like all of us have cooties and he's doing the devil's work with the flyers. But so far, you're the only one, so I can't see that it's bothering him too much."

Hamilton meets a woman in the hallway, and I watch them meet and flirt like they're in fifth grade. "Run, girlfriend, run!" I say to the closed door.

Lindsay scans me under the orange parking lot glow. "You're probably part of his penance, and now he has to feel guilty all over again." She starts to laugh. "Payback really is a female dog."

"I thought you said the class didn't accept man-bashing."

"Hamilton Lowe is different. He's a toad. One of those self-righteous, religious types who believe women are to blame for all things inherently evil in the world, and men are their innocent victims. I suppose it's not his fault for all the lies he believes daily. We're all harlots, you know. I think he lives to tell you the story of Eve eating the forbidden fruit first."

My eyes are as wide as saucers. I don't think the level of my anger against Jay quite rises to the heights of how Lindsay feels about Hamilton. Of course, that might help me in the long run, but even when Hamilton Lowe was asking me to sign my husband's rights back, he was never anything but polite. Maybe that's my problem. Maybe I'm too swayed by polite. Jay was always polite too, as he politely told me what to do and even where I could find my things after he'd tossed them out of the house.

Chapter 5

"Hop in." Lindsay chirps a BMW. I climb in, remembering just for a moment how luxury feels.

"Nice car. You get this in the settlement?" I ask.

"Not that it's any of your business, but yes I did."

"You don't pull any punches, do you? I thought people who went to a Bible study were generally nicer."

"If you want nice, wait for Bette. I'm having a bad day, but what can I say, I felt for you. Bette didn't get you. She's a great leader. Sweet and sincere as they come, but sometimes, she forgets what it's like on the outside because she really does see only the good in people. There's a lot of bad people, even in the church. Heck, sometimes especially in the church, but you can't let that dissuade you from seeing the good in life. We live in Southern California! Some people are neck deep in snow right now. We're getting our full count of vitamin D all winter long. Know what I'm saying?"

"Not really, no," I say, not feeling an ounce of gratitude and really bearing no guilt for it either.

"Convertible weather all year long; the Pacific Ocean with buff men in shorts; South Coast Plaza, the mother ship of shopping; Hollywood; entertainment capital of the world . . . these are a few of my favorite things!" Lindsay breaks into song.

"You're really a warped person, aren't you?"

"I *so* am! And don't act like you're not. Everyone acts like they're not and it just makes them more fun to tease. Remember this, no one ever actually graduates from the seventh grade. In our heart of hearts, we are the tiny, self-conscious geeks we were then, everything is just a façade."

"Your point? This conversation is making me question my sanity." Not that I have a great deal of it.

"My point is, no one really cares what anyone thinks. They only care what everyone thinks, and they dive into the pool that is the majority. You've got more of a brain than that, Haley, and that's why you don't fit in. The same reason I didn't fit in with all the wives whose lifetime job it is to ensure that their husbands come home at night because they can't trust them on their own."

"So what happened with you? If you have it all together. Why'd you marry a man who would kick you to the curb?"

She settles back into her driver's seat and extends her lanky limb to the stick shift. "Stupid choices. Some days I felt as dumb as a hamster. I just kept spinning on my wheel, hoping I'd get to a new place where I felt like all the other wives, who had it all together. I'm so grateful that ride is over." She gazes absently at the road.

"Are we having a conversation? Or are you just talking to yourself?"

She laughs. "Sorry, I was thinking that seeing you shows that the old feelings don't go away. I can go right back to that place where I feel out of control."

"There was this one time," I share. "When I felt on top of everything in the house. I felt like it was always clean when he came home, like I could stage a great dinner party at a moment's notice and knew what fragrance to put on, but inevitably, something was wrong. The hand towels in the guest bathroom weren't right for the event. That moment was fleeting. The right woman would have known and done it right."

She nods. "When I would look at my girlfriend, and I would see her husband come home from work, he was genuinely happy to see her. She'd have some bowl of slop in the slow cooker, and he'd beam like she'd made him a three-course meal naked. That is when I knew something was missing, and I would never get it right. It's all good until you know what you're missing. That's why the Bible says not to compare, I suppose." Lindsay gives a sneer. "She drove a Hyundai and lived in fifteen hundred square feet—that was the size of my closet. At the time, I thought how jealous of me she must have been." She snickers. "I came to find out she and her husband were praying for me to find unconditional love in Christ."

"When I noticed those happy couples around me, I thought it was just an act. They were better actors than us."

"Okay, we're getting way too depressed. Let's get a nonfat mocha!" she says with glee. "With whipped cream."

"Because we can."

"Because we always could and didn't know it."

The Coffee Bean & Tea Leaf is close enough that we should have walked. I imagine if Lindsay weren't wearing stilettos, we might have, but she locks the car door with a punch of a button, and we enter the empty shop.

"Two nonfat mochas. With whipped cream," she says as though she were placing her order for contraband. "Large. And don't skimp on the whipped cream."

The baby-faced guy behind the counter is rendered speechless and motionless while Lindsay speaks. I hadn't really noticed how truly beautiful she was until I watched this poor kid's reaction. His hand is suspended midair, his mouth awestruck as he tries to remember her order.

"Mochas. Nonfat. Whipped Cream," Lindsay repeats slowly. I imagine she's used to this.

I take out my wallet, and Lindsay pushes it toward my purse. "It's on me. It's the least I can do." The cashier finally recalls his brain and punches in the order, holding out his hand for the cash. Lindsay hands him a credit card. "Keep a record of everything," she tells me. "Every expenditure. If you have to, put the cash in an envelope and don't use credit. The payouts will feel huge until you start to live. Rent. Cha-ching. Grocery store. Cha-ching. Hair salon. Cha-ching. Cha-ching."

"I'm going back to my natural color," I tell her.

"I don't even remember what mine is."

"Do you ever want to be married again?"

The cashier jumps to attention. Lindsay ponders the question, focusing on a box of Ceylon tea. "Yeah, I think when I understand God more. When I'm healthier. Maybe."

"What do you mean understand God more?"

"This whole unconditional love thing, I'm still working it out for myself. People have higher expectations than God. If I can find someone who understands I'm not perfect . . . maybe . . . yeah, maybe. I wouldn't rule it out, but I would have to rework my entire notion of marriage, and I'm not ready for that."

"Bette never married again?"

She shakes her head. "It's too bad, really. She'd make a great wife. She's a widow you know. Not divorced."

"No, I didn't know."

"This is Trophy Wives Knowledge, so you can't use any of it."

I look around me, wondering exactly who I'd tell. "Didn't you tell me I was friendless?"

"Let's get a table."

"Why doesn't she want people to tell their real stories?" I ask.

"Bette is afraid of the truth sometimes. It's not her fault. She fears if she gets in touch with her anger, it will start all over again. She's worked hard to look at life through rose-colored glasses, and it's for real, but she hates conflict and wants her little chicks to fly again."

"It doesn't seem like the group would be that much help with her in charge."

"She's at her worst when we get someone new. She wants to teach everyone else how to live. She means well, but avoiding the emotions doesn't help most of us. The only way out is through the valley, unfortunately. We have to go in. We all come with a lot of anger, Haley. You're not alone."

"Did Bette's husband die recently?"

"She was a widow at thirty-four."

"She's upset by that?"

"Well, yeah. Believe it or not, most women consider that a tragedy. Just not us."

"I'm just clarifying, that's all."

"She's made peace with God that it was his time to go. She doesn't believe in remarriage, so she's devoted her life to making sure other women appreciate the men in their lives."

"Do we have to appreciate the ones who aren't in our lives?"

"She teaches a Bible study for 'real' married women, for people with healthy issues that can be solved. And then ours, which is for those of us in the process of rebuilding our self-esteem and our ministries."

"We're the troubled children."

"Precisely."

"I was always the good kid at home. How utterly ironic."

"Probably too good. You didn't learn to voice your opinion."

"I voice it now," I claim.

"A day late and a dollar short."

"True, but in my defense, when you live with someone who doesn't care what you think, you begin to question everything."

"So you have to get healthy. That's the point of the group."

"I'm healthy. I just lost 175 pounds of ugly."

"You'd be surprised how much ugly stays with you until you give it over to God."

"What's with the God stuff? You really believe that?"

"I know it's true, Haley. He loved me until I could love myself. I'm not good at explaining it. I'm only saying give it a shot before you decide it's like all the other self-help hocus-pocus."

Our drinks are called out, and the cashier goes beyond the call of duty and brings them to our table in tall glasses. He's probably ensuring his view won't leave anytime soon with a plastic cup. "Anything else?" He smiles.

"How old are you?" Lindsay asks.

"Age is just a number. I like older women."

"Well, if I see any, I'll let you know."

"I brought you a biscotti. It's on the house."

"Do you see this ring?" She holds up a gigantic cushion-cut diamond ring in a gleaming, pavé setting.

"You're married. It figures."

"I'm not married."

"Cool," he says as though it's a come-on.

"I'd love to tell you about my relationship with the One True God. Jesus is my husband now. That's why I still wear the ring."

He claps his hands together. "Enjoy the cookie."

Lindsay lifts her glass. "Cheers to your new life and learning to embrace it."

I lift my glass, reluctant to cheer something so miserable. She nudges the glass again, and I lift mine. "To a new and undefined future." I feel a lump rise up in my throat, like a whole, dry biscotti.

She holds up her ring again. "Jesus will be faithful to me always. A soft place to fall. That's what you need, Haley. A soft place to fall, so you can trust again, and He is forever faithful."

"Faithful. What does that even mean in Hollywood? That the alimony checks come on time?"

Chapter 6

I woke up this morning and gazed at my enormous wedding ring in an entirely new light. Being in a cheap motel, which accepts cash payment, it wasn't a great light either. In the back of my naïve mind, I always believed the woman with the biggest diamond was the most loved. In my case, it was about being the lead dog at the golf club. I never was good at math, and in this equation, I was downright ignorant. Or as Lindsay might say, dumb as a hamster. But today, I realize the size of that ring actually does give me power. I'm going to sell it and embrace my singleness.

I scamper out of bed to the mirror and try to yank the sucker off, but it won't come off for anything! I unwrap the minisoap and lather up my finger under the running water. "Come on, come on!"

Great. I think my hand is swollen. It looks like an uncooked chicken sausage topped with an obnoxious, gleaming diamond in the center. Not attractive. I lather up again, getting a good, sudsy layer of bubbles and grunt again as I try to pull. Nothing.

I catch a glimpse of myself in the bathroom mirror that's covered with someone else's toothpaste splatterings. *Ewww.* But what I notice, besides that, is my eyes look their normal size.

I didn't cry myself to sleep last night for the first time in months. From the time Jay went international, traveling to Monaco without me and, I guess more importantly, with Rachel. My eyeballs don't look like they're wrapped in two slices of raw bacon. That's progress. I do wish, however, I'd had my eyelashes dyed before I became an overnight credit risk. It looks like I'm sporting albino spiders—a fashion risk.

The motel phone rings, and I take my soggy finger and dry it on a board stiff towel. "Hello?"

"Haley, is that you?"

"Yes, who is this?"

"It's Bette, dear. From last night."

"Hi . . . Bette." I gaze at the phone. "How did you know where to find me?"

"Lindsay told me where you'd checked in. I must say, it's not a very good neighborhood. Do you need a place to stay, dear?"

"Um no . . . thank you. This place is fine. Free toothpaste and everything. My first settlement check should be arriving soon, and I'll move then." Yes, I have the financial ability to move now, just not the will. What if I run into someone I know? I shouldn't have told Lindsay where I was staying. I don't want to admit I have all this cash and no credit in my name.

"You're probably wondering why I called you so early."

It crossed my mind. "No, it's nice to hear from you." Anyone actually.

"We do this silly little thing," she goes on. "I'm almost embarrassed to tell you how it got started, but we were sitting around one evening, and we started lamenting how there just wasn't enough time in the day to do it all. Then, someone brought up how Jesus took time to wash the disciples' feet . . . and well, we have this monthly tradition where we meet at a pedicure spa and have our nails done and fellowship. There's no religious significance to it, it's just a chance for us to gab. I wanted to invite you for next week."

"Oh—"

"It's on Tuesday afternoons. We meet at Perfect Nail in Brentwood. Do you know the place? On San Vicente?"

"I do." I look down at my sausage finger. "Maybe I'll come."

"Two o'clock, next Tuesday. We hope to see you there. Do you have a cell number, Haley? So I don't have to track you down if you change motels, and I do advise that you consider changing to a hotel. A young woman like yourself should be in a hotel, where the access to the rooms is limited."

"Yes, ma'am. But I'm afraid Jay may turn off my service any day. I'll need to restart it."

"You do need to restart, Haley. Write down my number, in case you need anything."

"I don't think—"

"Haley, quit being so ridiculously stubborn and write down my phone number. Don't make me come down there!"

"Let me get a pen." I fumble at the desk. "Go ahead."

"It's 310–555–5674."

"I've got it." I scribble down the numbers, knowing I will never have any use for it but worried that I don't want to suffer Bette's wrath and have her come get me either.

"I'll call to remind you about the foot-washing ceremony." She laughs at her little joke, as though a church group getting pedicures is scandalous in nature. "Take care, Haley."

"You too, Bette. Thanks for calling."

Maybe the Trophy Wives Club helped in its own way. It felt

n getting invited to something again. Remember the days when everyone would get an invitation to a birthday party, and you'd be sitting there envelope-less? That's been my life in Hollywood. I suppose that's why I learned to throw such great parties—so I'd actually get to attend. Anyway, Lindsay really did seem to have some good information on renegotiating. I've made an appointment with Hamilton for next Tuesday.

My ring finally comes off and leaves a red indent where it sat for so many years. It clinks into the sink, but since it's so huge the catch stops it. The gem sits at the bottom of the scratched porcelain bowl, and I can't help but marvel at the dichotomy.

I rinse it off and hold it up to the mirror, watching it glisten under the fluorescent lighting that makes me a sallow shade of yellow. The diamond is incredible. No one can fix this situation but me. I ran Jay's life. He didn't just run mine.

And yet I'm here whining about not having a cell phone? Who picked the plan in the first place? The ring holds dozens of possibilities.

"I'll say one thing for you, Jay, you sure knew how to buy jewelry."

My father always said this rock could choke a horse, and whether or not that's true, it can't go down a cheap motel sink. Big stones have their privileges, but sadly one of them is not, she who has the biggest stone is loved the most.

I unwrap one of my outfits from the dry cleaner and slide into some fuchsia wedges I bought last spring at Bloomingdale's. My hands look like Scarlett's been out doing field work again, but I haven't got time to fix them. I think about checking out of the motel, though I don't know where I'll sleep tonight, but Bette's words suddenly brought up *Thelma & Louise* for me, and I imagine it isn't the best place for my budget. Especially without Louise.

Maybe I'll go higher end tonight after pocketing a little cash from the ring. I have to admit, I've been taking pride in being the victim. Driving a bucket of bolts rental car, staying in the cheap motel, it all makes Jay look like a bigger jerk, and I think I've derived a little pleasure from that scenario.

Arriving at Rodeo Drive feels different when you're not in a Porsche. I must admit, I never shopped here, even with money. It felt like such an obnoxious waste of money, and I never was into name brands. I suck in a deep breath and press the button to enter an estate shop. They check me out and decide I look innocuous. My hands are trembling under the weight of this task.

I'm buzzed in (I dressed well knowing I had to get in). No ratty tennis shoes today, though I couldn't feel much more ratty myself. To enter a high-end jewelry store by oneself tells a tale no one wants to tell. The shop is incredible, filled with baubles and precious gems from decades and centuries gone by. I have to wonder if each piece tells the story of a great love affair or a cold marriage of status. The classical piano in the background makes you believe it's the former, but of course, that's their job—to sell jewelry, am I right? Who wants to buy anything from a trophy marriage gone awry?

"Good morning, Miss. Are we looking for anything in particular today?" A man with an English accent greets me. He's Indian and has a strong, Bollywood chin. He could make a tax bill read aloud sound elegant. He's wearing a silk tie and a sharp suit, most likely from Europe.

"I'm wondering if you might help me. I'm here to see if there's some interest in my wedding ring." I hold up the ring.

"Do you have papers with it?"

I nod and pull the gold envelope from my handbag. It contains all the GIA information on my diamond and a diagram of the stone, showing its flawless credentials. He looks it over and back at me.

"You know I can't pay you what this is really worth. Maybe an auction might be the better avenue for you." He hands the jewel back to me.

I shake my head. "Too much effort." *Too much humiliation*. "I'm anxious to get rid of it privately."

"There are some fine auctions in town where your name needn't be announced, and they might be able to make special arrangements to do this quickly."

"The diamond is quite famous among my husband's colleagues. I prefer to do the transaction this way if you don't mind."

"If I can just examine the piece, my manager can create an offer and you can let us know if it's agreeable to you." He takes out his professional loupe and gazes into the diamond. "There's not a flaw in this diamond. I thought perhaps the GIA technician missed something." He sounds amazed.

"There is, it's just very slight. You'll see that on the documentation. It's not visible to the human eye."

"It's barely visible with the loupe. It's a gorgeous stone."

"The diamond's nearly flawless. There's just a giant flaw in the man who gave it to me." I laugh lightheartedly, refusing to acknowledge the pain underneath. "She weighs about 110 pounds."

"Well, you know what they say. Some men compensate with big cars, others with big diamonds." He smiles. "Do you mind if I take the ring back to the manager? I know he'll be quite anxious to see it. It's not often we see a diamond of this size in the cushion cut without flaws."

"No, take your time, I'll just look around." I wander through the glass cases, focusing on the elegant jewelry and electric sparkles coming from the backlit boxes. The security guard, a giant black man with a gun, smiles at me, and I smile back. I glimpse at all the unspoken promises here in the form of sapphires, rubies, and, naturally, diamonds. The cases are sparse, to allow a connoisseur to appreciate the fine Victorian, Edwardian, and Art Deco pieces.

I gaze at it all like a museum, admiring the beauty of the artwork but knowing its acquisition wouldn't change my life one iota. I think everyone should be wealthy at least once for that very reason, so you know if you're not content poor, you will not be content rich.

Lying in the back of the case like a sick afterthought, I spy Jay's wedding ring, and my heart pounds. I bend over the case and squint to see if it's really his ring and I see the engraving I had placed inside the ring. *To my beloved. Always.* The thought that he beat me here gives him the last word. A last word I'm not willing to let him have.

The Englishman comes out of the back room, his mouth straight. He holds up my ring, now shined to perfection, it glimmers like the North Star on the darkest night. "I cleaned it for you." He hands it back to me.

"Did you get a price?"

"I did, but I can't ethically allow you to sell it here. It's worse than I thought. You need to take it to auction. My boss is only willing to pay $12,000 for the ring; it has to be worth at least $20,000 at auction, $50,000 retail. My price is barely what a pawnshop might present you."

"I have to rent an apartment this afternoon, and I need what money I have to save for a down payment. I'm blathering, but I'm not proud, I need the capital. Just give me the money."

"I'm afraid I won't let you sell it here." He puts the ring in my hand and closes my grip. "I'll give you the name of someone reputable, and they'll handle it quickly and discreetly." I nod and place the diamond ring on my hand. The money from the car will have to do for now, but then I focus on Jay's ring again, and something snaps.

"Excuse me, can I see this ring here in the case?"

"The man's ring?"

I nod.

"It's Van Cleef & Arpels, very tasteful. Brushed platinum. Comfort fit. It has a Ceylon sapphire in it; a very rare one, which was the original owner's birthstone. It makes it quite unique. Is there someone you're thinking about for the piece?"

"No. I mean, there was. I used the money I'd saved for college to buy it once upon a time. How much is it?"

He looks me over. "It's fifteen hundred."

"I'll take it." *Again.*

"Will you need it sized?"

"It fits him now." It dawns on me how I came in here to make money, and I'm leaving with a purchase I can't pay for. "I'd like to sell my ring here, and purchase this with the money you'll give me for my ring."

"I've already told you, Miss—"

"Cutler. Mrs. Jay Cutler. The customer is always right, correct?" *Perhaps sadistic and slightly vengeful, but always right.*

He leans over the glass counter. "I'll have a check cut for you this afternoon and an agreement to sign, but you must know what I think of this. I'll not have it on my conscience." I slide my ring off and he puts it into a small envelope and labels it. "Let me give you a receipt for the ring before you go." He pulls Jay's ring out of the case. "Take this ring. Trust me, you've more than paid for it."

I clasp my hand around Jay's ring. "Really?"

"Come back after two for your check." He writes on a carbon piece of paper and rips off a receipt for me. "Bring this with you when you come. It's a pleasure doing business with you."

I clutch the piece of paper and the ring. "Who may I thank for this?"

"Nigel. The name is Nigel George."

"Thank you, Nigel; your kindness means a lot to me."

"I do wish you'd wait to sell that piece. It's an incredible stone and though Mr. Cutler may not be my favorite client, he certainly has good taste in rings. And wives."

"He's traded down, I'm afraid." This makes me giggle.

Nigel laughs aloud. "He has, and should he come in here, I'll make certain to help him accordingly."

"Oh yes, please do. Make sure her ring is just one-tenth of a carat smaller than mine. Better yet, try to sell that one to him, I doubt he'd remember he already paid for it once."

"Wait on this. Please." He holds up my ring. "You would receive quite a bit more money for it at auction."

"Money never solved any problems for me, Nigel, it only created new and more elaborate ones. This amount will get me back on my feet." I hold up the receipt. "I am suddenly my own boss."

Nigel puts Jay's ring in a fancy velvet box, and I shove it into my purse. "If you change your mind," he says, with his brow lifted, "you have thirty days to return the funds from your diamond."

"Like a high-end pawnshop?"

"That deal is only valid for you, because I don't take advantage of my customers. You'll remember that someday when you're back on your feet."

And with that accent, I find myself hoping he would take advantage. "Thank you, Nigel."

"Like I said, it's been my pleasure, Mrs. Cutler."

"I don't usually like that name for myself, but in your accent, it sounds quite natural."

"May God bless you, Mrs. Cutler."

Did he just say what I thought he did? We share a moment, and I feel my confidence bolster just an inch or so. I walk toward the glass door, and I swear, I'm just about to walk into it, thinking about that English accent and the weird encounters with everyone talking about God. No one talks about God in this town unless it's followed by a curse word. The security guard catches me and puts me back on the right path by stepping in front of me and opening the door.

"Thank you," I say, looking back at Nigel. My face flushes fuchsia like my shoes as he smiles at me. Clearly, my head is still in the clouds—ever so slightly.

As of this afternoon, Haley Cutler is back. And she's ready to shop!

Chapter 7

Against my better judgment, which indicates I have some, and I'm not certain that I do, I drive by the house . . . My house . . . My former house . . . Jay's house.

I'm in my junker, the rental car. I'm sure there are neighbors calling the police right now because a car worth less than $45,000 has entered the neighborhood, and I'm no one's maid. *Red Alert! Red Alert!*

When I was a child, I used to wonder what it was like to live in a house like this. How anyone cleaned it! (My mom informed me people who owned houses like that had maids.) I couldn't imagine the luxury of having someone else clean your house. It was unfathomable to me—and perhaps why I never learned to clean myself. Maybe I did have aspirations to be a trophy wife.

I pull up to the quaint gate, created to look like a home-style white picket fence, but as it slides into the property-surrounding wall, it's apparent to all, it's an iron security gate, not small town

Americana. I punch in the security code and it's just as I suspected. Without someone (me) to tell the staff to change the number, it's still the same. Which I actually take as a compliment. At least Jay isn't worried about me returning and stalking him. Though since I am here, maybe he should be.

As the gate slides open smoothly, my conscience tells me to turn around, but I always listened to my conscience, and look where it got me!

I pull up to the house, parking the sputtering junker in the middle of the two cars in the brick driveway, both new to me, and for a split second, I worry he's sold the house and never told me. One of the cars is a white 700 series Beemer and the other a small, black Porsche Carerra. I love seeing my Korean rental smack-dab in the middle of them.

I actually wish I had a camera. Wouldn't it make a great tabloid shot? My little economy car in the middle of their high-end vehicles? It's so symbolic, so Freudian!

I wander up the step, and I'm about to open the door. My stomach churns, and though I know better, I turn the door handle. My first crime, and it feels delightful!

The alarm sounds, and I quickly punch in the code and turn it off before the whole house system sounds. Jay always did miss the details. Change the locks, but not the codes and leave the front door unlocked. It's all the same scenario. Get married, tell the wife how to act and be, ignore any form of relationship.

Rosario instantly appears, shaking her head. "No, no. You shouldn't be here," she says, wagging her forefinger at me. "Go home."

"I have no home. Is he here, Rosario?" I scan around her.

She comes beside me and lowers her voice, "No, he's not here, but *she* is here. Very messy girl." Rosario gives her tsk-tsk sound. "Why do you want to come here?"

I hold up the ring box. "I have something that belongs to Jay."

"Go home, sweetie."

I feel the fight rise within me, and when I stop to realize *she's* in my house, this ugly, jealous green monster comes bubbling up as well. "Is he going to marry her?"

"I think so, yes." She says this as gently as possible, but I feel it like a knock to the gut. The woman who stole my husband and my life is in my home and I'm being asked to leave. "She has left bridal magazines all over the house. She is very valuable to him right now. It will pass, Haley. You know it will."

"Where's Darcy?" I ask, looking for my cat. "He didn't even let me get her, you know."

"Mr. Cutler put her outside."

"Just like me. She can't live outside. She's an indoor cat! She's been pampered her whole life, and he had her declawed."

"You are surviving. Darcy will too. You're both tougher than you look."

"Rosario, I think I've been reclawed, not declawed. Will you find the cat for me before I leave?" I walk toward the family room. "I'll be nice."

Rosario tugs at my arm. "He'll arrest you, Mrs. Haley, and fight for what little he gave you."

I turn on my heel. "How do you know he gave me little?"

She purses her lips. "He signs my paychecks, doesn't he?"

I run my finger along the foyer marble table. "Do you like her?"

"In my country, we have names for women like her, and they are not welcome in good society, not that my town has much good society, but she wouldn't be welcome there, regardless. But I need this job, so I smile and clean up after her dirty self. Does that answer your question?"

"I want to see her." I try to pull my arm away.

Rosario shakes her head. "Why, Miss Haley? She's not a nice person. She'll only hurt you more. You just need to move on and be happy. You weren't happy here. I'll get Darcy, and you two go and be happy." I keep walking, and Rosario tugs again. "She has to stay here with him, do you really think she'll find happiness?"

I square my shoulders. "Not if I can help it. I'll leave, Rosario. After I see her. I don't know why I want to look in the casket either, but it provides closure, I suppose. I want to see her." I march resolutely into the family room. It looks the same, its bleached wood beams and the casual elegance of the buff colors against the backdrop of a huge fireplace. The designer charged us a fortune to make the room look as nondescript as a psychologist's office.

"That's not beige, Mr. Cutler. It's Sahara sand," she'd said.

"It's ugly," I said.

"Mr. Cutler"—the designer took him aside—"no offense to you, sir, but your wife is young and I am a professional with twenty years' experience."

"And yet still only twenty yourself," I snapped back at her. But I have to give her credit, she realized who was boss.

I was excused about then. To brighten up the Sahara sand, our professional also brought in Burnt Ivory and Tawny Amber. Also known to you and me as beige number two and three. There's a giant screen that comes down from the ceiling. Jay has used it many times to screen his new movies for friends. *Colleagues.* I'm not sure we had what you would call friends. So why am I here, like a stupid lab rat who knows the way out?

"I don't think we ever lit that fireplace," I say absently, as I see Rachel sitting on the custom-made down sofa. It looks thirty years old already and it's only been here about three years. So much for quality. "I suppose there's not much use for fireplaces in Brentwood, is there? Odd that this place has four of them."

Rachel, my nemesis, stands and yarn drops on the sofa. She knits. How cozy. I have to admit, it gives me a little pleasure to see her keeping herself busy, like I always had to do because Jay was never around. That scarf will grow mighty long.

"What are you doing here?" She bolts away from the sofa, holding her knitting needles out like tiny swords.

"Great moves. Did you learn that as an extra on that Korean soap opera?"

"Did Rosario let you in? I knew I should have fired that girl. Of course she'd be loyal to you and betray me!"

"Betray you? Rosario? I think if you want to look for betrayal, you might think about calling here late at night asking *my* husband for assistance. Then, luring him to a foreign country into your lair. Is that the kind of betrayal you're speaking of? I was nice to you, Rachel. When everyone told me you were a no-talent hack, I stood up for you. I told Jay you deserved a second chance."

"It's not like that. You make it sound cheap!"

"No, cheap is posing topless on free Web sites. Plotting to take someone's husband borders on psychotic." I look over and see my picture is still on the mantel. "He'll never notice these pictures, you'll have to remove them yourself if you want them gone. I can't say I'd want to stare at a picture of you, so go ahead, take them down. You took the real thing down without much guilt. I don't see why you'd be stymied by a photograph."

"I do want them gone. Rosario!" she yells. Her voice is trembling. Her reaction calms me.

"Rosario didn't let me in; you haven't changed the codes, and the front door was unlocked. You'll have to do all that, you know. Jay just works. That's what he does. This house is your job. The parties are your job. He's missing the protective gene, so if you think he'll shelter you in any way, shape, or form, you're in for a world of hurt."

She backs up. I like that I scare her. For a brief blip in time, I feel powerful. "What do you want? If you want the pictures, take them!" she says in a panicked voice.

"I don't want anything," I reply in monotone, running my fingers along the mantel. "I actually came to give back something that belongs to Jay."

"Then leave it and get out." Her eyes go panic-stricken again. "Wait a minute, what is it?"

"Tsk. Tsk. One of the first things you'll have to learn as Mrs. Cutler is how to be sweet, even when people are rude to you, or you don't like them. It's simply not your right to have an opinion on someone. You probably haven't learned that being in the movies."

"Why would you come here?"

"I wanted to congratulate you on your Golden Globe," I quip, as I take the coveted statue in my hand.

"Put that down," she says with an outstretched arm. "It just happened. I never meant to end up with a married man. Sometimes, things are meant to be. Jay and I we're just—we're just soul mates, all right?"

"Jay doesn't have a soul. Maybe you don't either, and you're right, huh? Two soul mates without souls. How touching." I sigh, putting the coveted statue back on the mantel. "People are such victims these days. No personal responsibility. They can't help themselves." I look down at the coffee table. "You have to change the magazines out to keep them current. Rosario won't get rid of them unless you tell her to, in case you're saving an article. Sometimes Jay gets ideas for films from articles."

"Thanks for the tip." She's walking toward the phone as though she's invisible, and I can't see her.

"Who are you going to call, Rachel? Technically, you're in my husband's house, and I'm not going to hurt you, though I have to admit that would make very good tabloid material. A right pretty penny in my pocket. Go ahead, call. Personally, I think I could take you down pretty easily. You keep your figure by being twenty, I work for mine." I curl up my biceps for her perusal.

"Rosario!" Rachel calls. "Rosario!"

"Paparazzi are like vultures, and they're only around when you don't want them. I'll hold up the statue like I'm going to hit you with it. That is supermarket cover material!"

"You're legally separated, getting a divorce, whatever. Don't worry about me handling things, all right? I'm not like you, Haley. I have a career." She shakes her dark hair. "I have the intellect you lacked. That's why he left you, you know. He said you never thought for yourself, and he couldn't think for two any longer."

"Because every time I did think for myself, it ended up in three rounds. I'm not really much for conflict. And please. You're not trying to tell me you have the IQ of a genius, are you? I would think most geniuses know better than to take their clothes off on Web sites and call it a career."

"Get out of this house now! In case that statue doesn't tell you, I'm a serious actor!"

"Right. I could tell." At the moment, I feel like I could step into any heel and not come within a square mile of a wall! "You could have any man you wanted, why him? Did he write a big check to your favorite charity, make you think he'd meet your every need?" I flop on the couch and casually stretch out my arms. "He will, you know. He'll meet absolutely every need. Your wish is his command until he gets what he wants. You're nothing more than a conquest to him. Do you see that chair over there?" I point to the King Louis replica. "He'll look at you soon, just like he looks at that chair. An inanimate object."

"It's like Jay says, you didn't appreciate him." Rachel sounds more desperate than ever. "He wants to be needed, appreciated. All men do. You were too busy running off to the gym or getting your nails done. What kind of woman cares more about her appearance than her own husband?"

I let out a laugh. "I suppose the same kind who is told she's only valuable for her looks."

"When that's all you've got—what else is he supposed to compliment you on?"

"Didn't they teach you anything in that modeling school about men like Jay? It's always someone else's fault. Soon, he'll have you to blame, and I'll look like the sainted ex-wife. Mark my words, Rachel. You'll envy me one day because I'm free."

"Stop it." She points to the door. "I want you out of here. Jay said you were a psycho, and he's right."

"He probably is, but he had a good part in making me that way. Just like Norman Bates's mother."

"Why would you want to be with a man who doesn't want you? You come around here like a lovesick puppy. This isn't your house!"

"I'll ask you the same question in a year, Rachel. Some days I feel happy to have escaped, and others I think about how I have nowhere to go because I slowly lost all my real friends to this life. If I can give you one piece of advice, it would be to keep your life."

"That's not Jay's fault that you have no life."

I look her straight in the eye. "I suppose it isn't." I study my fingernails and focus on the red dent where my wedding ring used to be. "You're very beautiful, Rachel, even in person. I'm sorry for you that it won't be enough. Although why you would pick such an older man, a B-list producer by tabloid standards." Sure, he makes money hand over fist, but the culture he brings is worse than what you find in yogurt.

"Jay said if you talk to them, the settlement is over. He told me, and he prepared for your games."

"Only because he doesn't trust his own shadow. The settlement is half what I'd get from the tabloids, by the way. That's hardly a threat. Do you realize that? That he offered less than the tabloids would pay for even a pseudosalacious story. For such a brilliant man, he could use a little help in the math department."

Her face stiffens, like she's been Botoxed. She's way too young to be Botoxed. The doctor who started that, saying young women could ward off aging, ought to be shot. I realize that I want her to experience a little terror, and I don't like that I'm capable of such emotions. But, I want her to feel what she's done to my security.

I pull Jay's wedding ring out of my pocket. "Jay lost this, and I found it for him. I thought he might want it back." I put it on the coffee table, and Rachel picks it up and throws it at me. I catch it like a second baseman.

"Get out!"

Rosario comes in the room, her voice stern. "You no belong here, Mrs. Cutler." Rosario always puts on the deep accent when it's convenient for her, but the truth is, she speaks perfect English without the slightest hint of an accent. She only uses it to her benefit and always around Jay. I smile subtly at her, grateful she's giving me the opportunity for a smooth exit.

"I'm leaving." I pick up the ring and glance at Rachel. "By the way, you can ask Martin how to change the code on the gates and the house, and it will be done before dark. Not that I'm coming back, but that might make you feel safer. You know what they say about a woman scorned." I allow my eyes to flash.

"He's mine now!" she hisses. "We'll be married the day he's free of you!"

"Gosh, I hope you can act better than that in the movies." I shake my head. "Pathetic, really. Not believable at all." I know she can act. I'm the one who cast her. Dang, I'm stupid.

I see the corner of Rosario's lip curve, and I make my way toward the front door. It's over. For some reason, I just needed to know that and feel it for myself. Okay, I'm good. Time to move on.

Apparently, Rachel isn't quite as ready. She lifts up a crystal globe that we picked up in Mexico and hurls at me. It hits the doorjamb and, rather than shattering, leaves a dent in the wall and bounces back onto the carpet, unfazed. "I knew that guy wasn't really selling us crystal. Jay paid $400 for a glorified paperweight."

"He's Oscar worthy, you know. You held him back. I'm going to take him to the top."

I feel like my heart, once clutched in pain, is free to beat again. Rachel's words go for the throat, but in actuality, they only highlight the truth that I ignored for so long. First, that without a writer, Rachel's an idiot, and second, that Jay never truly thought of me as a person. Naturally, he would think nothing of kicking me out on the street. In his mind, I was never actually here to begin with.

"Good luck, Rachel. I mean that."

"Luck has nothing to do with it, girlfriend." She snaps her fingers like she's watched one too many rap videos. "Rosario, call the police." She looks at me again. "You're not getting away with this. You just can't walk into a house in Brentwood and call the shots. Rosario, now."

Rosario stands there like she doesn't understand. I almost expect her to say, "*No Ingles.*" Eventually, she makes her way to the phone and picks it up, giving me ample time to walk out.

I jump into my car and dial Anna to tell her what I think of her. Once again, she won't take my calls, so I dial Lindsay. As sarcastic and bitter as she may be, she's also all that I've got. If you're judged by the company you keep, this is not a good sign for me.

"It's Haley Cutler. I went by the house," I confess.

"You went by, or you went in?" she asks. I thought she might say who is this, but like any good sponsor, she knows me immediately.

"I went in," I admit.

"Did you sneak in, or ring the doorbell?"

I pull the phone away and look at it. *How does she know this stuff?* "I snuck in. Turned the alarm off and everything."

She gasps. "Did you see him?"

"No, but I saw her, and I left his wedding ring there. I found it in a shop when I went in to sell mine."

"Did you get a good price?"

"Not really, but it's gone now and I'm happy about that. Emotionally it was weighing me down. "

"Haley, that's exactly what we were talking about last night. You can't make rash decisions!"

"It wasn't rash. It was for the cash. That shows forethought."

"I'll loan you the money until you sell it at auction. Go get it back!"

I ignore her. "I've stockpiled a lot. I just need to spend some now. It's disheartening. She's really a dim bulb, and she told me Jay left me because I wasn't smart enough for him."

"What did you expect her to say? You probably scared the life out of her."

"I wonder if that's what everyone thought about me, too."

"You sound different. You don't sound angry today."

"I just realized something."

"That you don't walk into ex-husband's houses unexpected?"

"Well, that too, but I realized I've been waiting my whole life for Prince Charming to rescue me."

"Uh-huh?"

"Today, I walked into a jewelry store, sold my ring, snuck into my old house, confronted the other woman, and I survived it all. I can do this myself. Rachel didn't wait for anyone to make her a princess." I feel my stomach roil as I envy Rachel. Not only because she's taken over my life, but that she had her own to begin with.

"Oh, I think she did let someone make her a princess," Lindsay quips. "It's better known in contemporary terms as the casting couch."

"It never dawned on me. I can do it myself. It's my mother's fault. Yes, I'm definitely blaming my mother. She brought me up believing that a man would make everything all better, and you know, I really love my father, but my mother is still dysfunctional with him in her life. She makes teddy bears out of old clothes and goes to a church where they talk to rocks—okay cement statues of saints, but still. Someone else is not going to fix my life."

"Oh Haley." Lindsay exhales in exaggerated form; it sounds like a whale coming up for air. "I thought you had a God moment. I'd hoped you were ready to be a daughter of the King. You know, a true princess."

"Yeah, right now I'm just blaming my mother."

"Well, when you get to the part where you blame yourself, give me a call, all right?"

"No, I'll admit I've gotten myself into this, but I'm going to get myself out, and it's not going to be with another man. See, my mom thinks another man can fix this. I know better now. It's time I made some big changes."

"It's too soon to make any major decisions. You don't want to do anything rash. Need I remind you that none of the women in our group have used another man to fix things? You think that's a coincidence?"

"I just need to get all this out of my system first."

"Haley, come stay with me. I have an extra room in my condo, and if you won't need rent for a while, maybe you won't do anything stupid. And don't forget the pedicure party next week! If you won't come for us, surely you have to get your feet buffed. It's approaching sandal season."

"Next week I'm making a little visit to our friend, Hamilton Lowe. Don't worry, I'm announced, and I have an appointment. I go next Tuesday to say my piece."

"Haley, no!" she says with all the emotion that our great actress friend, Rachel, lacks. "It's better to use your energy for good. Stay away from Hamilton."

I should. But I'm diving in. "In the words of the infamous Jay Cutler, if you want something done right, do it yourself."

Chapter 8

Hamilton Lowe looks up from his desk casually. His eyes linger a tad too long for someone completely oblivious to us trophy wives, and he slides back in his chair, dropping his pen in one, smooth movement. "Haley, right on time. Wonders never cease."

"Where's linen girl?"

"She quit."

"That was fast." I look out toward the foyer. "I hope your dates last longer than that."

"She was fearful an angry client was going to storm the office with a machine gun. I tried to talk some sense into her, but Hollywood violence makes it tough on a guy like me."

I raise my brows. "Hmm. A gun. I didn't think of that."

He laughs. "I'm thankful for that. You looking for a job?"

"Not the kind I have to sell my soul for, no."

It's odd how comfortable I am in Hamilton's office, considering what I think of the man. I suppose that comes from living in a cheap motel after a cold mausoleum for years. Anywhere you can hang your hat, feels like home. I position myself in a black leather chair and wait until I have his full attention. I've been ignored for nearly eight years, I'm not putting up with it from Jay's lawyer. He makes too much money to ignore me. He finally folds his hands and looks straight at me.

"What can I help you with today, Haley?"

"You act like you were expecting something from me."

"I was. Jay said you'd been harassing him. Apparently, you scared his girlfriend by entering the house uninvited and left his wedding ring for him. A wedding ring he personally sold."

"No, no. You make it sound like I went back trying to get my husband back."

"Didn't you?"

"Of course not! Do you think I'm stupid? Wait. Don't answer that."

"You do realize what you did, that's called breaking and entering?"

"I scared her? I don't know how I could have scared her. She had the weapons. She's the one sleeping with my husband!"

He sits back in his chair, crossing his arms. "Weapons?"

"Knitting needles. Two of them!" I can tell he's still not convinced. "They were the really big, sharp kind. A girl could do serious damage with them." I thrust my nails out like claws.

"She could have had a gun, and it would have been within her legal rights to protect herself from an intruder."

"Please. She doesn't even know how to work the alarm yet; you think Jay is going to trust her with firearms? You give her far too much credit. Have you seen her movies?"

"You're avoiding the real subject."

"Maybe I should go to law school! That's what you do, right?

Avoid the real subject and blame the victim. I can totally do that! I learned from the very best."

"Are you through?"

"Not quite. The devil visited a lawyer's office and made him an offer. 'I can arrange things for you,' the devil said. 'I'll increase your income fivefold. Your clients will respect you; you'll work half-time, and you'll live until a ripe, old age. All I require in return is your wife's soul, your children's souls, and their children's souls for all eternity.' The lawyer thought for a moment. 'What's the catch?'"

"I assume you didn't come to tell me lawyer jokes."

"No, but that's a good one, huh?" I laugh. "I've been practicing on my way over. I'm not very good at telling jokes."

"You don't say."

"Listen, I didn't break anything, and Jay still hadn't changed the codes on the house, so it wasn't like it was difficult to walk into the crypt. If I were so threatening, you think Jay would have changed the locks to protect his precious girlfriend."

"Are you threatening Jay, Haley?"

My eyes go wide with feigned innocence. "Only if you're afraid of a little tabloid press. Some actors like it, you know. It's good buzz. Helps their career and keeps them in the public eye, especially when they've got a new movie they could use the buzz on."

"Rachel doesn't need buzz, and neither does Jay. It's very hard on her to see hateful articles about her."

"Oh, the poor baby. I feel for her having to read about being the other woman." I point a finger in the air. "I know!" I say in my most bubbly, cheerleader voice. "If you don't want articles written about being the other woman . . . maybe." I shake my palms. "Just maybe, and I'm only thinking out loud here, but maybe it's a good idea not to bed other women's husbands."

Hamilton taps something into his laptop, obviously trying to buy himself some time. *Lawyer stalling tactic.* He speaks without looking at me. "You do know what the draft of the agreement says about your talking to the tabloids. By the way, I'm assuming since you're back living here, you want the checks sent elsewhere."

"How'd you know I was back living here? Oh, the church—"

"You do realize he can sue to get the money back if you break the agreement."

"I do, and I also know Jay's story is worth a lot more to the tabloids now that he's dating an actress. A very popular actress; one who broke up our marriage." I bring my thumbs and forefingers along, framing my headline. "Wife Speaks! Rachel Barlin Stole My Husband."

"Haley, is this a ploy to get more money?"

"I'm the wronged wife. That makes me worth quite a bit of cash to the right bidders. More than Jay's offer, I'm afraid. I am a businesswoman, Hamilton. I wasn't married to Jay for so long without learning a few financial tricks." *Gosh, I feel so Alexis Carrington all of a sudden!*

This posturing is so slimy, but if I learned anything from Jay, it was to play it cool. Remain calm and go for the throat. That's what he used to say. Even if Jay doesn't acknowledge my tenure in his office, I did pick up a thing or two.

"What are you asking for, Haley?"

"He was producing bad television sitcoms when I married him. He was living in Studio City. It's simply not fair that he walks away and leaves me as though I never existed. He bought the house through his business to keep it solely in his name. You don't think a good portion of that is fraudulent to protect his assets from his wife when he knew he planned to leave?"

"Haley." Hamilton shuts his laptop. "Why do you even want the money? You never cared about things. Jay said you were upset when

I sold your Nissan for the Porsche, so why care about things now?"

I cross my arms. "You bought that car? I loved that Nissan, and I was heartbroken when I got the L.A. car du jour." Hearing Hamilton was responsible for the disappearance of my beloved car makes me want to spit on him, but Alexis definitely wouldn't do that.

"You got a Porsche!"

"I didn't want a Porsche."

"Everyone wants a Porsche."

"No one ever asked me what I wanted, and I am a human being. You, as well as Jay, seem to forget that. Suddenly, I had to worry about being carjacked, about checking behind me before I got into the car, if I parked too close to a car in the parking lot. With my Nissan, I just got in it and drove. I had the oil changed, and that was it. Suddenly, I became a slave to a car. I was already Jay's slave, wasn't that enough?"

"Do you know how much trouble I went through to get you that car in black? I had to have them drive it down from San Francisco."

"You should have left it there. I hate black. It's depressing, and shows every door ding imaginable."

"Now you're being vindictive. I took my job seriously, Haley. I'm a lawyer, I don't buy cars. But I did it for Jay because it was for you."

"Why?'

"Let's just say I thought you deserved the best."

"What does that mean?"

"I really made no impression on you whatsoever, did I?"

I shrug, not understanding what he's trying to say.

"Do you know that every time I came to the house on business, you greeted me at the door and offered me coffee, hung up my jacket, and offered me the sweetest smile. I always did think Jay was the luckiest man alive."

I hate to tell Hamilton I did that for anyone who came to the house. It's called common courtesy, but I can see by his expression he feels like he's unloaded this dark secret, so I let it slide.

"I don't need anyone making decisions for me. My head is not in the clouds anymore, Hamilton. It's firmly rooted here," I slap my hand on his desk. "In the present, and the present costs money. I've got an idea for my own business, and you have to remember, I gave up eight years of any career I might have had for Jay's business. I'm just as good a producer as he is, I'll have you know."

"You have absolutely no experience producing, Haley."

"That's what Jay tells you. But I can tell you what every film boasting his name cost him to make and how much it returned. I bet you Jay can't do that."

"He was gone for six months on that last film. Where were you if you're so integral to the business?"

"I was home doing the work, Hamilton. He didn't have distribution for the film yet, but he's off in Monaco acting like he needs to oversee the entire creative process. You know as well as I do that without distribution, that film was dead in the water. I don't care who was starring in it. He was on-site, so he could be with Rachel!" I have to work hard to keep the screech out of my voice. No sense in appearing the shrew that I feel like. "She thinks he's Oscar worthy, but you know as well as I do, there's no money to be made in artistic films when flatulence will buy him a vacation home in Spain."

"You're reading a lot into his trip to Monaco, Haley. He always goes on location."

"Look, I know you're religious and all, you're probably like my mother and believe the best in everyone, but study the facts. Can you do that for me? You're helping this man take what's mine." I pound my finger on his desk. "And you're telling me to back down because that's the right thing to do. When really it's the *easy* thing for me to do. It makes your job easier if I go away. What kind of justice is in that? Do you believe in a just God?"

This catches him off guard, and I watch him wince.

"He was producing bad sitcoms when I met him, Hamilton," I repeat.

"How did the Trophy Wives Club go?"

"Your fan club, you mean?"

"I didn't do what Lindsay probably claimed I did. I just asked a few questions of the pastor is all."

"See, that's why people don't go to church. You can't even get along in the church, and you want to teach everyone else how to live."

"People are flawed in the church, Haley, but at least they know they're flawed, and they're trying."

"I'm trying. I'm not 'in the church'"—I put my fingers up in quotes—"and I'm trying. I'd rather live decently than do what you do and try to justify my actions. I'm done being a victim, that's for certain."

"So why are you here?"

"You know why I'm here. I want $250,000, and I'm not going away until I get it. You can relay my message to Jay. He can afford it. The question is, can he afford the alternative?" I walk toward the door. "It's not that much for what I endured, and you know that, Hamilton. I suggest you let your client know he's getting a good deal." Shoot. I had to throw out the first number. Luckily, I made it a nice round one.

Hamilton rests his chin on his fist. "I'll tell him."

"Tell him that the tabloids would pay twice that. With pictures, even more." Of course, I don't mention that I have no pictures, but my dad didn't teach me the poker bluff for nothing. Seeing that wedding ring in the shop made me snap. *This is war.*

Hamilton stands and walks toward me, his voice gentle. "Why are you doing this?"

"No!" I hold up a palm. "I am done being swayed by charm. You don't have enough charm in this entire office to convince me that I should be a doormat and let Jay get his way. I'm a good producer, and I've started fielding manuscripts." I haven't, but he doesn't know that. "I know all the secrets, so don't even try me, all right? After all, someday you might want to work for me."

"I'm not trying to charm you, Haley. If you want to win this, I have no doubt you will, but think what you're losing in the process."

"I mean it, Hamilton. Quit with the nice guy act. Everyone knows what you do for a living. You act like you're Robin Hood, but you're much more like a tax collector. You have no idea what some of these women endure. Oh, I'm not saying there aren't a few who marry the guy for his money. There are, but I believe there are more of us who marry because we grew up believing in the fairy tale, and no one ever told us it was a lie."

He stands up and walks around in front of his desk, leaning against it with his arms crossed over his chest. "It's a lie, Haley."

"I've seen men who really love their wives more than money. They exist. Just not in our world. You might think me insane, but I am happy for those women, but as for me? I'm going the Ivana Trump route. I'll make my own money, and, more importantly, I will use it for things that matter. Not new Porsches."

"After you take *his* money, you mean."

His comment feels like a stinging slap across my face. I feel my brows furrow. A storm is brewing within me, and I hope Hamilton Lowe feels my thunder. "Did you just say what I think you said?

"If you didn't marry him for his money, why blackmail him for more of it?"

"Because I gave up any hope I had for a career, my education, and my hope of a family for his dreams, Hamilton. Do you get that? Do you get that I tried to be a good wife by giving up everything I wanted? Granted, that may have been stupid, but here's where I prove that I'm not stupid. Tell your client my offer." I snap up my purse and head for the door.

My heels click with resolve as I head to the elevator. The empty seat left by Miss Linen makes me pause. Feeling sorry for men is exactly what gets me into these messes. *Hamilton is a big boy,* I tell myself, and if he can't keep women around, even the ones he pays, he has only himself to blame.

Before the elevator comes, I hear Hamilton call my name. I turn to face him, and really, it is a wonder to see a man like him single with so many beautiful L.A. women. It doesn't add up. He's incredibly handsome, has a good job, seems to be a decent guy other than what he does for a living—which makes my skin crawl. There's really only one answer that I can see. This job has tainted his view of marriage. Just like Jay has tainted mine.

"Haley, whatever you think of me? Don't let that be what you think of God."

"You're thinking mighty highly of yourself. You're comparing yourself to God now? Don't worry, Hamilton, I'll separate you in my mind, though it will be hard." I punch the elevator button again.

"Haley," Hamilton grasps my hand tightly, and he towers over me as he steps closer. "That's not what I meant."

I hate that his proximity makes it difficult to breathe. *I hate it.* Will I never learn? I avoid his eyes and focus on his expensive shoes. *Please, elevator, come. Come quickly!*

"I'm not here to assuage your guilt. I'll get through this." I punch the button again with my free hand. The poor button; it's feeling my wrath! I meet his gaze. "Are you going to let go of my hand?"

He drops it like a hot potato. "I'm sorry. I didn't realize—"

The elevator door finally opens and inside is my soon-to-be ex-husband. "Well, isn't this cozy?" Jay asks as he steps off the elevator.

Jay appears short standing alongside Hamilton. I don't know why this makes me feel better, but it does. He looks like Mini-me standing next to Austin Powers. Okay, maybe not that extreme, but it still makes me rise up on my heels and stand to my full height. Jay studies me, as if to notice if I pass his inspection. I clench my hands into fists as I watch him take inventory. How many days did I wait expectantly for his approval? It inflames me that I was so pathetic, and yet truthfully, there's something within that's waiting right now.

"Didn't your mother teach you not to stare, Mini?" It comes out before I can help myself. I realize he has no idea what I'm talking about, not being a fan of late-night reruns, but it feels good not to be edited by him, what can I say?

"Pardon me?" he asks, as though he's not checking me out for any and all flaws. I imagine Rachel is better at hiding her flaws, or more accurately, paying to have them hidden, but hopefully, she's better at not signing ridiculous pre-nups as well.

"Quit staring at me. I don't belong to you, Jay. Not anymore."

I step closer to Hamilton, shielding myself from Jay's view, before realizing Hamilton is no friend of mine. I'm on my own, and I'm deep inside enemy territory.

"Do you see how moody she is, Hamilton? Yet she wants all my money." There's not an ounce of shame on Jay's face. If anything, he *blames* me. He actually blames me for not being what he wanted every minute, of every day, over the years. He blames me that he has to add divorce to his résumé because I couldn't cut it. I know he does. The only difference now is that he blames me as his ex instead of his current wife, and I don't have to stand up to the daily scrutiny.

"Funny how us wives cop an attitude when our husbands move new women into the house before we're divorced."

"Our marriage was over a long time ago, Haley." He says this with the calm of a newsman's delivery. "Cut the drama. What do you care?"

"According to *you* our marriage was over. If you knew that, I do wish you had shared it with me, because I was in this 'til death do us part. That's what I learned marriage meant. Not until you didn't feel like it anymore, or you might have to pay out more money, or until someone younger comes along. Until death, Jay."

"And that's exactly how you would have liked it, isn't it, Haley?" Jay smirks at me as though I've been caught. "You would have liked to watch me keel over from a heart attack while you ran off with a younger man and my money." He shakes his hands out in front of him. "I can't take this! I'll talk with you when you're reasonable."

"Have we met?" I ask him. "Jay, how can you—" But I'm talking to a wall. I recognize the expression as he ceases to hear what I have to say. Not another word will permeate this invisible barrier I've come to know so well. Stonewall Cutler.

"You won't get another cent! Our divorce is almost final."

It's at this moment that I realize Jay is not playing with a full deck. Maybe if I hadn't walked into one too many walls, I would have figured it out years ago. It's an amazingly weightless sensation, like I have helium in my shoes. As I look over to Hamilton, it's clear he's realized the very same thing about Jay, but his shocked expression immediately goes back to the lawyer's poker face he's perfected, and he gives away nothing more. If only I'd known there was something within Jay that prevents him from seeing reality; it never dawned on me it wasn't all my fault.

I have a feeling Jay came to read Hamilton the riot act about my coming into the house, and now that I'm here, he doesn't have the guts to mention it for fear it might hurt his case. I try to steel myself from his words, but it's like a new sun has dawned. All these years, and it never occurred to me that perhaps it wasn't all me with my head in the clouds and my face in windows. Maybe my best defense is letting Jay dig his own grave.

The image of Jay on Rachel's arm keeps flashing before me, and I still feel it as a loss. I want to be smarter than that, but every self-esteem issue I ever had comes out to dance, as Jay looks at me with disdain. *I only ever wanted you to love me, Jay. Can't you see that?*

"So did she sign it?" Jay asks Hamilton.

Hamilton coughs, and I turn to find him shaking his head at Jay.

"Did I sign what?" I ask.

"Mr. Cutler has asked that you sign one more paper to finalize all this."

I look at Jay. "What else could you possibly take from me?"

"Give her the contract, Hamilton. I've got an appointment in ten."

"Hamilton?" I search his eyes, but once again he looks away.

"I'll be back." Hamilton jogs into his office.

Meanwhile, Jay and I stare at the tiles individually. He's as cold as this floor. How on earth did I miss that? What happened to me? Hamilton comes back, trying to look as dignified as possible with a single sheet of legal paper. "Halcy."

"Just give it to me!" I grab it from his hand.

Permission to reverse—" The blood drains out of my face, and I read the heading again, trying to comprehend. "Jay, you had a vasectomy?" I finally sputter. "When?"

Hamilton, bless his heart, he tries, but I can tell he feels like something at the bottom of my shoe. I'm shamed to have him look at me, and I can see he's trying to say it gently, but he knows. He knows my ugly truth that my husband not only has said he doesn't want me. Now he must make sure I know exactly how much.

"I had it done when I was twenty," Jay says dismissively. "I didn't want kids. I told you that, Haley."

"When? When did you tell me that, Jay? Because it's definitely something I would have remembered!"

"I'm sure I told you, and you won't get another cent just because you didn't know. Can you sign that, and I'll be on my way?"

Hamilton puts his hand on my shoulder, but I can only count tiles on the floor. "Jay wants to reverse the procedure he had before you were married. He needs permission from you for his doctor. This urologist doesn't perform them without consent when the patient is married, and he's apparently the best in the business."

I thrust the document, unsigned, back at him. "There's no way Jay could be paying you enough to do this for him, Hamilton. Not a chance. Take my advice. Get out while you still can and be sure and let him know I'm not signing that thing." I look right at the man who I wanted to father my children. "You can wait until the divorce is final. It's the least you can do in fact! May you pine for ages, like I did." I pull away from Hamilton's hand.

"Haley, enough of the drama," Jay deadpans, rolling his eyes. "Just sign the thing."

"I wanted a baby, you know? I wanted—" I blink back tears. "I wanted a baby, and there was never a chance, was there?"

Hamilton grabs my fingers, "I'm sorry, Haley."

I look into his eyes, which are tinged with liquid. "There's only a month left until the divorce is final. This is just cruel. No wonder you have no faith in humanity. How could you?"

I step onto the elevator, thankful for its solace, even if I do have to hear Nickelback as Muzak. Hamilton gazes at me as the doors close. I feel soiled, as if there isn't enough soap on earth.

Chapter 9

It's been almost a month since those words cut deeply into my soul. It was like Jay tore something open, and my hopes and ambition drained out around me. Sure, I knew now what kind of person he truly was, but something about that moment when I realized how I truly was living a lie, it was like I'd been set free from prison and couldn't get my bearings. Before I knew about the lie of the operation, I had the desire for revenge. Now even that motivation was gone.

"Haley, where have you been?" Finally, my mother appears on the doorstep of the motel where I'm staying. Yes, I checked back in. Even with money, I couldn't bring myself to spend it, for fear I wouldn't be able to find work. "You can't be serious," Mom says, as she barges into the room. "How long have you been staying in this rathole? Rent an apartment, Haley. For goodness' sakes. What a dump. Here I brought you this—" She thrusts a teddy bear in neon pink flower fabric toward me.

"I have to find a job before I can afford . . ."

"Well, as I've told your brother Mike, you have to look for a job to get one. They don't come looking for you."

"I think I want to produce," I say weakly.

"You're producing a lot of nothing. Haley, it's been months since Jay kicked you out, it's time to start your life again. You're just going to sit here in this motel room and watch daytime TV and blame Jay for everything, aren't you?"

"I'm going to get a job, Mom. I just don't want to make a mistake."

"You have to make a mistake. Making mistakes is how we learn. You'll learn you don't like a particular job if you get one. You got married and learned someone else can't fix things, right? That's a productive mistake."

"Albeit a costly one."

She opens the curtains in my room and starts to pick up the chocolate wrappers on the nightstand.

"Mom, the maid will be in this afternoon."

"Get your things together. You're leaving. You've had more than enough time to wallow. If you don't find an apartment by tonight, you're coming home with me."

No, not the teddy bears! "I don't want to leave here. I've grown accustomed to it, and I have enough money to think about what it is I'm going to do next."

"Look around you and see what you've grown accustomed to. Mushrooms grow accustomed to the dark and having fertilizer thrown on them, do you see what I'm saying?"

"Mom, I haven't thought things through yet. I just don't know what to do next."

"Of course you don't, and neither does Mike. And all this chocolate is probably fogging your brain." My mom straightens the chair. "I did too much for you kids; that's the problem."

"Sort of like you're doing now?" I ask.

She purses her lips. "I never let anything hurt you or get in your way, and look what happened . . . neither one of you can handle your lives! I'm a failure as a mother."

My mother finds a way to induce guilt every single time. "Because I failed? Didn't you say that's how I'm supposed to learn?"

"One of you not working, not married, not walking with the Lord, I could say it was a fluke, a personality flaw. Two of you, and that's batting a thousand. I'm going to tell you this once, and it's not pleasant, but you have to hear it because Grandma told me I had to say it."

"It's not about Daddy being virile, is it?"

"Get dressed," she says as she throws my jeans, which were lying on the chair, at me. "Haley, look at this room. It's like you're sixteen years old all over again!"

"It doesn't matter."

She sits down on the bed beside me. "You were always the good child. You always did what you were told, never gave me a day's worry. You came home with excellent grades, you were the teacher's pet, and the kids loved you, too, voted you Homecoming Queen, remember?"

"This isn't a pitch for Gavin as a husband, is it?"

She pinches her lips together. "This isn't a pitch for anyone as a husband. I used to brag about how perfect and compliant you were as a child, do you remember?"

I nod.

"It's only after seeing you in that marriage to that self-absorbed man who never cared a whit about you that I realized I hadn't prepared you for the world at all. You learned to please everyone on the planet, except yourself. You used to like sparkles, remember?"

"How could I forget? It led up to one of the worst nights of my life."

"If there was an outfit with outlandish colors, maybe a little garish sequin at the hem, you were all over it. It made you happy to wear it, and you didn't care what anyone thought. You used to tell me they were just jealous because they didn't have the guts to wear those clothes. Where did that girl go?"

"I grew up, Mom, and I saw pictures of myself. I was . . . I was tacky."

"You were happy." My mom shrugs. "More people should be tacky and happy. Look at Dolly Parton, she's happy."

"More people should decorate with teddy bears and 1960s-style TV trays, right?"

"Exactly!"

She's got me there. I personally had way more fun with the TV trays and *Full House* than I ever did at an Oscar after-party. "All right, Mom. I hear you." I lay back against the headboard.

"If I could have given your brother half the drive, and you half Mike's ability to have fun, I would have been the perfect mother."

"You're not blaming yourself?" *Because what a coincidence, I've been blaming yourself!*

"I am blaming myself." She pounds the pillows like she's going to find much more life in these cheap motel pillows. "You're not handling this, Haley. I didn't teach you to handle upsets. Everything came so easily to you. You were always beautiful." She shakes her head. "I think that was to your detriment. Your personality was always like morning sunshine. Boys flocked to you like ants to a picnic."

"Your point?"

"Life isn't like that. You never learned about mean people, or bills that don't get paid, or what happens when your sewer line is stopped up by a tree."

"Do I need to know about sewage?"

"Sometimes life is hard and you still have to pick yourself back up and walk." She is trekking around the room, nervously folding things and putting them into my suitcase. Even when my mother is taking responsibility for her lack of parenting, she makes me feel guilty.

It's disconcerting to hear my mother offering advice. Firstly, because she never has before, and secondly, because she's married to my dad, and they hardly have anything I want to emulate. At least I thought so nine years ago. They have about as much marital advice to offer as anyone in Hollywood. Two people who live their different lives under the same roof, but the fact is, each of them is their own person. I can't fault them for that. Neither of them tried to change the other. Oh, I could argue they probably should have, but they didn't waste their time on pointless activity.

"I never thought I'd be divorced. It feels like the ultimate failure."

"Why? Because you believe Jay was the perfect husband, and you let him down?"

"No, of course not." But when I have time to think it over. "Well, maybe."

"See, that's my point about sewage. If you can't discern sewage, you're always going to think you were the only problem. Because you believe you should be the one person alive without sin, save Jesus."

"I made my mistakes. I see that now. When someone doesn't care how you think, it's not enough to let him have his way until you forget what you'd want, is it?"

"No, it's not. His job was not to necessarily agree with you, but he had to listen at least." She comes toward me and wraps me into a hug. I feel myself stiffen at the touch, not realizing how long it's been since anyone showed me affection. It makes me bristle, and I can't relax, but my mom doesn't leave me, she just clings tighter. She stays there until my body finally crumples into hers, and I feel the tears start to flow again.

"You wanted children."

I nod against her shoulder. "I did. I don't see how that can happen now."

"You say you want to produce."

Again, I bob my head up and down.

"If you want something, you have to go out and take it. No one is going to bring it to you anymore. Not me. Not Jay. Not even Jay's money. It's up to you now, Haley. God is in control. Take the life He offers you and run with it."

"Mom, I don't believe in all that."

"Shh! Don't say that." She cowers under the ceiling. "He hears everything, you know."

"I asked Him, Mom. I asked Him to fix things."

"Maybe He did, did you ever think of that?"

"He fixed things all right. Rachel Barlin is in my house, living my life, and I'm in a cheap motel made to grovel at the feet of the only tall man left in Hollywood."

"See, that's exactly what I'm talking about. You're going to play this up for all it's worth, aren't you? He was a callous jerk, Haley. He was always a jerk; you just chose to overlook it. Do you remember what he said about the dishes you had picked out since high school?"

"He didn't like them."

"What kind of man picks the china, Haley?"

"I just thought he had a strong preference."

"You had a strong preference way back in high school. What happened to that?"

"It was just china. What did it matter?"

"It mattered because that first time you gave in, you told Jay exactly how things would be. Now he's done something you can't overlook, so it's time to take some action for yourself."

"You should have seen her sitting in my family room and knitting, like everything belonged to her. They even have my cat, Mom."

"So go get the cat, Haley. No one is bringing you the cat."

"How did you find me, anyway?" For a seedy motel, people sure seem to find me easily enough.

"Someone named Lindsay called the house to tell us you hadn't been out of the motel in a long time. She's been inviting you to something at church, she said. You even missed a pedicure appointment, and that's when I knew I had to step in. It's not one of those weird California churches is it? Where they talk to rocks or wear strings?"

"No, Mom. In fact, I don't think they have one famous member. You'd approve."

"Well, that's something, I suppose. When we found out where you were, your dad got me an airline ticket, and I flew down."

"Daddy did that?"

"He's worried about you." She rests her hand on my head.

Truthfully, it's hard to believe my dad even knows I've gone missing. He's not exactly one to pay attention. To me, or to life in general, unless it involves the 49ers or the Giants.

"It's time to wake up, Haley. I'll make you a new sparkle dress."

I laugh out loud. "That's all right, Mom. I think I've been laughed at enough times for my taste in sequins. My interest has sort of waned. Are you going to make me go home?'

"Have you been listening to me at all? I'm not going to make you do anything. It's time you did it for yourself. Go buy yourself a car today. The broker called the house; he's had that mini you wanted for two weeks now! Rent an apartment and get some furniture. Apply for credit in your own name and find yourself a job or start producing something. I bought you some Suze Orman and David Bach books on money. I saw them on *Oprah* with that debt diet of hers. Very good stuff. I have money in my name now. If anything happens to your father, I'm ready."

"You make it sound like you're too ready."

"Don't worry, he's safe for now." She laughs.

"You read a Suze Orman book?"

"I did."

"What's a HELOC?" I ask her.

"A home equity line of credit," she answers smugly. "Not smart in this day and age with fluctuating interest rates and with the Fed, you never know what's going to happen to rates. They could rise any day now."

"You're scaring me."

"Our house is paid in full. We have four income-producing properties. We have absolutely no debt, own our cars outright, vacation where we want, buy what we want, live how we want—"

"But Mom, you and Dad don't go anywhere on vacation, and how do you live like you want?"

"We like to stay home. I sew; your Dad subscribes to a dozen or so sports channels, that's how we want to live. Maybe you need to embrace the simpler side of things. It's time we taught you and Mike to do the same because you have to be ready to do right by us in the end."

"Mom, what are you talking about? You'll outlive us both."

It's like this woman is an alien posing in my mother's skin. I thought all she did was go to Goodwill and find old clothes for teddy bears. She owns her house outright? Rentals?

"Jay is not doing this to you, Haley. You're doing this to you. If I sat around and let your father handle everything, we'd have nothing more than our house payment, do you know that? Now go get dressed."

My body doesn't want to move. "It's almost time for *Judge Judy*," I plead. I try to pull my jeans on, but the fact is, I've put on a little weight since this divorce business started, and I sort of want to breathe too. "I'm just going to get another pair of pants."

I slide into my favorite UCLA sweats, and my mother shakes her head. "You're not getting a job in those. We'll go shopping if we have to. But you're paying for yourself. I would have taken that settlement and had it in various CDs coming due at different times so I always had money. Did you do that?"

"No." I pull my sweats back off and get into a breezy summer skirt that fits loosely. I find a pair of sandals and slide them on, only to realize it's been some time since I shaved my legs. "I think I need a shower."

"I think you do," my mother says.

I unwrap another small chocolate on the way to the bathroom, and my mother plucks it from my fingers.

"I think you've had enough."

I enter the bathroom and start the shower running. Looking into the mirror, I can see the dark circles under my eyes. It looks as though it's been ages since I slept and really, that's all I have done. And my roots? Ugh, don't even get me started! I see my natural color, and it's not pretty. "Mom," I open the door a crack. "What day is it?"

"It's February 23. Friday."

"I'm almost officially divorced."

"Yep," she answers.

A weight falls away as I realize I'm three weeks away from being free. It's over. I need a life. One of my own.

Chapter 10

Is it just me? Or are there an awful lot of women willing to be on daytime TV admitting their ignorance as to who fathered their children? You know, a mistake I can understand, a literal platoon of women lining up for their fifteen minutes to admit sleeping around, not so much. Maybe it's human nature, but it makes me feel better about my own life. For five minutes, anyway. I click off the television set as someone knocks on my door. It's probably my mother again with homemade clothes to make me feel better. I thought I sent her home last night with the promise that after our day of shopping, I was ready to find a new place. I look through the peephole. *Oh crap, it's Hamilton Lowe.* The last person I want to see me suffering. I wonder if I'm quiet if he'll just go away.

"Haley?" he calls again.

I run to the mirror and behold a frightening vision. I have no mascara on! I look like a cadaver on *CSI* before the testing. I slap some water on my face and dampen my hair, but quickly realize it would take a miracle to erase my current state in an appropriate span of time. I slap more water on and spray on my Dior foundation. Skin in a bottle, and thank the French for ingenuity! I try to focus on the under-eye area so I don't look like a Tim Burton character.

"Haley?" Hamilton calls again through the door, with another rap of his knuckles.

"Just a minute!" I yank a brush through my hair, but there's little difference, so I grab a rubber band and shove it into a ponytail. I frantically apply mascara, and my eyes reappear. I run to the door, and I'm about to open it, when I notice two empty frosting tubs on the nightstand. One, a person might understand. Two borders on insanity. I grab them up and toss them into the bathroom. "Be right there!" I call again. I smooth my tank top and realize I have no bra on. Sheesh! I run to the bathroom and wrestle myself into "proper underwear" as my mother would call it, throw on a sweater and take a deep breath. Opening the door, I put on my best party smile. "Hamilton, how are you?"

He looks behind me. "Everything okay?"

"Perfect," I say, sliding my fingers through my ratty ponytail. "What can I do for you?" For some reason, it dawns on me that I might have frosting on my face, so I start to wipe my face as though I'm a diseased animal in the zoo. Of course I sprayed on skin, so if I do, it's caked underneath it. Nothing I can do about it now.

"You're sure you're okay?"

"Just not expecting anyone, that's all."

"Your phone's off the hook."

I look back at the phone tossed on the floor. "Yeah, I was taking a nap."

Hamilton nods. "I'm sorry to come without calling first. I brought you the money from your wedding ring."

"My wedding ring?"

"Lindsay went down and bought it back for your price and sold it at auction for you. The store called me to verify her story. You put me down on the paperwork to certify the ring was yours?"

"Oh . . . yeah I did."

He pulls out a check from his chest pocket. "It's a cashier's check, so don't lose it."

I hold up the check. "Thanks, huh?" I start to shut the door when Hamilton edges closer.

"Why don't you get dressed and come to Friday night service with me?"

I feel my hair, "Oh I couldn't. I'm—busy."

"Haley, you need to get out for a while. Just church, maybe a little dinner afterwards. I'll wait in the car for you. Take your time."

"Hamilton, I hardly think I'm ready for an outing—and church?"

He rolls his eyes, "You really haven't got anything better to do, have you?"

I look at the television, willing myself to come up with an excuse. "No. Not really."

"Get dressed. You're going to start to discolor if you stay in here any longer, it's like you're pickling. I'll meet you in the car."

He walks out into the sun, and I slit open the curtain to steal a peek. "In another life, Hamilton Lowe, in another life . . ." Too much bad television. I'm getting hallucinogenic. But the man did get me to agree to church on a Friday night.

I'm ready in twenty minutes. Hair washed, brushed out, and everything. If Jay taught me anything, it was that he wasn't waiting, so I'd better be quick about it. Hamilton's waiting in a Lexus sedan. He sees me coming and gets out of the car to open my door. Jay always opened my door too. Someone might see him!

"You're sure about this?" I ask as I meet him.

He opens the door. "Absolutely. We can be adults, Haley. We can be friends."

How I wish that were true. If Lindsay sees me with him, she's going to kill me. Small talk proves . . . well, small. Neither one of us can think of a thing to say. And me with all my experience in shallow discussions. It's useless at the moment.

"It seems money is just falling from the sky," I finally say about my check for the ring. "Of course I'll have to pay Lindsay back what they gave me already. Luckily, I didn't spend it. This windfall is going to end soon enough. I'm not being irresponsible with it."

"No, you wouldn't be."

"My mom was down to visit."

"I'll bet that was nice."

"She wants me to find an apartment."

"That's a great idea."

"Yeah."

And that's it. All we have to say for the duration of the forty-five-minute trip (ten without traffic). We capture small glances here and there, but then snap our heads toward our respective windows. I'm comforted by Hamilton's presence. He has this way about him, a smooth walk and deft touch, always the gentleman except where it comes to law. We arrive at the church ten minutes early, and the congregation is gathered out front. Fear boils up within me.

"Maybe this wasn't a great idea."

"Don't be silly. I'm anxious to introduce you to some of the members." As we get out of the car, I see a good portion of the milling people turn toward us and act as though they're not interested, but there's a buzz across the group, and no one's eyes have veered.

"Please, Hamilton, let's go."

He stops walking and faces me. "Really? You want to just go to dinner?"

"There's a coffee shop across the way. How about if I go and wait for you? I could grab a coffee and read the paper. That way you can get your church time, and we can meet up afterwards. I won't put you out. It was really kind of you to rescue me from my hovel tonight."

He stretches out his arm toward me. "They won't bite."

"No, but they might sting a little."

"You really don't like churches, do you?"

"I had a bad experience as a child. My parents used to drop me off, and more than once, my mom forgot to pick me up. She gets busy with things, you know?"

"I promise, I won't leave you anywhere." He pulls me toward the church. "I'll stay right with you the whole time, and everyone can see I'm the one with the trophy date tonight." He winks when I try to protest. "That was my attempt at humor. You can see why I chose law."

I breathe in a deep breath as we approach the group. I try to focus in on faces so I don't get overwhelmed at what they must think of Hamilton bringing some woman with him. Hamilton introduces me to an older lady named Ethel Wyeth, and she proceeds to tell me she's known him since he was in diapers. I think he actually blushed. "A pleasure to have you, young lady. You know, we think the world of Hamilton here."

That doesn't speak well for the rest of the night since I'm not familiar with anyone who'd speak well of him.

Then the first lightning strikes. She's a brunette about my age, wearing what can only be described as a frock, boasting big pink flowers and a skirt the size of Texas. I want to shake her down to see if she's hiding weapons under there. She's a bitty little thing, lost in the atrocity she calls a dress. Now that is a crime against fashion. To make matters worse, she's wearing pageant makeup. But I shouldn't judge. Right? Isn't that what they say? Never judge a book by its cover or a person by her dress. Maybe she likes floral frocks like I preferred sequins.

"Priscilla, I'd like you to meet Haley." As Hamilton says this, he doesn't tear his eyes off me. The interaction between them is one I've seen at many a Hollywood party. She only has eyes for him, and Hamilton—well, he doesn't have the first clue.

She gives me the fake smile that only women see. "Haley, welcome. Aren't you a pretty little thing?"

I think that's meant to be a diss as I'm about a foot taller than her, but I smile graciously. "Thank you."

"How do you know our Hamilton?" She pinches his cheek. Really. Like she got her dating tips from Great Grandma. There's a part of me that wants to take her aside and give her seduction clues. But I don't think they do that type of thing here in the church. It's a different frame of reference. She probably bakes him a pie or something.

"Your Hamilton," I say, giving her full ownership as she's more than welcome to him. "Your Hamilton is my ex-husband's lawyer."

"Ex-husband?" Priscilla face is bewildered. "Well, honey, you're too young to have an ex-husband."

"Oh if that were true, I'd be folding shirts merrily and the chocolate frosting shelves would be safe."

I get the rightfully confused look. She pulls Hamilton aside as if some magical wall has just been built between us. "Hamilton, you're mixing business with pleasure? That doesn't sound like you."

I smile at those around me, trying to act completely natural while Hamilton answers for his frivolous choice in women. His brow darkens and he whispers something and comes back, smiling too broadly. Priscilla huffs off. "Haley, shall we go in?"

"Hamilton, go talk to her."

"Haley, you're my guest, and as such, you should be treated accordingly."

"She wants you, Hamilton. Is that something lost on you?"

"Priscilla? Haley, don't be ridiculous, I've known her since seventh grade."

"Then, there's most likely a Pee Chee folder with your name in hearts scribbled all over it."

"You just want to avoid being seen with me. I know what this is about."

Every fiber in my being wants to run. I can't bring my feet to place one in front of the other. "I can't do it."

"What do you mean? It's church. It's not the gallows."

"I'll catch a cab." I walk toward the busy street. "Hamilton, go get that girl and either take her in your arms and act like you mean it, or let her go. She's too old to be chasing you for something that won't happen."

"What are you talking about?"

"I appreciate what you're trying to do for me. You're trying to get me back on my feet, and I completely applaud that. But maybe this isn't the best venue for me, if you know what I'm saying."

"I don't have any idea what you're saying, actually. I'm looking forward to having dinner with you. I want to hear everything you're doing now and how you've managed. I want to know what you're up to."

"And what about Priscilla? If she's been your friend since seventh grade, maybe it's time you actually noticed her."

I'm sure Hamilton means this with the best of intentions. He's not devious enough to be doing it for anyone else, but Hamilton Lowe is single, handsome, and available. It wouldn't matter if we were in college, a bar, or this church. The women have staked their claim, and I am an interloper. Just like Rachel.

Hamilton stands there with his mouth ajar. He's so handsome, so very filled with innocent ideas. I hate that it's my job to slap some sense into him. I walk toward the coffee shop. "I'll catch a cab. Thanks for the nice visit!" I call out, and I'm gone. The church is once again safe from the likes of me.

Chapter 11

I'm a snob. It sort of snuck up on me. I thought I did all the self-pampering for Jay's approval, but in truth, I am dying for a good color and cut. Facial. Eyelash dye. Wax. I need the works. I don't even remember how to cut my own toenails (in fact, I don't think I own scissors to do it!). I *so* have to get a life because the fact is, I am a wee bit spoiled and now that I've emerged from my cave, the sunlight is revealing every flaw I've hidden for the last nine years!

One has to be proactive in warding off ugly, and that costs money.

I want to shop, too. Not for brand names, but definitely for higher quality, and I'm broke. Well, not broke, but let's just say I'm not used to plopping down cash for purchases. But my new life has to start somewhere, and I can think of no better place to give birth to a future than at the mall.

Shopping always gives me a sense of purpose, and that's just what I'm missing. So maybe I am shallower than I thought. I want good shoes. Am I really so different from anyone else? Who wouldn't select Giuseppe Zanotti's over Payless Shoe Source if given a choice? But as I take a pair of jewel-encrusted stilettos in my grip, I realize three things.

1. $700 will pay for eleven days in my motel.
2. I can't walk in stilettos.
3. I have no need of stilettos at the Motel Del Mar or in any other facet of my lifestyle right now.

I place them back on their pedestal while mourning all three relevant points. People were nice to me when I shopped. I felt important. I came home with shoes and handbags and everyone was happy. For a little while, anyway.

Jay never held anything back from me when we were married, except himself. If I wanted it, I slapped down a credit card, and he paid the bill. I totally see why I fell victim to daytime television and QVC to cope in my crisis. Without the power of money, my shallow relationships have caught up with me. That's just wrong. I need a fix.

"May I help you, Madam?" He's handsome. He's gay. He wants me to buy these shoes! The pressure mounts . . .

"I . . . um . . ."

"Do you have an event you're shopping for?"

"No." I shake my head.

"These heels are to die for! Let me get your size. Seven?"

"Eight," I say, enjoying the little game where the salesperson makes my feet smaller than they are.

"You have to get to the root of the issue," my mother told me. Jay was not the root, the origin, though it could be argued, he was certainly one of them—on ample doses of Miracle-Gro.

The experts (Dr. Phil) say I taught Jay how to treat me. "You teach people how to treat you!" Well, this proves I should never have a dog because a trainer I clearly am not. And I don't have it in me in this lifetime to train another one. So I need to be thinking cat. Of course, Darcy is AWOL, so maybe I should cut my losses.

"Those are genuine Swarovski crystals on the toe," the salesman prods. "Halle Berry wore a similar pair to the Oscars. Of course, none of them are exactly alike. These shoes are custom with each pair."

I'm salivating. Eleven nights . . . Free toothpaste, I try to reason.

"The sole"—he runs his manicured fingers the length of the shoe—"is perfection."

Free Maury Povich . . . Free Dr. Phil . . . how will I know my life isn't all that bad compared to others without them? I may not have a baby daddy, but I'd know who he was if I did.

"They look hard to walk in—"

"They're Zanotti's, darling. Perfectly balanced, a feat in engineering as well as Italian beauty."

I lick my lips. What would it hurt to try them on? Since Jay didn't pay attention to me, I paid salespeople to do so. That's the height of pathetic, isn't it? No one will be your friend unless you're doling out the cold, hard cash? I didn't know it was a problem until I was broke and couldn't pay my friends.

"I shouldn't. I won't be able to walk in them."

"I have just the thing." He jogs over to another display and brings over a teal suede wedge with small crystals on the elegant straps.

"Gorgeous, but still too high for me."

"The white leather medallion thong with a fuchsia and teal inlay."

"Did you say fuchsia?"

"On sale for $330."

"That's not even six nights!"

"Pardon me?'

Oh gosh. "I'm late. I have to go." My hands are in a cold sweat as I run out of the shop and brace myself against the wall outside. *Breathe in. Breathe out.* I need support. Now!

I haven't been back to the church for the Trophy Wives Club even though I promised Angry Lindsay. I figured she was mad enough on her own, what more could I do to her. And I implied to Bette I'd be at the foot-washing ceremony and blew that off. Maury was a continuation that day, I had to know who fathered Deidre's baby! But they kept calling. Kept nagging. I tried to imply I was so busy with friends, but neither Lindsay or Bette seemed to believe me. It was either give in finally, or get caller ID and since I hadn't found an apartment yet, that seemed unrealistic.

The monthly foot-washing ceremony had come around again, and in all honesty, I'm desperate to talk to someone, and $40 for a pedicure is a bargain for friendship at this point. Not even one night's stay. Maybe I need a little preachin', who knows?

Bette has rented out the entire pedicure salon, Perfect Nail, for the afternoon. And hey, I may not remember much from my Sunday school days, but I'm pretty sure this isn't exactly what Jesus had in mind. Then again, I'm all for a religion with good hygiene.

There are five spa chairs, each with its own cauldron of bubbling, blue water and a personal disciple at the ready. "Do you have room for me today?"

Bette lights up. "Haley, what a pleasure to see you! We've been praying for you."

Deidre needs prayer more than me. Dwayne the dirtball was her baby daddy. I take my place between Bette, the boss, and Helena, the gorgeous redhead with the personality of stone. I wish Lindsay were there. I look around the salon, but she's nowhere to be found.

These women are nice and all, but I need someone a little more real. Someone who's seen the darker side of life and come out the other side.

"You're looking beautiful and refreshed," Bette says in her overly warm, not sure if it's real, way.

"Thank you." I'm feeling homely and haggard, but I'm glad to hear it doesn't show. At least if I'm to take Bette at her word, and for now, I will. "I've had a time of respite."

"We don't mean to mock Jesus' washing of the feet ceremony, but this is something we can usually gather for, and I always like to provide a Biblical reference," Bette overexplains.

"Yeah. Did Jesus prefer a particular color?" I ask.

"Oh." Bette laughs. "Good heavens no. Nail color wasn't invented. I don't believe. Helena, do you know if nail polish was invented during Jesus' time?" She looks back at me. "The Greeks and the Hebrews were very inventive."

"It's okay," I put my hand up. "It was just a joke."

"Oh," Bette says, as though I've offended her.

"I'm going to get something that sparkles, anyway. In honor of finding the real me." I select a fiery red that has specks of glitter in it, and it's free with the price of a pedicure

"Actually, the origin of nail color is still but a mystery," Helena pops in. "It is believed to have started with the Chinese or the Egyptians, but direct answers remain unclear. The earliest form seemed to be a combination of floral petals, mashed and left on the nail beds overnight. The Chinese used an early form of lacquer."

My mouth's ajar. I'm trying to shut it, but it just keeps flopping open. "You should totally be on *Oprah* with that."

"That's fascinating, Helena," Bette offers.

"Nail polish as we know it, or varnish as it was called, started in America when automobile paint was invented."

"How do you know all that stuff?" I ask, truly mystified. I was lucky if I remembered my pin number.

"I have a photographic memory. If I see it once, I happen to remember whatever the information is. I once read a set of encyclopedias in high school, and the data stayed with me."

"You must be great at cocktail parties!"

Helena laughs, an odd sound—sort of like part farm animal, part teenager. "Actually, I don't get invited to many cocktail parties."

"Where did you meet your husband again?"

"At work." Her face changes, and I wish I hadn't brought the memory up for her.

"So he was brilliant, too?" Again she looks downtrodden, and I'm wondering if I should have just bought the shoes and put myself out of my misery. You can't say the wrong thing to a guy selling you $330 shoes! "I meant, brilliant in the IQ sense, not the personality sense. Clearly he can't be that if he left you."

Shoot me now.

"I meant—"

"Don't worry. I've made peace with the fact that I married an idiot."

"Helena!" Bette chastises.

She shrugs. "I don't lie, Bette. Have you ever heard me lie? If I know anything, it's that I married an idiot. But now, he's where he belongs, and they will make bonehead children together. I wish him the best. Really I do."

"I could tell."

"Well, let's talk about something positive, shall we?"

Climbing up into the chair while trying to take my shoe off at the same time proves too much for my balance, or lack thereof, and I splash my foot down into the water, like a drunk in the Chateau Marmont water fountain. I pull my soggy shoe out and try to remain composed, while Bette jumps up to help me, and Helena takes careful mental notes.

"I guess it's starting to show why I wasn't a great trophy wife, huh?"

"I hope those were cheap shoes," Bette says.

I look down at my Donald Pliner flip-flops. "They weren't, but they'll dry out." I don't want to elaborate on how I know this. Let's just say it's not the first time my shoes were intimate with the pedicure chair.

"The statistical chance of a trophy wife wearing cheap shoes to get a pedicure is almost nonexistent," Helena says in a tone much like Spock. I wonder that Helena understands enough about makeup to apply it. She doesn't seem to know there is any power in beauty at all, so it seems an odd dichotomy. Maybe she learned a thing or two from Cleopatra.

"I have a friend who brings rhinestone-studded cheap flip-flops to all her appointments," I offer. "Well, I had a friend who did that. You know, before—"

"How's life going on your own, Haley?" Bette asks, as she sits back down. "I've been praying for you daily."

"You have? What do you pray? I mean, if you don't mind my asking." For how strange this group is, I'll tell you it means something to me that Bette prays for me, and I haven't had to pay a dime. There was a study on *The View* that stated people who were prayed for had a higher rate of recovery. Maybe that's why I was able to resist the shoes.

"I pray that God would surround you with His love and let you be at peace. I ask that you might receive His forgiveness, so you in turn, can extend that forgiveness to others."

"Meaning Jay?"

"Forgiveness isn't for him, Haley. It's for you."

"Like you said, can we talk about something uplifting?"

"So what are you doing with yourself?" Helena asks.

The warm water is like a truth serum. "It's sort of lonely. Not because of Jay. I don't miss him," I admit. "He would just come home and tell me what I'd done wrong all day. There's not much to miss in that. But I miss the companionship of the maids, the cook, just people. I miss people. I've watched a lot of television. I've picked up the phone to call QVC a few times, only to realize I have to watch my pennies until I know what I'm doing. Not only can I not afford the sixty-nine-dollar caramel apples, but I probably shouldn't waste the dollar on the phone call, either. I'm still in the motel you know. Jay finally canceled my cell, and I just never restarted it. I figured what was the point? I didn't have anyone to call."

"Surely, you're not that poor, are you?" Helena asks. "Do we have to pick up her pedicure tab?" she asks Bette. "Because you know, I don't believe in that kind of charity. She has to pick herself up off the floor to be helped. You know what Ben Franklin said about God helping those who help themselves. She hasn't even got a plan yet."

"And she is right here," I say.

"Does it matter, Helena? I'm going to pay her tab because I invited her, and I'm glad she's shown up. She didn't last month, so let's give her a reason to come back. That's the Christian thing to do, dear." Bette pats her hand. I'm glad it's someone else's hand being patted and as far as I'm concerned, Helena is much more in need of hand patting than I am.

I watch Helena's gaze cloud. I think this Christian thing might not come all that naturally to her, which makes me like her a little more. Being kind is harder than being right, and I don't think she gets that. She's has all the grace of a steamroller. Definite friend potential here.

"I mean, you got some sort of settlement, didn't you? He was richer than you, right?" Helena prods. "Have you started looking for work? What do you do? You might have to rethink your education like I had to do." She looks at her nails. "I have my Ph.D., you know?"

"Yes, you told me." *But no job either. I may not have a photographic memory, but I seem to remember that.*

Lily Tseng walks in, and I have to say I'm glad to add someone else to our little warped group. Bette is trying. She really does make you feel like she's willing to bake you a fresh batch of cookies anytime, anywhere, but Helena doesn't seem to understand how the world operates. Small talk doesn't seem to be her gift.

"Hi, Lily," I say with too much enthusiasm.

"You remembered my name."

"Wasn't that my job for eight years? To remember everyone's name when Jay couldn't." That sounded spiteful. I didn't mean it that way.

She laughs, and sways her hair over her shoulder. "Oh, I need to pick a color. Hold that thought, Haley." She clicks over in her high heels and picks a pale pink, then puts the bottle back. "On second thought, I'm just going to do French today. Hey, May, how's your week?" She pats her pedicurist and climbs into a chair and turns toward me. "I'm telling you, what a day! It's like *Twelve Angry Men* in my office. I didn't think I was going to get to come." She switches on the massage chair, looks at me again, and her well-groomed brows flash. "Haley, you wouldn't be looking for a job, would you?"

"I am, but I don't know what I do, besides fold shirts."

"Well, you have to do something," Helena says. "Did you go for the throat on your divorce like Bette warned you against? Apparently, you didn't do all that well if Bette has to pay for your pedicure. Are you ready to let God guide you?" She smiles at Bette, like she's passed some sort of test.

"Helena!" Bette gasps.

Helena's face falls. She can't imagine what she's said wrong.

"Well, Helena." I turn to mortified Bette. "It's a fair question, Bette. I'm not offended." I turn back to Helena. "Today is the first time I've taken a shower in three days. I shaved my legs this morning and could barely get the razor through the stubble, which grew like tree stumps on all the chocolate I've been eating. I think magnesium must help hair growth. Anyway, you know that spreadable frosting for cakes? I've been buying the fudgy kind and eating it right out of the tub with a plastic spoon that I pilfer from the deli section at the grocery store. In addition, I've been eating a variety of takeout and watching a lot of Jerry Springer—oh, and I could barely zip up my jeans the other day. So for now, I'm not aiming real high, but I do hope to graduate to makeup tomorrow. How about you? Are you well?"

"So, Haley," Lily interrupts. "About this job. I have a position I need to fill quickly, and I think you'd be perfect for it. I'll bet you know a great many people in the industry already."

"Lily is the human resources director at CMG, a big talent agency."

"One of our big talents is Rachel Barlin," Lily explains. "Would that bother you?"

"Would it bother her?" I grin. "If so, sign me up."

"You'd probably never see her. You wouldn't work for her agent, and she's at a point where he goes to see her. She doesn't generally come in."

"I would get paid?" I ask.

"Oh yes. It's a real job, Haley. We have this one agent, who is any number of different diagnoses, including but not limited to ADD, OCD, and probably a good portion mental perfectionist."

"He sounds like Jay."

"Exactly what I was thinking. You'd be perfect! He needs to be handled, and he needs an assistant. Actually, he needs an assistant about every six weeks, but by then, something better would probably open up at the agency, and I could find you a decent boss."

"He's not Rachel's agent? You're sure."

"Positive, and for as insane as he is, he's brilliant, and he's got the Midas touch when it comes to talent. He just can't pick an assistant for beans because he has so much work. He piles too much on them before they know what they're doing. He always goes for the lookers, but of course, they can't handle all the requirements. You have both!"

"I've never actually been an assistant, so I don't know—"

"So what would you call what you did in your marriage?"

"I shopped a lot. No, that's not true, I did a lot of detail work to make sure the movies got produced."

"A detail person is exactly what I need, and it sure doesn't hurt that you're gorgeous. I can't go wrong!"

"What would I have to do?" I ask, like it matters. *Right now, the only talent I'm using is my remote finger.*

"Handle him. If he tells you to do this, but he really needs something else done, you handle it. You smile pretty to his face, then do what needs to be done. Do you understand?"

"Sadly, I understand perfectly."

Lily takes out a card. "Be here at three o'clock today. I'll set up the interview."

I grasp it. "I will. Thank you!"

"Do you have a job for me?" Helena asks.

"Helena, you're in the sciences. What would I have for you?"

She shrugs. "Probably nothing, but I'm bored and tired of looking for something."

"You know, Helena, you probably could use a little coaching in your interviewing skills. You know, subtly keeping the truth to yourself sometimes? I could help you with that this week, if you like," Lily offered.

Helena lights up, "You'd help me with that?"

"Just get me a description of what kind of job you're going for, and your résumé, and I'm happy to help."

Bette rubs Helena's back. "We're all going to be working soon. I can feel it! This is our year!"

Chapter 12

Penny, the dark-haired yoga gal, walks in with a double stroller inside which are two toddlers hitting each other and crying. "Hey, sorry I'm late. My mom canceled, so I brought the twins. Sorry, I had to get out though."

The twins, two boys, are wailing, and though they seem to be in abject pain, they continue to inflict havoc upon one another. One of the boys grabs the other's ear and starts to pinch, while the other twin takes a clump of hair and practices his version of a saltwater taffy pull. The screams get louder and Penny, with her yoga body and sense of inner calm, looks as if she might pull her own hair out. There aren't enough downward dogs and cobra positions in anyone's routine to quiet the souls of these two screaming toddlers.

I step down from the massage chair (without getting wet), as no one has started on my pedicure yet, and kneel before the stroller in my bare, wet feet and smile at the boys. They look to one another and wail louder. I hand them each a fishy cracker on their stroller trays. "Are you hungry?"

The boys are towheads sporting bright blue eyes, which have already developed a sense of mischief. They stop torturing one another and look at me, tears still on their cheeks and watery eyes flowing. I touch their cheeks with the back of my fingers. "They're gorgeous, Penny. How old are they?"

"Eighteen months," she says with a heavy sigh. "It only *feels* like six years."

"Well, they probably need a little exercise."

"I think they've already had eighty laps around the house this morning."

"They're walking, right?" I start to pull one of the boys out of the stroller. Maybe it's my biological clock, maybe the lack of affection, but I want to cuddle these munchkins and not let go. Even their screaming doesn't put me off. "Truthfully, this is how I feel when I've been in the motel too long. Maybe they just need some good, ol' vitamin D sunshine."

"Don't do that, Haley! They'll be all over," Helena objects, lifting her feet out of the water like I'm letting rats out of the cage.

"I'll just take them for a little walk. There's a park right up the street. Jay used to run there every day." I look to Penny. "Would that be all right if I took them for a walk? It would give you a chance to relax, and it would give me something to do. Relaxing isn't exactly a big need at the moment, and who is going to see my feet?"

"Just don't wear open toe shoes to the interview today," Lily warns.

"You don't mind?" Penny asks. "I suppose you heard my husband was sleeping with the nanny, so we're in counseling, and I'm out a nanny. Some days I wonder what's harder." She laughs, but I can see the truth in her eyes.

"I can have a pedicure anytime." I slide into my sandals, one soggy, one not, and take a toddler with each hand. "What are their names?"

"Jonah's on the left. He has a mole over his right eye and Micah there, doesn't. Jonah starts things and Micah's happy to finish them. Here, take my cell phone, so you can call if you need to. Everyone else's number is programmed in, so you can find us." I grab the phone and place it in my back pocket.

"Come on, boys, let's go for a walk. I'll bring you right back to Mommy after we go to the park for a while."

They both look to their mother and start to cry, so I bend down again, and their whimpering soon slows with my gentle words. "We'll go to the park up the street and let Mommy get her feet washed. Do you like swings? Then we'll come back when Mommy is all done, and she'll be happy again." After some careful finagling, the boys come with me as we walk out the door and toward the sunlight. "Anything I need to know?" I ask Penny.

"Keep your hands on them so they don't run into the street. They're very fast. Faster than you might think them capable." She climbs down from the chair. "I should go with you."

"Penny, I ran Jay Cutler's life for eight years, I can handle two toddlers for a half an hour."

"You're an answer to prayer, Haley. Thank you." She climbs into the chair, and I can see her Zen moment is about to come. Without any yoga moves whatsoever.

I'm too tall to walk with both boys on my hands, so I kick off my sandals in the doorway and walk barefoot up the street.

Their touch is like a slice of heaven as they grasp my hands with their chubby fingers. There's power in having a warm grasp hold on to you like that, and my mood lifts. I talk peacefully to them the whole way to the small park. Once there, I put each of them into a baby swing and launch the ride gently.

Their giggles are infectious and I find myself singing to them aloud and stopping to listen each time they laugh. Wouldn't it be great to laugh like that? To laugh from the belly with reckless abandon and not know there is anything painful out there waiting to pounce?

"I'm not a praying girl, boys. But I pray your mommy and daddy make it, because you two are worth the trouble."

"Talking to yourself, Haley?"

I turn around and see Jay in his running shorts that I purchased for him at Nordstrom on sale. They were $33.88 in fact. I look at him, then to the boys. What might ours have looked like? Jay appears healthy—fresh and rested, like he's been on vacation. His skin is a luscious, golden brown, and I can see why I fell in love with him in his warm smile. In his boyish charm he has this amazing ability to erase all the evil he's done. It's like a magic potion to me, and it erases so much.

I think about how when I was reading the Bible in my motel room, while waiting for *Jerry Springer* to come back on, it said that part of the curse on woman, besides pain in childbirth, which I'll apparently never know, is that thy desire shall be to thy husband, and he shall rule over you. Well, I'm cursed something awful. I could fall all over again if he'd give me the time of day. Some part of me will always belong to him. I *should* hate him. A smart woman would hate him. A woman with a lick of sense would hate him.

But just like always, when I look at him, I want his approval. I want him to tell me he's made a mistake.

"I'm talking to my friend's boys. This is Jonah and this is Micah."

"How can you tell?"

"Jonah has a tiny mole over his eyebrow. See here?"

Jay slows the swing and looks at Jonah. "No, I don't." Jonah starts to cry. Jay's charm doesn't translate to toddler.

"Jay, don't get so close. He doesn't know you."

Micah starts to wail at his ride being over as Jay studies him too. Jay pushes the swing with a little too much force. I still it. "What are you doing, Jay? They're children! Take it easy."

"It's a tough world, might as well prepare them," he screams over Jonah. "Whose rugrats? Feisty little buggers."

"My friend Penny's. Look at those faces, Jay," I say, when the twins are calm again. "Doesn't that make you want to believe in God? Look at their hands, the work of beauty they are. Like prized works of art."

Jay has that caged animal look he gets when he doesn't like where the conversation is headed. Which translates, anything veering away from his favorite topic: him. "Yeah, I guess."

"What are you doing here, anyway?" I ask him. "You never come here on the weekdays." The park is his normal jogging route, but during the week, he usually jogs at the beach or a park by the studio. At least he used to. I suppose I'm not an expert on Jay Cutler's routine any longer.

"I'm at home reading scripts today. I'd love to know what you think about this one. It's serious. I think it could be a contender, Haley. I'm ready for that, don't you think?" He looks at me expectantly. "The Golden Globes lit a fire under me that I could be doing more with my life. I got it right on that last script."

"I picked that script," I say, and he looks puzzled. "The one that won Rachel her award."

"No, you didn't."

"I did, Jay. I picked it, and I hand-selected Rachel Barlin for the role when I saw her on a television drama. *CSI: Miami* to be specific."

"Haley, you don't know the first thing about what I do. Rachel was never on that show."

The way Jay says things, it's no wonder I am afraid to have an opinion. I know I picked that script. I know I found Rachel, and yet here he is making me question these very facts, like I'm living in some sort of alternate universe. I know just what he needs. He needs Helena, a woman with a photographic memory who can tell him he's full of crap. Not a mouse like me. I find the familiar anger stirring within me.

"Why would I say that if it weren't true?"

"You're trying to get more money out of me, and don't think I don't know that you can captivate Hamilton Lowe. He's easy prey for a woman like you, but that agreement is rock solid, I made sure of it myself because I know how good you are." He looks at the boys, whose eyes are glued to him. "You look beautiful, Haley. Maybe putting on a little weight."

"I'm eating a lot of chocolate. Not working out so much," I say like a rebellious teenager.

"Why would you do that?"

"I'm pregnant," I blurt. Which of course, I'm not and in fact would be a miracle if I were, but I want to see if there's even a smidge of jealously. I want to hear that Jay cares something about me and not just my image.

"Wow." He checks out my figure. "Whose is it?"

"I'm not sure." Now that sounds Hollywood.

Nothing. No jealousy. Not a flash of the eyes. Nothing. He is inhuman. It's that simple. Then . . .

"It's not mine. You know that, right? Don't try to extort—"

"I know it's not yours, Jay," I say simply. "That would be impossible, wouldn't it?"

I used to watch Jay's strong legs run and think how lucky I was to have such a gorgeous husband who cared enough to take care of himself. I wish I'd seen that he *only* took care of himself. Some people are like giant SUVs, they just require more effort, more energy, and leave an indelible carbon footprint on your backside.

"You should take this movie, Jay. I think you can do anything you want. You can be a contender if you wish."

"I trust your opinion, Haley. You always did have a good head for business."

"Only when it agrees with yours, Jay."

"You won't give this script a read-through? For old times' sake?"

I look back at the boys and blow them kisses as I push the swing. "I can't help you anymore, Jay. I have to help myself now. Besides, didn't you just say I didn't know anything about what you did?"

"Hamilton said you were going to the tabloids. You won't do that. I told him you wouldn't."

I won't. He's right. "How do you know what I'll do?"

"You're a kind person, Haley. You may try to act like me, but you'll never be like me. It's one of the reasons I married you. I knew you'd always be there for me."

"And the reason you divorced me?"

"It wasn't personal."

I start to laugh.

"No, really. I don't like who I am with you. I'm better with a more independent woman who knows what she wants."

"I always knew what I wanted, you just told me it was ridiculous." Micah and Jonah start to fuss, and I pull them out of their swings. "I need to get back. Penny will be worried about the boys." I look Jay directly in the eyes and he looks away, like he always does.

"Rachel is pregnant, too," Jay blurts.

"I thought—"

"It's not mine," he says, as naturally as you please.

"And you're okay with that?" My eyes fill with tears as I see he is okay with it. I am not okay with it. I've been sucker-punched. I'm not good enough for him, but some tramp carrying another man's baby is what he wants? Just when I think I know Jay, I realize I don't know him at all.

He shrugs. "Why shouldn't I be? She's with me now. She's a smart girl. I have nothing to fear, she has the best now."

I live in an alternate universe, and I think, in this case, that's fine by me. He runs off as soon as he's done with our lightning-quick conversation and I take the boys and we toddle back to the salon.

Lindsay is finishing up her pedicure when I bring the boys back to Penny, and Lindsay smirks at me. "You're supposed to be here getting to know us. You did bail on your promise, but I forgive you."

"I was getting to know these handsome fellas instead." I kiss the boys on the cheek as they scramble to their mother. "I always did do better with the boys." I wink at her.

"Me too. That's why I'm going back to my husband," Lindsay tells me.

"You're what?"

She nods. "I prayed about it."

"Do you want that?"

"I need to. I asked God, and I just need to do this."

I nod.

"He's sick."

"Sick?"

"He's had a few ministrokes. And I think the pressure of being alone is more than he can take. He doesn't have the energy to be a workaholic right now."

"So will you nurse him back to health, so he does?"

Lindsay laughs. "That's not my intention, no."

"You sound like you're going to the gallows, Lindsay. Shouldn't this be a happy thing if you're going back to your marriage?"

"It's a duty. I don't expect you to understand, but I've been selfish my whole life. I have a chance to do the decent thing here. I want to be the person who does the decent thing even if it isn't appreciated here on earth. I know God will appreciate it, and that's who I want to impress, not anyone here. I'm not trying to fix anything for God. I'm only trying to make me a better person."

"You offered to take me in off the street. That makes you a better person in my eyes. Maybe you could ask God if that's enough goodwill for the day."

Lindsay giggles.

"What does the priest say about this?"

"He's a pastor, and he thinks I should go. That I'll feel guilty if anything happens to Ron."

"I might feel guilty too, but maybe I'd get over it."

"For all his faults, he never left me out in the cold, Haley. The condo is proof of that. He continued to support me. It may not be much emotionally, but he gives whatever he's able to. I can appreciate that more now. It's the decent thing to do, and he's not a believer, so now it's my turn to rise above my humanity."

"The decent thing would have been to honor his marriage vows and not work himself to death, but it's all a matter of degree, I suppose."

"I want you to take the condo."

"What do you mean?"

"You don't have a place to live. I have a place to rent, and we can use the write-off, so take it."

I look around the room at this bevy of beautiful women. In the span of an hour, they've offered me a job and a place to live, and friendship. But more importantly, they've offered me hope. It's something I didn't have a few hours ago.

"Thank you, Lindsay." I can barely get the words out. "I just told Jay I was pregnant."

"Jay?"

"I saw him at the park."

"Why would you tell him that? You're not, are you?"

"No, I'm not. But I think I'd like to be." I look over to the twins. "I want to be a mother."

"Wait a minute, Haley. Hold up. You're freaking me out. First thing when I met you, you were saying you never wanted to be married again."

"I meant that."

Lindsay sighs. She's exasperated with me. I thought telling my mother this idea would be tough, but Lindsay is not exactly the pillar of support I was looking to test it out on.

"When did you come up with this stupid idea?"

"At the park with the boys."

Penny rolls her eyes, "Girl, you need to come to my house and spend the night. I'll grant you, they're darling for an hour or so."

"I've been taking care of Jay for eight years. At least with children, they would love me back."

"Haley," Bette says. "Obviously, you haven't heard of teenagers. Why don't you ask your own mother about teenagers and how much they love you back?"

"You are all doing to me exactly what Jay always did. I made a decision, don't you see?"

"You had an idea. There's a difference, and we're just telling you it's a stupid idea. We're telling you because we love you, not because we want you to feel bad about yourself," Helena adds. "We're all about positive self-esteem here."

They love me? They don't even know me! Do they know I walk into walls? That I have a cat who I abandoned? That I hate driving fancy cars? Do they know any of that? No, so their opinion doesn't count! But the fact is that Helena said it, so it's got to be true on some level. Last time I checked, Vulcans couldn't lie.

"I've got to run to the motel and get dressed for this afternoon. I want to practice being professional. Lily, are there any glass walls in this office?"

"I don't think so," she answers, then after a pause, "Why?"

"No reason. Just asking."

"I'll meet you at the door at three o'clock on the dot. Don't be late!"

"I won't."

I pause at the door. "You all really think being a mother is a bad idea right now?"

A loud collective groan comes up. Apparently, it might be a bad idea, but I glimpse over at Jonah and Micah, and they offer me a smile as big as sunshine, so I'm not thoroughly convinced.

"Haley!" Lindsay calls.

"What?"

"Take my cell phone. The number is written on the inside of the case. I can never remember it." She presses it into my hand.

"'Take my cell phone, take my condo.' Is there anything else you'd like to give me?"

"A piece of my mind, but there's plenty of time for that. Go get a job."

I haven't been on a job interview in nearly a decade. I am so glad I shaved today.

Chapter 13

CMG is a giant conglomerate in the talent industry, and its modern "green" building demands the respect it deserves. The roof is tilted upwards to make room for the solar panels, announcing their commitment to Hollywood's "issue du jour." As I walked in from the parking garage, in the "Employee of the Month" slot was a brand-new hybrid. I have to wonder if it comes with the label.

Believe it or not, there is a lot of talent in Hollywood. I think when Paris Hilton is on television, the general population forgot this town gave rise to a worldwide entertainment industry. The lobby is all marble (slipping potential high and not sure how that fits in with global warming).

The expansive room is filled with hopefuls, some reciting lines to themselves, one doing some form of deep meditation where his arms are capturing the light, outstretched to the ceiling, and all of them looking around to check out their competition. I spy one girl take her fingers and try to "measure" a nearby hopeful's waist.

Lily, unlike Helena, doesn't have a photographic memory because the building is nearly all glass, and I talk to myself about focusing.

Keep your eyes ahead of you.

Listen with your ears. Watch with your eyes.

"Haley, perfect, you're on time!" Lily comes out of the elevator, and all the hopefuls looks as if they might rush it. When they see her speak to me, their chests all collapse in disappointment.

"Of course I am. I am more punctual than a Blackberry. I thought you said this place wasn't glass."

"Did I? Sorry, my mind wanders on details."

"I wore heels."

"So?" She looks down at my feet. "Those aren't heels." She slides her foot to the side, and she must have five-inch stilettos on. "These are heels."

"Never mind."

"Bud Seligman is the agent you'll be meeting today. He's crazier than a loon, so if he says something off the wall, just smile. He's probably ticking off things he needs to do this afternoon. Without an assistant, he's lost."

"Why did the last one leave?"

"We don't generally publicize our jobs because most people who take them are just aspiring actors trying to get an 'in.' This particular girl bucked the system. She was a friend of someone in accounting."

"But why did she leave?"

"She didn't know what she was doing. Bud is actually very kind if you do your job and cover any mistakes he might make. Nothing is ever his fault, all right? If clients call up, and he's screwed up or forgotten a meeting, it's your fault, you didn't write it in his calendar."

"Sounds familiar."

"He's very busy. Spends his life on a cell phone and can negotiate like Satan himself, so just know that going in. The only time he'll pay attention to you is if you do something wrong."

"Hey, sort of like my marriage."

"Keep that out of it. He probably knows Jay, and it might be better if you don't mention your marital status."

I hold up my ring finger. "My diamond is paying my motel bill, so I'm good."

We take the elevator to the top floor, and when the doors open, a view of the surrounding buildings comes into view. All glass. Every last wall. I look down at the travertine floor. All slippery, all the time. "I don't stand a chance here."

"What?"

"I don't think I can focus on this job and walk at the same time."

"You're not even wearing heels." Lily looks down at my shoes.

"These are heels. If I wear tall heels, I can't talk either."

"What skills do you have? What did you do before you got married? I told him you'd been your producer husband's assistant, but if he asks you about your professional history—"

"I can fold a perfect shirt."

Lily pulls her clipboard to her chest. "Let's just not mention work experience, all right?"

"I was never late. Had perfect attendance. And I can size someone just by looking at her."

"We'll focus on the fact that you're detail-oriented." Lily walks ahead of me with a self-assured stride (in heels). She's got that *Vogue* confidence most women only dream of. She raps quietly on the door, and inside there's a man pacing while talking on his Bluetooth headset. He's got TV preacher hair, dark and dyed, too full for his age. I can tell he's not married. No self-respecting woman would let her husband go out in a toupee that bad. He's a wadded-up ball of stress. You can see it in the bulging veins in his neck.

Stand back everyone . . . he's gonna blow!

His lime green business shirt is open at the collar, to reveal rashy, bologna-colored skin. His tie lies loosely around his shoulders. He rubs his temples as he shouts into thin air, "I don't care how you interpret the contract. You're not a contract lawyer. I only care how the courts interpret the contract, and I'll tell you exactly how they're going to interpret it, because there are a thousand precedent cases that show you've got nothing here."

He paces toward the window and back. Clearly, the windbag on the other end of the line is having his turn yelling. It's no wonder these types hate women in the workplace. They employ absolutely no manners in business and don't want to be reminded of that.

Of course, he might be perfectly amiable. I should wait five minutes before I hate him. Seeing Jay's personality in a paunchy old man with a bad toupee makes me question just how vain I am. I heard Jay yell exactly like this, but I'm embarrassed to say I found it a little hot. How depressing.

I am a snob.

And I really do like to shop.

My best friends are still at the other end of a credit card transaction.

Hmmm. Maybe Jay was a trophy husband for me too?

"I told you the script isn't ready. She's not taking a role with substandard writing. You have two options, you can get a screenplay adapter in there to fix that mess, or you can say good-bye to my client!" He punches his ear button and stares at me, open-eyed and lizardlike. "What do you want?"

Lily steps forward. "This is the assistant I was telling you about. May I present Haley Cutler?"

He nods. "I know her. You're Jay's wife?"

"Ex wife."

He snivels. "Well, no loss there. You type?"

I nod.

"Fast?"

"I do. I used to type people's papers in college." I have a skill! "And I worked briefly for a loan broker before I got married."

"Did you hear that phone call?"

I nod. "Anaheim Stadium heard that phone call."

The corner of his lip lifts into a grin. "You're not afraid of me."

"I was married to a producer for eight years. I'm not afraid of anything."

He nods. "We'll get along fine. You're first job is to arrange it with Human Resources so that you have a job. I hate all that paperwork. Can't be bothered with it. You figure out how to hire yourself, then get back to that desk and answer the phone. We got ourselves a partnership."

"Right now, sir?"

"We're not getting any younger."

"Yes, Mr. Seligman."

"Wait a minute," he says as I start to walk out of the door.

"Yes?"

"You don't want to be an actress, do you? She's too pretty to want to be an assistant," he says to Lily.

"My ex-husband is living with an actress. I have no use for them whatsoever. I'll be nice to them if I have to."

He snickers. "Lily, good job on this one. Now go," Bud says to me. "Don't disappoint me."

"What's my salary?"

"What are you worth?"

"Well, you can't afford that," I tell him.

"Start her at the top, Lily." His eyes narrow at me. "You're fired if you're not worth it."

"Got it, but I am."

I have a job! Not the kind I have to marry for, but a legitimate, you-do-the-work, you-get-a-paycheck job. Haley Adams Cutler is back.

I have a job. I might have a place to live. I have the Jay Cutler Memorial Scholarship Fund for the next six months, and I think I might even have friends who would pick up the pedicure tab.

The world must be ending tomorrow.

"I have a job!" I squeal into the phone as I get into my sorry rental car, that I'm so getting rid of immediately. Do you have any idea what it's like to drive a car that's worth less than most people's shoes in this town?

"Who is this?" a man's voice answers.

"Oh sorry," I nibble at my thumbnail. "This is Haley Cutler. I punched the button programmed 'home' and thought I'd get Lindsay. Does Lindsay live there? I'm on her cell phone."

"Well, I'm pleased you acquired a job, Miss Haley Cutler. Lindsay has told me so much about you."

"She has?" I pull the phone away from my ear and stare at it. "Who are you?"

"She's so pleased you're going to take the condo."

"I never said –"

"Of course you'll take it. Where else are you going to go?"

He has a point. "Who is this again?"

"This is Ron. Lindsay's husband."

"Right. Congratulations on your marriage?" I didn't mean for it to come out as a question, but I'm not sure what the etiquette is for "not divorcing" status. I have yet to see a Hallmark card for the occasion.

"Yes, well my marriage is convenient for both of us, Haley. I get my wife back, and you get her lovely condo."

"I got a job. I have more options now, so I don't need to bum off Lindsay," I say enthusiastically.

"Not many more options without established credit. I can help you with that if you like."

"Why?" Do I sound like I need help? Because I'm thinking I'm the very air of confidence at the moment.

Ron laughs. "Why would I help? Because Lindsay can't say enough nice things about you, and my wife is an excellent judge of character."

Which is odd, since she doesn't like his, in particular.

"I think pretty highly of her, too. She picked me up when I was down." Of course, I don't mention that a lot of strangers have done the same thing when I walked into a wall, or the like. This was different. This was personal.

"She told me you were the reason she decided to come back home, so I have to tell you, I'm eternally grateful."

"Me? Lindsay said that? I think you might have the wrong friend. Those gals have been together a long time."

"No, it was definitely you. I may have forgotten anniversaries and birthdays, but I don't forget the name of the woman that my wife says convinced her to come back. So if I can help you get a portfolio started, I'm more than happy to do so."

"Ron, is Lindsay there?" *Because you are too happy for words, and it's sort of scaring me.*

"I didn't pay enough attention to her. I know that now. What an imbecile I was. I see it all so clearly now. It took a stroke or two to bring me back to my senses."

"I'm sorry to hear that."

"She's my world, Haley. You have no idea. As Lindsay says, Lazarus got a second chance, and so have I."

There are two sides to every story. I realize that. Example: I thought Jay was controlling and emotionally unavailable. He thought I was a doormat. Well, I was a doormat and yet, my assessment of him still holds true. I can't make heads or tails of what Ron is trying to say, but I'm sure his side is in there somewhere, and he certainly sounds appreciative to have his wife back. I can't imagine Jay ever uttering the words that I, or anyone else besides him, was his world. My muscles stiffen with envy for Lindsay's ability to captivate Ron as I realize that I will never have this. Looking up at the fantastic building that houses my new job, I wonder if I can ever be grateful for what I do have.

"Would you have Lindsay call me when she gets in?"

"She's at the condo cleaning it out for you. Why don't you go over there? She's really excited to introduce you around the complex." He then proceeds to give me the address and, before I know it, my cheapo rental car is chugging toward Bel Air. I wonder if *they* have a neighborhood watch.

The Trophy Wives Club is too convenient. I'm still very leery. Women don't usually like me. I think it's because I'm tall. I enter a room, and people just stare, like a giraffe has walked in. I've gotten used to it, and maybe it's because I've had more than my share of other women's boyfriends rescue me from walking into something. But I meet these women, they buy me pedicures, and give me a job and a condo? I'm thinking they'll be passing around the Kool-Aid at any moment and asking me to swig, long and deep.

Lindsay is taller than me. Lily, Helena, and Penny are all prettier. Bette is smarter than me. I daresay I could walk in next to any one of them and be completely ignored unless I knocked over a Tiffany lamp or family vase. I look down at the scrap of paper where I'd scribbled the address and up again at the address, which has the number in bronze on it. *This can't be it. If this is what she gets when she divorces a guy, I can't imagine what happens when she's married to him.* She's probably going to get her own island.

I'm still focused on the house number when I miss a step leading up the pathway's gentle slope. I go down so fast, I don't even realize it until I'm on the step, bum first. I look down to see my toenail bleeding. *Darn it!*

"You all right?" a deep voice asks me as he extends his arms to help me up.

The sun is blocking his face. "Is this 8030?" I ask, hoping whoever he is, he doesn't notice my toenail. Ugh, is there anything grosser than a toenail issue? I have to turn the page when I see a magazine page advertising some fungal cure.

"Not sure. Looks like it might be. You took a hard fall, are you sure you're all right?"

"Oh, I'm fine. That wasn't that hard." I push myself up off the bricks. "I've done a lot worse. Ruined a pair of Donald Pliners just this morning. Well, they'll dry out, hopefully."

He looks at me oddly. Hey, he asked. Well, maybe he didn't.

I look up toward the house, ignoring my throbbing foot. This collection of condos was clearly built in the late fifties and has that modern, retro look, with lots of glass and clean lines. This look is so sought-after, since Brad Pitt bought that ugly house and famously furnished it with uncomfortable sofas. *Clean lines,* Hollywood said, and formerly unpopular older buildings suddenly became coveted property like the rat pack had come to life again. The lawns leading up to the entrance are meticulously landscaped, the hedges from a bygone era are freshly trimmed.

I head up the next step, when I remember my rescuer. "Hey, thanks."

In that instant, rather than a simple you're welcome, he starts to belt out a show tune from *Les Miserables*. He stands, feet well apart, legs perfectly straight, and hits each note with a sweeping hand motion. I look around to see if there's a camera hidden nearby, or if Lindsay is playing a great practical joke, but she doesn't know I'm coming, and the guy just keeps belting it out.

After my initial shock, I'm able to see he's good-looking, at least. Maybe Ashton Kutcher-like, with bigger teeth (if that's possible) and a slighter frame. I'm still looking for the camera as I start to back away. After a tap dance that clicks his way up the steps following me, I'm in for a treat with a big finish that lands him on his knees, outstretched, his arms in fists over his head.

At this, he stands and waits for some sort of response. I'd really like to give him one, too, but my mother taught me if you can't say something nice . . . "Javert."

"Right!" He points at me. "You're a fan?"

"I was. What the heck was that?"

"Javert's lament before his suicide."

"Sounded more like after."

"That's just cruel."

"I don't have any change," I say, as I dig around in my purse. *I sure hope this is Lindsay's place! If not, I'm going to make myself right at home in whoever's house it is.*

He comes alongside me and reaches in his back pocket. I lace my single car key, through my fingers, but instead of some sort of weapon, he flips out a CD. "It's my DVD."

"Yes?"

"Get it to Bud Seligman for me, will you?" He pats me on the shoulder. *What is it with people patting me? Am I suddenly wearing a collar?* "If you enjoyed my performance in the slightest, please give Mr. Seligman my regards and let him know how hard I worked to get this to him." Then he bows at the waist and clicks his heels together.

"This was a sales pitch? Are you psychotic?" I pull my key higher, and he backs up.

"Who doesn't like a little *Les Mis* after a long day?"

"In the first place, I did not enjoy your performance! One is not normally looking for a show tune performance after a first day on the job with a boss like Bud Seligman." I catch my breath. "Secondly, why would I do you any sort of favor when you scared the daylights out of me?" I shake my head.

"How could that possibly have scared you?"

"Really, you should warn a girl if you're going to break into song—because I thought you were some new type of serial killer that only L.A. could create."

"Serial killer? What kind of serial killer has both formal and classical training in the arts?"

"I don't know. I don't know any serial killers personally." My eyes bore through him, as though I might need to remember details. "Do you?"

"Of course not. I'm a dancer. Dancers are happy. We don't kill people."

Now that I know why he's here, he doesn't look nearly so frightening, and I start to relax. "What else you got? Javert's suicide lament is too big for the street."

"I can juggle."

"People hate jugglers. Almost as much as they hate mimes."

"You're really a buzzkill, you know that?"

"You introduced yourself as a dancer, so that's how you see yourself. Lose the Broadway vocals, that's my advice." I walk around him again.

"You're a secretary for an agent and not even for a full day. Why should I listen to you?"

"Exactly. So use your ingenuity that you put into stalking me and think up a better brand. You can do it; you're creative, or you wouldn't have thought to follow me."

"You certainly have a lot of opinions for an admin."

"I do have a lot of opinions, it's just that no one has ever actually listened to them. So why start now?"

"Because you work for one of the most powerful men in Hollywood, that makes your opinion count. Even if it sucks."

"I'll have you know, I've been assistant producing for close to a decade. It's not enough to be as good as everyone else. That's what you might think, huh? I'm better than Justin Timberlake or James Blunt, but most likely, you're not. So you have to do something different, better. Be original. You have to look at what makes those men special and find that in yourself. What do you have that no one else can offer? I'm thinking it's got to be something different."

"You're not a very likeable person."

For some reason, I take this as a complete compliment and grin from ear to ear. "Thank you. That's the first time anyone has ever said that to my face."

"I'm sure it's not the first time they said it behind your back." He laughs. "But I appreciate the advice. I'll work on it."

"Do that, and I'll look at it. If I like it, I'll get the DVD to Bud. I promise. But don't you dare stalk me again. You freaked me out, and women do crazy things when they freak out."

"Deal."

I look up at the doorway, and Lindsay is cracking up while wearing rubber gloves and holding a bottle of bleach.

"I'm so getting a gun," I tell her as I pass her into the house.

"So, does this mean you are going to take the place?" Lindsay is donned in an apron with red chili peppers, and she's got her hair tied back and a rag in her hand.

"It's really good for my soul to see you look this bad."

"Because I want you to have everything perfect. You're moving in?"

"Believe it or not, I really want to shower again with a whole bar of soap. It's the little things you miss. You didn't clean this place yourself, did you?" I let my eyes run up and down her getup.

"I did," she says proudly. "I can clean, you know. It's not rocket science, and a bottle of bleach goes for an eternity and makes everything seem cleaner than it is."

"Not rocket science, but it is a skill. I can't clean for the life of me. Things always look worse after I start." I push through the foyer, which is beautiful, with an iridescent blue glass tile on the floor. "Italian?" I ask her.

"You know it."

"How do you clean them?"

"It's best with a toothbrush and Windex for deep cleaning, but a rag works for normal touch-ups. I have this environmental stuff for when I have my green friends over, but Windex works best."

"I was banned from cleaning at the house. One time I tried to wipe the stainless-steel fridge down and used furniture polish by mistake. I didn't read the label. It never did recover, and my maid told me if I touched 'her' fridge again, I'd never hear the end of it. So I decided to embrace my slovenliness that day."

"I clean to ward off anxiety. It calms me."

"Well, you're welcome to come over and get relaxed anytime you feel like it. This will be like a spa date for you." I wink. "I'm kidding. I'll hire someone and take good care of the place. There are truths you learn about yourself in life. Like maid service is not a luxury for me and that once I start a tub o' frosting, I am not putting it down until I scrape the bottom of it."

"That is nasty. Don't admit that." She puts the bleach down in the hall closet. "Don't hire anyone. I'll come clean it. You can scrape the iridescence off this if you scrub too much. Maids always want to scrub too much."

"Right. Just lend me your million-dollar condo, then come over and clean it while you're at it. I'll hire whoever you want me to. Did you want to cook for me, too?"

"I can't cook."

"Good. I can. Now, we're equal again, we can be friends." I try to take in all the visuals around me, but there is a complete absence of buff or sand or whatever you want to call California-can't-trust-myself-with-color beige.

The condo is awash in this incredible underwater, tropical blue with iridescent tones and silver accents. It sounds tacky, but it's luxurious in a way I never thought possible. It's warm and relaxing and yet clean and sparse. The blues are warmed by a honey-colored wood floor and a Persian rug that ties all the colors together subtly. "This place is incredible."

"It's the first place I decorated totally on my own. No designer involved. I tried everything, and I thought if it didn't work, I could always change it later, but I loved it from the very start. It makes me feel like I'm in Hawaii all the time." She points to the French doors. "Look on the patio, I had that Queen Palm put in, and it's like my own lanai."

"Lindsay"—I walk around and gaze at the artwork and vases she has about—"this is beyond simple decorating, you have a gift! Why don't you charge for your services?"

She grins. "I don't think I could be reined in by someone's rules.

This place . . ." She runs her hand along a wall. "This place was my refuge when Ron and I separated. I put all my angst into tile selection and paint chips. "

"It worked for you. I just got fat eating chocolate frosting and ruined expensive shoes in spa chairs."

"Shut up. You look fantastic. If you're fat, the rest of us should all shoot ourselves."

"What am I going to do, Lindsay? What am I going to do with my life?"

"Working at CMG and living in Bel Air doesn't sound like all that bad a life!"

"Oh I know that, but it doesn't really solve my problem."

"Your problem?"

"Never mind. You don't need to hear me whine. I want to cover your mortgage on this place with rent. I can afford rent, you know. I'll have my money working for me because I've been getting great tips from a friend. Your husband."

"Yes, he called and said you were on your way over. There's no mortgage. Ron pays for everything with cash."

"There's taxes. Let me cover the taxes at least."

"We need the write-off. Ron said so. Come take the full tour."

"Ron is someone I have to meet. He's beside himself that you're coming home."

Lindsay looks off into the distance. "Yeah."

That was convincing. Marriage is like calculus. Complicated and inexplicably remote. People think it's about loving one another and riding off into the sunset, but no one tells you the horse is lame or that it's an eclipse, and there won't be a sunset that day.

Loving someone more than yourself takes more than effort—especially when they want something different from you. Especially when the something different is a sleazy actress. The truth of what goes on inside any marriage is really only for those involved to know.

"All I know is Ron would buy you an island."

"What are you talking about? This is the living area—" Lindsay points like Vanna. "I redesigned the place when I bought it. You should have seen it, oh it was a mess. Ron begged me not to take it. It was like Dean Martin meets Elvis's jungle room. But I saw its potential. It wanted to be given a new life and maybe in the process, I'd get one too."

"Maybe that's what I need? More of a purpose."

There's a floating circular staircase in the middle of the room as the place was the height of chic in 1960. It blocks the straight view to the kitchen, which is amazing. I run right to it. "Oh Lindsay! What do you mean you don't cook?"

"I don't cook, but I know enough about real estate to know it's the heart of the sale."

The cabinets are a painted silvery blue lacquer with small glass tiles as the backsplash, and all of the appliances are top-of-the-line, stainless steel.

"Lindsay, why on earth would you lend this place out? Are you nuts?" Standing in the tropical warmth of this house, it's all too much to take in how my life is slowly turning around. "You don't even know me that well. Why are you doing this?"

"Lending you the condo while you get your life back on track?"

"Well, yeah."

"God told me to."

"That is not an answer."

"It's not an answer you believe, but it's the truth. Seriously, when you walked in that first night, and we had coffee? That's when He told me you'd live here. I didn't even know Ron and I would get back together, so at that point, I thought He meant we'd live together as roomies."

"Well, if God wants me to have a million-dollar condo in Bel Air, who am I to argue?"

"My point exactly. So I take it by your dancing stalker, you got the job."

"I did! And what's better? I think I'm going to be good at it. It's nothing more than what I've done for eight years, only I get paid for it, and I don't have to sleep with the boss, Bud Seligman."

She laughs. "Thank goodness for that. I've seen Bud Seligman."

I run back into the living room and plop myself on the couch, kicking up my stocking feet on the coffee table. I've been here two minutes and feel more at home than I ever did in the Brentwood house.

"I'm home."

Lindsay smiles broadly. "I knew when I designed this place, it wasn't for me. I'm glad I get to see who it's for, and I'm glad I like her. Nothing worse than handing a house over to someone you don't like—even if you do like their cash."

"Lindsay, I can never make this up to you."

"You can."

"How?"

"You can read this." She hands me a Bible, and it's got my name inscribed on the cover. I hate to tell her I've been reading the free one in the motel for nothing, but I've never had a Bible.

"I've never owned one. We used to read booklets that had the Bible printed in sections for the sermons," I muse before noting she's waiting for an answer. "I'll read it. Thank you."

"Start in Matthew. It makes the Old Testament make more sense later."

It creeps me out that it's so imperative to her that I read an ancient text, but all the religions I've ever heard of ask for money, they don't give you million-dollar condos to live in, and Lindsay has been nothing but there for me. So for her . . . for this condo, I'll honor the agreement. Besides, it's cheaper sleeping medicine than Ambien.

Chapter 14

After two months, and the end of a long, cold winter and a chilly spring, May arrives. The hardest part of my job has been learning who is important enough to get through to Bud, and who isn't. Most people aren't, so I start with that assumption. If they're brandishing the name Hanks or Spielberg, common sense kicks in, but every once in a while, someone without a famous Jewish name calls, and I incur Bud's wrath. Like now.

"Don't you know who that is, Haley? You've been in this business for ten years, how is it you managed to dismiss Bill Messing?"

"I just did, that's all." I add Mr. Messing's name to my list of important people to put through. "Won't happen again. See?" I hold up the list.

"See that it doesn't. I had to listen to him for twenty minutes about how I couldn't get a decent assistant to save my life. I don't have twenty minutes, Haley."

That makes me want to cross his name right off my list. Sometimes, I think Bud just has to get out of the office and roar at someone. Prove he's still a man. Still alive. Still virile, as my mother would say.

Speaking of my mother, I called her on Lindsay's cell phone and she trilled that Gavin is dating someone. Was I planning a visit home soon? Ugh. Does she not see that I am man poison? Only selfish, arrogant men are immune by their own wickedness.

Bud sticks his head out again, "I'm on a call for the next hour. Hold my calls." He slams the door to his office, and I salute the door.

I look up and there's a wall of a chest sitting on my desk. I look up to his face. Handsome features and a strong jaw meet my gaze.

"Can I h-help you?" *See? I am looking for Trophy Husband material, this proves it!*

"George Stanley." He thrusts out a hand. "Bud's my agent." He sits back on my desk. "I'm starring in a new Western out next year, and I'm the new face for Melotti Underwear."

"Right." *Do not create a visual. Do not create a visual.* "I'm Haley Cutler, Bud's new assistant." I shake his hand, which is strong and firm.

"I can see that. Says right here *Assistant*."

He can read. That's a plus.

"I don't have you down for an appointment, Mr. Stanley. Did you want to see Mr. Seligman?"

"No appointment today. I'm just in to pick up a check. The little Asian hottie in HR has it waiting for me. Just wanted to say hi."

"Lily. Her name is Lily Tseng."

"You're not one of those women's libbers, are you? Haven't met a woman yet who didn't appreciate being called a hottie."

"I'm sure you haven't."

"Hey, I'm a virile man—"

"Haley, is that you?" Outside the door, standing in the hallway, is Hamilton Lowe. Speaking of virile. *Ugh. I did not just think that. Bad Haley! But oh my, he's like a steamy vision after seeing only Bud and his cronies important enough to get to the sanctuary.* Even Underwear Boy isn't tempting. Especially Underwear Boy isn't tempting. There's a world I could do without: public underwear showings. There was a time in my lifetime when you had to open a J.C. Penney catalog to see people in their underwear. Now it's like the national pastime, hanging out in your underwear. I don't see why they have to pay anyone to model it.

Hamilton steps inside the office and stands over my desk, completely ignoring Bud's client. He picks up my nameplate. He's still tall. I love that. Not that I care anything about him, you understand. I just like tall men. The norm is for me to tower over men, so it's a sweet surprise when I don't. It would be better still if this man weren't the devil himself. He's good eye candy regardless. More evidence that I am indeed shallow.

Hamilton's wearing a red-and-navy pin-striped shirt. *Facconable*. It's paired with a red silk power tie, so he must be here on business. Maybe he's here to ruin some new woman's life. He looks like the cover model for a Barcelino catalog. Facconable is one of my favorite brands on men because it's classically fashionable and doesn't look like he tried too hard, nor is it too metrosexual. I used to make Jay wear it when he had an important business meeting because it made him younger and more hip while being all business.

"I have a job," I finally say, since he doesn't seem to be willing to offer any cordialities of his own.

"I see that. Very impressive. Bud Seligman is not just any agent in this town. I suppose you know that."

"Yes, he's my agent," Underwear Boy says.

We both ignore him. "Bud turned Rachel Barlin down, so I'd have to say that's true. He has taste. He doesn't regret it, by the way. Thinks she's a shooting star who will die out fast, either in a scandal of some sort or make one bad movie too many," I say, with a tinge of spite in my voice. "That's impressive enough for me to work for anyone." I stack papers that don't need stacking, just to look professional.

"How'd you get this gig?" He nods toward the door.

"Tell Bud I stopped by and let him know I'm not impressed with his assistant." The male model stalks off.

"Already making friends I see," Hamilton says. "Did Jay give you the connections?"

"Believe it or not, Jay's not really into doing me favors at the moment." I sit up straight in my chair. I couldn't have a better job for myself if I were paid millions. I was a great assistant to Jay Cutler, but I'm a better one to Bud because I'm simply not in love with the man. Love changes the equation. For me, it's usually a negative number.

"It's a pretty high-end position." His face clouds. "I mean, for someone who hasn't worked for— no—" He stops to collect his thoughts. "I mean for—"

"Never mind. I know what you mean. I see why you're not a trial lawyer." The phone rings, and I put a finger up in the air. "Bud Seligman's office. Haley speaking, how may I help you?"

Bud has two lines of defense from callers. First, he has the downstairs' operator, then he has me. He has a private line for those people in the know, but I answer that generally because he's always on the phone.

"I'm not sure where he is in his production schedule, but I can check and have Bud get back to you . . . right . . . most definitely, it will be today. And thank you for calling."

I hang up, and Hamilton is walking around the office, checking out all of Bud's awards and recognition plaques.

"So what are you doing with yourself, Hamilton? I saw you at church a few weeks ago for Bible study, but you were in the sainted section, and I had to head to the sinners' room."

"You're still coming?"

"Not regularly, but I still keep up with the gals. Did you expect a heathen like me to drop out?"

"I didn't know if you were ready to hear what those women had to say."

"Those women?"

"Stop it. You're trying to catch me stumbling over my tongue. Can you assume something decent of me for one minute?"

"Not really, no." Again, he gives me that wounded animal look.

"You're making me answer to you to get money that rightfully belongs to me. That production business was at least 30 percent mine. If you think I should be decent to you, you underestimate your presence in my life, Hamilton."

"I'm not representing Jay anymore if it makes you feel any better. He dumped me for someone more sharklike. Someone Rachel recommended."

"Ah, so we both got dumped for the likes of Rachel. Pretty shrewd of her to get her own lawyer in place before any pre-nups."

"Naturally, I'm still handling your case and the ones I wrote contracts for, but Jay says I don't have the edge anymore." Hamilton has the verge of a smile. "That should brighten your day."

"Nothing is ever his fault, is it? That's just what he'd have you believe, that you've lost your edge because he's found someone better. Jay gets everyone around him to question their competence. Well, now you're right alongside me. A castoff. You be the professor, I'll be Mary Ann."

"What?"

"I knew you wouldn't get it."

"I get it. *Gilligan's Island*."

This makes me smile because I can't for the life of me imagine Hamilton Lowe was ever childish enough to sit through a sitcom. Any sitcom, much less *Gilligan's Island*.

"Maybe this is a sign you've grown a conscience. Maybe you believe that Bible verse on your wall now, huh? I don't remember what it said."

"It said I can do all things through Christ who strengthens me."

"And can you?"

He ignores the question. "So the Trophy Wives Club is working out well? That Bette really has a heart of gold. She can teach you a lot about servanthood."

I roll my eyes. "I think I could teach them all a thing about servanthood myself."

"I meant servanthood in a good Biblical way, not a dysfunctional way."

Hamilton is more nervous and fidgety than I've ever seen him before. Maybe it's because we're not on his turf, but he can't sit still, and he keeps rolling a pen in his hand.

"Is something wrong, Hamilton?"

"What?" He looks to the pen and drops it back in his pocket. "No, nothing's wrong. Why?"

"I owe you a debt of gratitude. Even if you didn't mean for anything good to come of it, the women in that group rescued me from a very bad daytime TV addiction and chocolate frosting fetish."

"Huh?"

"One of the gals found me this job. I moved into another's town house, since she's going back to her husband. One of them reminded me how much I wanted to be a mother . . ."

Crash!

Hamilton knocks over the pen receptacle and disappears behind my desk to pick them up. "Are you all right, Hamilton?" I stick my head over the desk.

He looks up at me with those incredibly large eyes and immediately looks down at the pens. "Fine."

"I thought you'd be happy about the women helping me find my worth again. Doesn't it assuage some of your guilt?"

He stands tall again. "I have no guilt. I protected my client's assets. That's what I'm hired to do."

"Well, I credit the women for giving me my life back—you know, the one that was stolen from me so you could protect your client's extramarital affair? This is a better life than the one I had because I'm not looking over my shoulder any longer."

"And the money? What did you do with the money from the first checks?"

"Not that it's any of your business, but I put it in separate CDs that mature every three months so I always have cash on hand. And, I'm putting as much as I can from my salary into a 401k. It turns out the fantastic redhead Helena is quite the stock expert. And Lindsay's husband is no slouch either. So with all their help, I'm well on my way."

"You look happy."

"I am brilliant."

"Jay says you won't go to the tabloids. Is that true? If so, I can just mail your next check." He nonchalantly stands up and places the pens back where they belong. "Why don't you write down your address?" He takes out a pad from his chest pocket and opens it to a clean page. He plucks a pen from the bucket and hands it to me.

"I thought you had to see me. You know, approve that I wasn't going to rat Jay and Rachel out to the tabloids, which by the way, I see they're doing enough of themselves."

"I trust you. People in glass houses and all that."

"What?"

"Right there." He points to the pad, and I scribble my new address.

"What about you, Hamilton, are you happy?"

Bud bursts out of his office. "Haley, I need those docs on my desk in ten minutes. Did you get them signed?"

"Yes, sir. They're right here." I hand him the manila folder. "Jerry Bruckheimer just called. He's interested in Hugh Jackman's availability for the fall." I rip off the message sheet and hand it to him.

"Hamilton," Bud nods. "Everything okay? You're not here to serve me, are you? Don't sign anything this man ever gives you," Bud says to me. "He's a piranha."

"Don't worry, that's what got me into this mess. Signing Hamilton's documents will only lead to trouble."

"Good girl, Haley."

"Just a personal call, Bud. I saw Haley as I finished up some business down the hall. We're old friends." Hamilton smiles, obviously glad to see he still strikes the fear of God in someone of stature.

"Then what are you hanging around for? Don't sign anything and don't date him either, he'll probably make you sign a contract giving him power of attorney. See you later, Hamilton. Quit flirting with my assistant. She's a knockout, ain't she?"

"That's sexual harassment!" I call to Bud.

"Tell it to my lawyer." He slams the door behind him with a snigger.

"I see you have a good working relationship with him."

"He's great. A little gruff, but nothing I can't handle. So, you're dodging my question. Are you happy?"

"Why do you care?"

"Because that's something I realized about myself. I could take satisfaction in a job well done each day, and I could try to please Jay and make the numbers work for a production, but I never had any fun. Fun is underrated. Do you have fun, Hamilton?"

"Does it matter?"

"Yes, it matters. That's why I'm asking. What's fun to you?"

"I don't know, Haley. I've got to get back to the office."

I nod. "Well, always a pleasure seeing you, Hamilton, especially when you don't have any documents in your hand."

"Yeah. Nice to see you, Haley. Maybe when things calm down we could have dinner together."

"It's all right, Hamilton, you don't have to offer up any mercy dates. I do appreciate your handing me the Trophy Wives flyer. When I make enough to keep my own husband, perhaps he'll need to start a group of his own."

"A mercy date? With you, Haley?" He laughs aloud. "Am I missing something?"

"You're missing a lot, actually, but that's beside the point. You would never end up with a girl like me. I'm tainted. Divorced. A sinner by all accounts."

He pauses. I knew he'd pause. He still can't bring himself to see me as anything more than a client's wife who brought him coffee. "The Bible says to marry a divorcee is to make her an adulteress."

"I am an adulteress. At least from what I've gleaned in the little Bible knowledge I have." I nod. "But I understand, you can only do what you can do. You're standing up for what you believe in, and I totally admire that. But be honest with yourself, Hamilton. Don't play with fire and have some mercy, don't flirt with the likes of me." I flip my hair for emphasis.

I get up to file some paperwork when Hamilton speaks.

"I was brought up to believe divorce doesn't happen."

"So what would you have me do, Hamilton? In my case? Would you have me ask Rachel to scoot over so I can get into my bed?"

He doesn't answer.

"No one gets married planning to divorce. Except for maybe people who make up prenuptial agreements. Even women who marry for money see more money in the marriage than the divorce. Did you ever think of that?"

He clutches his briefcase. Hamilton Lowe is not a risk-taker. That much is evident. He methodically plans everything in his life. I bet he knows what he's having for dinner tonight.

"Sure, I see where people think that way, but then the reality of divorce happens, and that's where I come in. I make the breakup less painful because everyone knows what will happen, and there are no unfortunate surprises," he finally answers.

"Like finding out your husband couldn't father children, for instance?"

"I didn't know about that when you were married," he claims.

"A man can protect his money, but he won't walk away unscathed, regardless. You might think Jay is unscathed, but wait and see if he'll marry again."

"We'll just have to see."

"Hamilton, I don't care if you've made up a new airtight contract, or if she earns more money than him. I know Jay, and marriage required something of him that he can't part with it. There's something in him that can't deal with the emotional pressure. He looks at it like a business relationship, and when it ceases to be beneficial to both parties, he's outta there."

"My client went into this marriage with good faith."

"That is a bald-faced lie, Hamilton. You cannot go into a marriage in good faith when you don't mention to your beloved that there will be no children."

"Good day, Haley." He walks toward the door, but I scamper after him in my heels.

"Marriage is like a wall, Hamilton. Someone has to bring the bricks; someone has to bring the mortar. Without either, you have no wall, and you have no marriage."

"How profound," he says sarcastically as he continues down the hallway.

"You arrogant son—"

"What did you say?"

"You stand here smug and so full of yourself, the great expert on all things marriage. But you haven't spent one day committed to anything more than a cell phone contract, have you? Did you ever think for one moment, you may have it wrong? That life may not work out as well as Hamilton Lowe deems it does? Those are words on a contract, they're not life. What if I were maimed in a car accident? What if Jay had a heart attack running? Do you think you can really be married with an 'out' if things don't play right?"

"It's not my rules, Haley." He rolls his eyes at me. Just like Jay used to do.

"You hold it right there!" A group of people stop to check out the scene and quickly get out of the area near the elevator.

"Why do I infuriate you so, Haley?" he asks smugly as he presses the elevator button. "I just thought when you'd calmed down it would be nice to talk about you in a casual dinner setting."

"Why do you infuriate me? Because you're completely wrong in this, and you sit upon your tower and dare to judge me. What if you married a woman and she was your world and you wanted nothing more than to make her happy? And suddenly, that woman decided she could not live without her college sweetheart and she'd made a mistake marrying you and left?"

"I'd fight for her. She's my wife."

"But ultimately, you cannot control another human. Free will, isn't that what you Christians are always preaching? Jay had free will. All of us have free will and all the ironclad contracts in the world can't protect you from someone else's free will, Hamilton."

He steps into the elevator.

"You're not even going to answer me?" My temper flares as I follow him in, and the doors shut behind us. "Do you think there's a reward in heaven for staying together for fifty years, but not once thinking about the other person's needs?"

"I don't know, Haley. I think there's a reward for staying together."

"But staying together where you kill each other emotionally, do you think there's a reward for that?"

"I think people always have options, and if they choose to humble themselves—"

"What? The other party won't run off to Monaco with a leading lady?"

"I would never do that, Haley. That's all I can answer to. I would never do that."

"But you won't have to, right? Because no one's good enough for you to risk it all, are they? That's your problem you know, not being willing to risk anything you can't control. And that's the real problem with love, isn't it? You can't control it."

"My problem? Look I didn't stop by for a free analysis, I was only trying to be cordial. I thought when you got over the passion of this situation, you would see—"

"Answer me this, Hamilton. If I was to have avoided this fate, what could I have done differently, besides realized at twenty that love doesn't come in the shape of goods and services rendered?"

"I guess maybe you should have been better prepared."

"God forbid, because then I'd be you, Hamilton, and I'd be alone forever."

"Right." He plays with a pen in his chest pocket. "So I guess I'll see you when you come in for your next check."

"I thought you said we were done with that charade."

"I want to continue this conversation. At some point, maybe we'll understand one another. I look forward to it."

I watch his expression, and he means it. He has not heard a word I've said. "Why? If I'm not good enough, that's not going to change. I've spent my whole life trying to be good enough, and Jesus says I am. I have to cling to that." Even if there's nothing else about the church I cling to. I punch the next floor and escape when the elevator stops.

"Haley!" my boss bellows into my radio.

"I'm coming, sir."

I swallow my emotion as I watch the doors close on Hamilton.

Say it. Say something, Hamilton. Show me that your religion goes beyond rules. *Show me there's a heart beating in that broad chest of yours*. His hand reaches through the doors.

He steps out. "I'm glad you found the Bible study. I'm glad they showed you how to get back on your feet."

"Me too, Hamilton. Thanks again for the referral." We go back to the surface, where he's comfortable.

He looks down to his shoes. I can't explain why I want Hamilton to break free of his ridiculous prejudices, but for some reason I just can't let him walk away without understanding. I have this desperate need to be heard by him. Maybe it's for all the women who will come after me in his office. For all the women who find out their husbands didn't care enough to tell them to their faces that all those late-night phone calls and lipstick stains were exactly what they feared. While her husband came home and took off his suit, hung it over the chair, and asked her to take it to the cleaners, he was, at that very moment, planning a romantic getaway in some quaint little island village with her.

"Hamilton, I—"

"If you need help planning for the baby, I can help you with that. Pro bono."

"The baby?"

"Jay told me about the baby. He wants to help if he can."

I clasp my eyes shut. "You're pregnant?" Bud comes out of the conference room on the lower floor.

"What are you doing down here?"

"I'm not training the perfect assistant to go on maternity leave!" Bud yells.

What have I done?

"You can't fire her for that, Bud. It's against the law," Hamilton says.

"I wouldn't have hired her if I'd known she was pregnant."

"That too—illegal."

I know I should just shout that I'm not pregnant, that only another miracle, in the form of a second Immaculate Conception, could make that happen, but I can't bring myself to protest while they argue over me. Over the innocent life I will never be carrying. Tears sting my eyes, and I watch Hamilton slip away onto the elevator.

"Hamilton, it's not—"

"I hope you'll raise the baby up in the church, Haley. You owe the child that much."

It's no wonder Hamilton doesn't believe in me. He thinks I'm sleeping with someone else already and that I've got myself a baby daddy out there somewhere.

"What do you mean, taking this kind of high-pressure job being pregnant?" Bud yells.

"You're pregnant?" Lily appears in the hallway.

There's a reason you're taught not to lie in preschool. I do wish I'd thought of that standing in Jay's presence that day, but I only wanted him to hurt. I'm the one who ended up being hurt yet again, because he acted like I told him the plant in the bathroom needed to be replaced.

"Bud, can you excuse us?" Lily asks.

"You're fired!" he yells at me.

"I am not fired!" I yell back.

"You can't fire her, she's pregnant!"

"I wouldn't have hired her, if she was pregnant."

"Doesn't matter; you still can't fire her," Lily explains.

"Would you all relax? I am not pregnant!" I finally shout, as we all get into the elevator to ride back up to the office. "Not that it should matter if I was, Mr. Seligman! And you would have been guilty of upsetting the baby if I was. You certainly upset me!" I shake my finger at him. "But I'm not." *I need a good shopping spree. Just a few hours in the Sephora aisles, and I'd be right again.* "You can't fire me because I'm the best assistant you've ever had."

"Bud, may I take your assistant to lunch?" Lily asks.

"Please do." He checks out my frame as I stand. "You don't look pregnant."

"That's because I'm not pregnant!" Why are people so much quicker to believe a lie than the truth?

"We'll be back in an hour," Lily says.

"Don't forget to call Bruckheimer back. He sounded anxious."

"Right."

"And you've got lunch today at the Ivy in twenty minutes, call him on your cell phone." I press the codes into the phone so that the calls are taken downstairs and grab my purse and Lindsay's cell phone.

Bud does just as he's told and gets his jacket from the office. Lily has her long, jet-black hair in a straight ponytail, cinched with an expensive clip. She takes long, elegant strides to the elevator and punches the button hard.

"Wait for me!" Bud says, as he runs in before the doors close.

We all ride in silence until the door dings to open into the lobby. Security rushes to protect Bud from the throngs of hopefuls, and Lily and I walk by unnoticed. We get to her car, a Mercedes SLK, and she unlocks the door. I slide into the seat, and she gets in, her expression drawn.

"What was that about?"

"Remember at the salon? When I had Penny's boys?"

"Yes."

I tell her the sordid tale, and she turns on the car and presses the accelerator, until the G force makes me feel like I'm getting a face-lift.

"Haley, you can't be lying like that. If you're over Jay, prove it to us. Move on."

"I know. I know. I felt like slime as soon as it tripped off my tongue, but it just came out. But look at it this way. At first I wanted to lynch Jay and take him for everything he had. I figure a little white lie is nothing compared to my first thoughts. Believe it or not, this is improvement. I want to believe something different now. Something better about Jay."

"Thinking the best of someone is one thing. Living in denial, quite another. You might recognize Jay's character by the fact that he changed the locks on you and kicked you out of your own house with a fraction of what you helped him earn."

"Well yeah, there's that."

"Or maybe that he was having an affair with some skanky starlet and thought nothing of moving her right into your place, what about that?"

"Okay, enough already."

"This job is a good job. Haley, I have no doubt you could be one of the best agents in the business with some training. I didn't bring you on here to be an assistant forever. You're far too smart. I could tell the first night when you sized us all up that your mind was constantly working."

"You think I could be an agent?"

"Everyone seems to believe in you, but you. You keep going backwards because you choose to listen to Jay over us. Over the Bible and even over reason, and I'm telling you, it's time to stop going backwards!"

"I'm grateful, haven't I said that? I sent you flowers to show my appreciation!"

"Haley, you're misunderstanding me. I'm not picking on you. I'm only trying to point out if you continue to play games like you learned with Jay, like trying to make him jealous for instance with a false pregnancy, you'll reap what you sow. That almost cost you your job!"

"He doesn't hurt yet, Lily. I wanted him to hurt!"

"And you wanted him to love you, and you wanted him to appreciate you, and he didn't do those things either. Did you ever think that he doesn't feel the appropriate responses because he's just shut out of his emotions, period? Imagine if you put this kind of energy into a healthy relationship. You might actually enjoy your life."

"I enjoy my life."

"What do you like to do? For hobbies, I mean?"

"Besides eating tubs of chocolate frosting, you mean? I used to like to run on the beach and in my neighborhood. I could go for miles, and all my problems were left behind in a cloud of kicked-up sand. I'd plug in the iPod and go. Once in a while, I'd get lost in the neighborhood and have to ask for directions back." I sigh wistfully.

"So what stopped you from running?"

"The motel wasn't in the best neighborhood, and I just could never get motivated to drive to the beach, so it just sort of faded into the background. Underneath the frosting."

"Can't you go get real chocolate at least?" She shakes her silky tresses. "From here on out, you don't do anything to hurt Jay that hurts you, you promise?"

"I guess so."

"If you get fat and out of shape, does Jay hurt? Or does he say, 'Oh, I dodged that bullet.'"

I'm not saying the answer to that out loud. "So you want me to start running? That's why you brought me to lunch? I'm getting dessert, by the way."

"I brought you to lunch so that I might show you living well is the best revenge."

We drive to the south side of town, and I have to say the neighborhood is getting a little dicey. Gone are the neatly manicured lawns and brushed-silver address numbers, and now we're seeing a lot of wrought-iron gates and bars on the window, and I don't even want to know when the last gallon of paint was sold here.

"You do realize we're in an SLK in the hood?"

"I do," she says calmly.

"And that this is L.A.? The southside? And that carjacking is a relatively normal scenario?"

"Yes, yes, and yes."

"And you feel safe because of the 352 under the front seat of the car?"

She laughs. "Yeah, right."

"We only get an hour for lunch," I say, worried about my growling stomach as much as getting shot for our ride.

She pulls to the side of the road on a street that has no sidewalks, where the houses are all slightly larger than the one-car garage that makes up the curb appeal—or lack thereof.

"Do you see this house?"

It's sallow green, the roof has places where it's missing shingles, and the windows are covered in thick, jail-like bars. The grass is totally dead, but makes a final resting spot for an old Chevy on the former front lawn. There are greasy tools lying about and several, let's say underemployed, men in barrio jackets leaning on the car.

"I rented a room in this house after my divorce," Lily explains.

"Why? And can you tell me while we drive, please?"

"Because I didn't have any money, why do you think?"

"Fascinating, let's get to the living well part of the story."

"I paid $150 a month, and I got a job at an Italian pizza place to make the rent, took my son with me, and we got to eat all the pizza we could during the day." She shivers. "I still can't abide the stuff."

"You have a son?"

"Jason," she nods. "He's twenty now attending UOP, majoring in architecture."

She does not look like she could possibly have a twenty-year-old, she barely looks thirty herself. "You had a son here?"

"It was all we could afford."

"Okay, I'm appreciating all that's been given to me. I will bow down and kiss the glass tiles in Lindsay's place when I get home. Can we go now?"

She stares forlornly at the building. "I've come a long way, baby." She looks to me. "You have to learn how to dream again, Haley. How all things are possible."

"I'll daydream all afternoon at the office. Let's go. You never told me how you got a divorce. Did you get a divorce? I mean were you married to Jason's dad?"

"I got married at eighteen to my high school sweetheart. He was a quarterback and had big dreams of playing at Texas A&M, but when he didn't make the cut, he took me to Ohio, and we got married instead."

"So your parents didn't approve?"

"No, they did. Other than he was a Caucasian, they liked him well enough. We both went to the same church, we were baptized together, we had a lot of history together. They were upset they didn't get to plan a church wedding, but life went on."

"So what happened? And this is the last time I'm asking before I step on that gas pedal myself." I'm feeling the beat of other people's music in my gut.

She puts her foot to the accelerator again and now I'm no longer worried about being carjacked, but I am worried that the car will take off into the air the way she uses the road like her personal runway.

"Long story short, he decided he didn't want to live like a Goody Two-shoes anymore, left the church, left the faith, and started a business selling tools out of a big truck."

"That's it?"

"That's not tragic enough for you?"

I shrug. "I just thought you were going to tell me he bit the dust doing cocaine or something. Selling tools?" I sigh.

"How would you have liked to live in that dump? With a little boy who doesn't understand why he can't play in the yard?"

"Oh that's easy. I wouldn't have. I would have gone to his tool-selling self and told him to give me my share."

"Sure, you would have. That's why you lied and told Jay you were pregnant because you're such a tough girl." She shakes her head. "I raised a straight A student in the hood all by myself, and I drive an SLK and work in the best agency in Hollywood. Don't be telling me you're tough, Haley, I got a black belt in being kicked to the curb—without money for diapers."

"So did your son ever meet his dad?"

"Yes, Robby's parents tried to forge a relationship with Jason, but they felt weird having an Asian grandson, and their prejudice eventually destroyed the relationship. Robby met his son once at an Easter brunch, but"—Lily shrugs—"that was it. So I tried to marry for money and do the trophy thing. I thought my son would have a dad, and our problems would be solved. Unfortunately, I could not live up to my husband's high standards, and it wasn't long before we were worse off than where we started. Now I'm a two-time divorcée, and it was then that I decided to rely on the faith of my childhood. No one is going to fix things for you, Haley. You have to fix things for yourself or you'll just stay an eternal trophy wife."

She gazed ahead of her as we continued back toward the office. "Anyway, the whole reason I'm taking you out is to tell you that Rachel Barlin is pregnant."

"I know that."

"You never said anything."

"Jay told me. It's not exactly something I wanted broadcast."

"It's not his baby."

"I know that, too. But Jay doesn't know whose it is. What is with men that they want to be with a woman who is carrying another man's baby, and they don't know who the father is? Don't they read the paper? Don't they know every man can come out of the woodwork, like with Anna Nicole Smith and demand a DNA test? I mean, I know Jay thinks I'm the one who is dull-witted, but hello."

"I do," Lily whispers.

"You do, what?"

"I know who the father of Rachel's baby is. She told her agent, and I overheard."

My eyelids feel heavy. I'm tired of getting hit. I need a respite. "Don't tell me, Lily. I can't move on if I continue to obsess over this. I don't want to hear anything more about Rachel Barlin. America continues to love her, as does Jay."

"They won't when they hear who the father is."

I'm tempted. Oh so very tempted. "I don't want to know."

"So you're not going backwards?" she asks me. "You're going to fight for your career?"

"I've got the message, I'll be clean and sober. No more lies, no more tubs o' frosting, a little more running, a lot less Jay. Happy?"

"Ecstatic. See you at TWC tomorrow."

She drives me back to work without food. Have I mentioned that I am extremely grouchy without food, or that my boss is currently at the Ivy?

Chapter 15

June comes in like a lamb. Stays that way. This is Southern California, after all. I've skipped the Trophy Wives Club for months now, and though I'm flaky as all get-out, someone calls every week to invite me. As if that weren't enough, Lily comes into the office and nags me every Tuesday. And Lindsay makes me feel guilty by asking how far I am in the Bible she bought me. But Bud keeps me so late, and all I want to do each night is get to the condo and go running to shed the day's stress. The last thing I need is to hear other people's troubles. I've got enough of my own. Well, I've got enough of Bud's at least.

I have, however, been attending church. In the back pew and reading my Bible, it brings me comfort.

I bought a treadmill. And I finally picked up my car from the broker after he sold the first one when I didn't pick it up. It's darling. A Mini Cooper in blue with a Union Jack flag on its roof. It's rumored to have once belonged to Rod Stewart, but the broker couldn't tell me for certain because of confidentiality clauses. I ravaged the glove compartment looking for a leftover Oil Changers' receipt or abandoned registration paper, but there was nothing. So it's Rod's. I've decided and besides, it makes me sit up straighter when I drive it.

I pick up my next check this week, and with it comes the knowledge that I don't need it as desperately as I once thought. Lindsay and Ron will come over to help me invest it properly, as they've done with the others. My threat for the $250,000 went unheeded. Jay knows me too well. I don't have the strength to fight for money. I'm not like him; as long as I'm clothed and fed, I'm happy. Maybe a little spree at Sephora here and again . . . some online shoe purchases at Zappos during lunch hour, and, really, it doesn't get any better than that.

I only wish I didn't have to see Rachel's belly grow on the tabloids. I feel as though its been sent from below. As though this ache will never go away. And please, could she have some dignity and lose the cropped shirt with her naked belly on display? But like I said, I'm content with my settlement. Didn't Anna ask me that question eons ago?

At this rate, I can put a down payment on this condo soon. Perhaps not this one I'm living in, but *a* condo. I can look up Lily's old neighborhood, perhaps. Though I'm tempted to keep living here if Lindsay will have it. Even if it is a little lonely. The neighbors are complete snobs who want nothing to do with me (most of them are ancient former actresses, and at least one of them has some type of bandage from plastic surgery on at all times.) However, I'm within walking distance of the grocery store, coffee shops, and especially restaurants, if I get home too late.

I tried at first to be a good neighbor. I offered to feed one of their cats when she was gone, and she just snapped she wasn't going anywhere. I'm sure that meant she'd be only gone for a few days to the rehab center after the face-lift, and the cat could fend for itself. I don't know who these women want to look beautiful for—they never leave the house—but I can say quite plainly that I have more wrinkles at twenty-eight than they do.

My doorbell rings, and I arrange the stuffed mushrooms on the platter. "Just a minute!" I call.

I put the plate back in the oven to stay warm and wipe my hands on my apron before opening the door. It's not Lindsay; it's a messenger.

"Delivery for Haley Cutler."

"That's me." I sign for it and I tear into the envelope. The doorbell rings again, and Lindsay and Ron are on the front stoop. "Come on in," I say absentmindedly.

"What's that?"

"It's my check from Jay. The rest of it, not the ten thousand from the agreement. It's all twenty thousand that's left." I look up. "I think I'm free."

"Not free if you got all that," Ron quips. "Well, it's a good thing we came tonight then. You owe taxes on that, and we should pay them here and now before it's gone." Ron pulls out his glasses. "The best thing the government ever did for themselves was get taxes prepaid out of a paycheck. People have no idea how much it really hurts. When you physically have to write the check, you see how much it hurts." He takes out his specialty calculator that no human, without his brain, can operate, and punches a few numbers. He lets a long whistle out, which I can only assume is my tax bill.

"Don't bother, Ron." I sigh. "I'm not in the mood to talk money. I won't cash it, don't worry."

"Haley, what's the matter? This is what you've been waiting for. It's all over."

"Why didn't he bring this to me himself?"

"Who, Jay? Probably because he's following jail bait around to movie sets while she incubates," Lindsay says. "Duh. It isn't easy to keep up with a child at his age."

"No, not Jay. *Hamilton*. It was supposedly part of the contract that he see me in person to deliver each payment." I drop the check onto the entry table. "What changed?"

"Did you ever check the contract? He probably made that up to get close to you."

"Hamilton? He doesn't want to get close to the likes of me. Trust me."

"Well, doesn't he think you're pregnant with another man's baby?"

"That was a misunderstanding."

"It's not really a misunderstanding men understand," Ron says. He sniffs the air. "What's cooking?"

"There are stuffed mushrooms in the small oven and lamb chops in the big one. Help yourself."

"What? No fanfare? No, Martha Stewart presentation?" Lindsay asks. "I live for that. It makes me feel inferior in all ways domestic, and you're just going to let me down because you're feeling sorry for yourself? No, no, no. Unacceptable. I came all the way over here with my money magnate husband. I want service!"

"I thought he liked me."

"Hamilton? He doesn't like anyone but himself, Haley."

"He said he was sorry when Jay did what he did, and he never gave me the operation form, even when Jay had ordered him to."

"What's he supposed to say? Here, sign this so I can make money off your pain and suffering?"

"It's not Hamilton himself. It's that I can't read men at all. When I first met him, I thought him a decent guy. Just like I thought Jay was decent. They both turned out to be complete dogs, and I was clueless until they both had me for breakfast!"

"You've lost me. When's dinner?"

"I have this high school boyfriend. Gavin is his name."

"What does Gavin do?"

"He sells windows and doors."

"Scintillating."

"But he's the one guy I know is true and decent."

Ron coughs. Ron looks like one of those news anchors who specializes in money. He wears bow ties twenty-four/seven with pinstriped shirts and probably hasn't had hair in this decade.

"Besides you, Ron, but you're already taken."

"Thank you."

"So my question is, why can't I be happy with a man like Gavin? What is wrong with me that I wait for the sizzle of a man who will totally reject and humiliate me?"

"I thought you wanted to stay single forever anyway."

"I did. I do. But I want to learn something from this. What did I learn?"

"You learned that you made a stupid choice in your twenties, and it had long-term consequences." Lindsay calls out the last part as she enters the kitchen and opens the ovens. She grabs a pot holder and gets out the mushrooms. "These are dry. Haley, you're slipping, girl."

"But how am I a better person after all this?"

"You lost two hundred pounds of LDL, the bad kind of fat: Jay." Lindsay pops a mushroom in her mouth.

"Why am I the kind of woman who can't be attracted to the right kind of man?"

"You're not that kind of woman. Is she, Ron?"

"You overestimate men, Haley. Most men will believe anything you tell them to get next to you."

"Ron! Lindsay, I don't know how you get anything done with this guy's sweet-talking."

"He talks sweeter to his calculator, but eventually I figured him out." She winks at Ron.

"Deep in my heart, I thought maybe . . . just maybe . . . if I had a little more sense, kept my head out of the clouds, my face out of walls, I might find someone else and get a second chance. But that was it, wasn't it? You can't ever say my husband. You have to admit that it's your second husband, and that implies failure. You're always a failure. I will always be a failure. Even if I married Gavin."

"You are not marrying the window salesman. You're not marrying anyone, and you don't have to say 'second husband' if it bothers you."

"But even if I stay single. I'm not single. I'm divorced. It's like having your middle name be failure. Haley Failure Adams Cutler."

"Do you need another sermon on grace?"

"I don't. You've told me it can all go away in God's eyes. That might be true, but it never goes away in people's eyes. Look at how the Trophy Wives Club is treated! We're given a room in a corner and told to stay out of the way. Our roster is kept quiet."

"That's because we don't want the husbands to feel bad. Do we, Ron?"

"A secret Bible study. How wrong is that? It's not like we're living in the middle of a Communist state."

"You don't even come, I don't see why you're complaining."

"I'm complaining because if it's true what you tell me, that the old is washed away, there's got to be a major clog in the sink! Because the old doesn't go anywhere. Debbie Reynolds is still the woman that Eddie Fisher left for Elizabeth Taylor."

"Rachel is no Elizabeth Taylor," Ron says.

"All I can tell you, Haley, is that God isn't His people. And you've got to make your peace with Him and yourself. You won't ever find complete acceptance here. This is not heaven."

"I think Gavin accepts me for who I am."

"That's because Gavin hasn't lived with you and gets to play Superman when you need him, what, once a decade? Even Jay could probably muster up the commitment that requires."

"He calls and checks on me since the divorce. That's more than Jay ever did."

"It's still how you use him. He's not God, Haley. Gavin has expectations of you; they just aren't very high. He's probably completely emotionally stunted and can't handle relationships, so talking to a beautiful woman is payoff enough for him to believe he could get married anytime, and there's nothing wrong with him."

"Thank you, Dr. Laura." I open the oven and set out the warmed dishes on the table and give the salad a final toss. "I still feel like a piece of furniture. Jay and Hamilton redecorate, and I am no longer a part of the décor."

"Stop using Hammy's name in the form of manhood. It's emasculating poor Ron."

Ron has my check and his calculator. He hasn't heard a word of this. "Huh?" He looks up at the sound of his name.

"I can't trust someone who will stomp on my heart again, and because I can't read Hamilton, I can't ever trust myself again. Don't you see? It's not Hamilton. It's that if Gavin is my only option for trustworthy, I am doomed to being single because he bores the very life out of me."

"I thought that's what you wanted. To stay single."

"So did I until I got in this house with all your crabby, old lady neighbors and realized that's what I'll become. A woman with cats, and the cats won't even eat my food! What is wrong with this picture?"

"All I'm saying is that you really need a better test subject than Hamilton Lowe."

"It's not about Hamilton. Lindsay, you're not hearing me."

"That's because I'm smelling lamb chops, and I'm hungry. They smell Greek."

"They are. Focus with me here."

"I am. You're telling me that Hamilton Lowe was your test rat in your laboratory of love, and he didn't respond properly to the bell. Do I have it right? How did you have time to make lamb after work?"

"Lamb doesn't take long, just the marinating does. I did that this morning. Could I have your full attention?"

Ron guffaws. "Good luck with that. I don't think Lindsay ever did one thing at a time in her life."

She smirks at her husband. "I'm listening," she says softly, like a bad counselor. She puts her elbows on the counter, and her chin rests on her fists. "Lay it on me."

"This spark. The chemical combustion that happens with only a handful of certain people—I'm very particular that way, and—"

"Maybe you just had indigestion. Hammy will do that to a girl."

"Would you not call him that? I can't take this conversation seriously if you're calling him Hammy."

"It's because he's not kosher. Get it?" Lindsay slaps her own leg. "Seriously, I can't take this conversation at all. He flirted with you, Haley. Now, maybe you've been married too long, perhaps you're clueless to the effect a nearly six-foot blonde has on men in general, or maybe you're feeling desperate for attention and admiration. Whatever it is, this too shall pass. And so will your obsession with why Hammy, the self-righteous, does anything. In the meantime, you need to teach me to cook like this." She grabs the pot holders again and put the chops on the table.

"I'm going to watch the news," Ron deadpans. "All this girl talk makes me nervous."

"You want a beer, Ron?" I ask.

"No!" Lindsay pulls my hand off the fridge handle. "No, he doesn't."

"Lindsay, let the man answer for himself."

"Haley, Hamilton can't date you, so what does it matter? It's not personal."

"Why not? Jay's not his client anymore."

"He's a believer. You're not. The Bible says that is a no-go, and Hammy loves the rules, doesn't he? He probably wants you so badly, he's ready to pluck his own eyes out, but you're off-limits, and if I know anything about Hamilton, it's how he does love the law. He always errs on the side of it versus grace."

"I believe in God." I grab the plates from the cupboard. "Sort of. I just believe in being a good person and that He loves us all as His children."

"It's different. I know sometimes it doesn't feel different, but it is."

"He's not a better person than me. For crying out loud, he's really sort of a jerk. Don't you think?"

"Yes, I do. I think he's an incredible jerk, in fact. If I had a dollar for every jerk sitting in the pew, I'd be a rich girl."

"She loves you. She preaches at those she loves." Ron moseys to the table, and I place the plate in front of him.

"Because I want to see my friends in eternity! What kind of friend would I be if I believed this were the way to heaven and didn't tell you how to get in? It's like I didn't put you on the waitlist for a party at Sky Bar." Lindsay scratches her head. "You're not getting in without your name on that list." She stares at me. "Okay, well you'd probably get in because you're hot, but if you were normal, you would totally be standing out on the street without my say. Get it?"

"That's a terrible analogy."

"I know, Ron!" Lindsay says, clearly frustrated. "I haven't been a Christian very long, I'm not that good at this. I only know it changed my life, and I want it to change yours too, Haley, because I love you. I see my former self in you, and it makes me want to cry."

"I've prayed for what you have, Lindsay, but I'm a slow learner, all right? But we need to feed your husband."

She nods.

"Oh, I forgot to let the wine breathe."

"No wine, Haley," Lindsay says gruffly.

"With lamb?"

"What she's trying to tell you, as subtly as a freight train, is that she's married to an alcoholic, and I can't have a beer and I can't have any wine or I will officially fall off the wagon and perhaps have another stroke."

I look at Lindsay, and she nods. I stare at Ron like a monkey in a cage. "You, Ron? I think of you as the epitome of sober."

"You're confusing sober with boring. I am boring."

"He's sober, too. Been so since the stroke. Sixty-three days and counting." Lindsay beams proudly at him.

"Congratulations. But I thought you were a womanizer." I place a lamb chop in front of him and grab for the salad. Sheesh. "Speaking of subtle."

"I sort of implied that," Lindsay says in a voice barely audible.

"Why would you do that?" I ask.

"Yeah, why? That's why I get all those dirty looks from those women when I drop you off at church. They probably think I'm hitting on them." Ron rolls his head to his chest. "Do I look like a womanizer, Haley?"

"Is there a type, really?" I ask.

Lindsay breathes in deeply. "I never said why we separated, Ron. They just assumed, and I never corrected them." She looks at me for support. "Beautiful women attract men who care too much about beauty, less about substance. Right, Haley?"

"I thought we just picked badly."

"Lily's in the class, Ron, and I didn't want it to slip that you were a drunk or you'd never get work with Hollywood big money again. You had a lot of business at her agency. It was selfish, but I've grown accustomed to the lifestyle. I didn't think you could lose your job and be all right."

Ron takes his wife's hand, and he looks deeply into her eyes. The love they exchange in that momentary gaze is more than I ever shared with my own husband in eight years of marriage. My heart tightens at the thought that no one will ever love me like that. I am a third wheel at my own dinner party.

"I know why you did it," Ron says. "You're not fooling anyone; you were protecting me."

"No, it was solely for me." She smiles at him. "There was a sale at Gucci."

"I know better, Lindsay. Don't I, Haley?"

"I guess." I shrug. "Let's eat. Before I puke on the both of you."

Later that night when I'm lying in my bed, I realize I just need to find a new lab rat. I stare up at the ceiling and think about the men at work. There has to be somebody out there.

The women in the Trophy Wives Club all deal with something

intense, I'll give them that, but they're not trophy wives. If the definition is a younger woman who married an older, affluent guy for security and became little more than a bauble, taken out and polished up for the right moments in life, then I may well be the only true Trophy Ex-Wife, present. And that? Well, at the risk of sounding sixteen again, that just sucks, quite frankly. I'm deathly tired of being in relationships of one.

Chapter 16

Running along the beach in the morning hours is my solitude, my place of rest, my only break from the voices that tell me how incredibly hectic and altogether pointless my existence has turned out to be. It used to be cooking, but now I have no one to cook for, and that too, feels futile. Maybe I should start feeding my neighbor's cat. He looks a little scrawny.

Here, on the beach, with a destination of two and a half miles, I am in control with the wind at my back.

Until . . . that poorly placed piece of driftwood.

"Are you all right?"

If I had a dollar for every time I was asked that question! That has to be the number one introduction line of my life.

"I'm fine," I say with annoyance, but as I rise, I feel that isn't quite true and fall back into the damp, morning sand with a grunt.

"You don't look fine. I saw you fall. You may have twisted something. Do you mind?" He reaches for my ankle.

I look up against the sky and capture a vision of a man who looks as though he's surrounded by a halo of sunlight. He's got short, cropped hair and baby blue eyes, nearly Bahama blue by any account. He's wearing running shorts and a breathable, muscle T-shirt with tiny vents and a solid chest—and most importantly, no wedding ring.

"Are you a doctor?"

"No, just a former soccer player. I've broken everything in this lifetime, and if not, I've watched it be broken on someone else."

He rotates my foot, and I squeal. "Yowza, that hurts!"

"It's not broken," he says plainly.

"Tell that to my aching ankle!"

"Sorry about that, but you couldn't rotate it like that if it were broken. But it's going to swell. Badly. I don't think you fell hard enough to do anything hairline-wise." He shakes his head. "If you don't want to trust a stranger on a beach, you might want to get to a clinic for an X ray. A sprain can hurt as bad as a break, depending on how you do it."

I still can't move. "Yeah, thanks." I size him up and wonder what kind of lab rat he'd make, but the truth is, I don't have the strength to try flirting. My only peace of the day has been wrecked by driftwood. I look around and see not one other piece on the beach. I should have odds in Vegas at my rate of failure. "Do you mind if I ask you a question?"

"Shoot."

"If I were to flirt with you, and this is a hypothetical question, but if I were to flirt with you, would you flirt back?"

"Aren't you flirting with me?"

"No, I'm in too much pain to flirt. I'm much better when I flirt purposely."

"Give me an example. What is different about when you flirt versus now, when you're just hypothetically flirting?"

"Oh I'm nicer, and I shake my hair a little bit, maybe touch your arm—you know." I shrug. "Girl stuff."

"When's the last time you did that?"

"Can you tell I'm rusty?" Disappointment flares in my chest. "I told you, I'm not flirting, this is only hypothetical."

"Maybe you meant to trip on that piece of wood so I'd come to your rescue?"

"No, I'm just klutzy. That part is real. Flirting doesn't include game playing, I was never into that. Besides, life on my feet is too tenuous ever to toy with for a man's attentions."

"Well, Miss –"

"Adams. Haley Adams."

"I think I should ask you first, if I were to flirt with you, would you flirt back?"

"That's not fair. I asked you first."

He shrugs. "A guy has to protect himself. You could be after me for my money."

"How would I know that you had money?"

"I don't know; don't you women smell it or something?"

"So you do have money."

"If I didn't, would you flirt with me?"

"If you did, I wouldn't flirt with you. Rich men have issues. I'm looking for a poor man with a heart." I stare at his cocked eyebrow. "Not that I'm looking. As I said, this is a hypothetical scenario."

"It's not often I get to rescue a gorgeous blonde off the beach and have her ask me questions about flirting." He bends down and lifts me off the ground. "Wait a minute, you're not asking me because I have that 'friend' look. Do I look innocuous to you? No harm, no foul?"

"Not in the least. Very handsome. Strong flirtation potential with devastating good looks, so I wouldn't call you harmless."

He grins. "Put your arm around my shoulder, and we'll hobble to your car. Can you drive?"

"It's not my driving foot, but I'm parked that way." I limp to my car, alongside my new, I'm guessing six-foot-three, lab rat and I do my best to sway my hair and touch him on the forearm without completely losing my balance.

"Are you a Brit then?" he asks, upon seeing my Union Jack car.

"No, it used to be Rod Stewart's. So they say. He bought a Prius," I embellish. "Sorry to have broken up your run, but it was a pleasure to meet you. I didn't catch your name."

"Sam Jacobsen at your service. Always glad to help out, and if you have any klutzy friends looking for poor flirtation partners, please send them my way."

"So aren't you going to ask for my phone number?"

"Of course. I'm looking forward to really being flirted with because we're still in the hypothetical flirting scenario."

"But you're not rich, right?"

"Do you want to see my W–2s?"

"I don't think a poor man would know what that was."

"On the contrary, us poor guys have to pay taxes too. It's the law."

I narrow my eyes warily. "How old are you?"

"This is L.A., that information is more private than my W–2s. How old do I look?"

Oh no, I'm not getting caught in that trap. "I'm twenty-eight," I announce. "You're not more than ten years older than that, are you?"

"What if I'm younger?"

"Perfect!"

"Haley, I feel as though I'm in some odd experiment for you, but you do have the bluest eyes I have ever seen, and I'm a sucker for blue eyes and legs that go on forever."

"Tell me what you do for a living, Sam."

"I'm a soccer coach. Is that poor enough for you?"

"Absolutely. When I get back on this foot maybe we can run a few laps?"

"So it sounds as though I'm flirtation-approved. Do you have a pen?"

I hand him one, and he writes my phone number on the palm of his hand. I don't even remember the last time a guy took my number, but it feels very, very nice. I'm giddy, in fact. My ankle is killing me, but not for one second do I let my guard down and stop smiling. Everyone should have a lab rat that looks this good.

I settle into my Mini, feeling quite pleased with myself, when my cell phone rings. No one ever calls me, except Lindsay, Bette, and Lily and I don't recognize this number as any of theirs. "Hello?"

"Haley, it's Hamilton Lowe."

My stomach actually churns. I will never learn. I am sitting in my car watching my new lab rat run up the beach, and yet, here's my body reacting to the old, and desperately confused old lab rat. I haven't seen him in weeks, maybe months. Why would I obsess about a man who I haven't seen in months and who helped rip my life from me?

"I'm not getting stuck in this maze again, Hamilton."

"What?"

"Never mind."

"Haley, I need to talk to you. Do you think you might be able to meet me for dinner?"

With every fiber of my being I want to jump at the chance, but my voice of reason speaks first. "I can't do that, Hamilton."

"You don't have to answer right now, just—"

"That's my answer. Have a good day." And I snap my phone shut. Exhibit A is getting smaller as he disappears down the coastline, but somehow I don't have the same rush of excitement I did five minutes ago. I think I'm perfectly untreatable. I will run the same maze for the rest of my days. I stare down at the phone clutched in my hand. *What have I done?*

Looking out over the crashing waves, I realize how much my life has changed in the past few months. Lily, Lindsay, Bette, Penny, and Helena have become integral in my life. They've taught me that people don't always abandon you when you don't do things correctly. And more important, that God will never abandon me, no matter how much I screw up.

Watching the soccer coach disappear into a speck along the shore, it dawns on me that Mrs. Kensington had it right all those years ago. No Prince Charming ever did come along to rescue me. Only the King.

I want my faith to grow ever stronger. As the man disappears from sight, I realize how tentative my belief system is. How willing I've been to hand over my power to someone else. Not to the One who matters.

I punch a few buttons in my phone. "Bette?"

"Yes, Haley."

"It's time I was baptized. Don't you think?"

"Absolutely, I do." She rambles on excitedly about plans and I watch the waves roll in, as if they are seeking me out. God never gives up, they say to me.

Chapter 17

"Haley!" My boss yells and then focuses on my foot. "What did you do now?"

"I fell on the beach. I'm fine. Thanks for asking." I pad over to my desk and sit down.

"How does one fall on the beach?"

"I just did, all right? You have two meetings this morning, one at CMG's boardroom, that one is in ten minutes and one at eleven thirty at the Ivy. Don't you ever go anywhere else for lunch?"

"I do it to taunt you." He goes through his messages and hands one to me. "I can't read this."

I roll my eyes. "You don't want to read it, it's from your ex-wife, she says you owe Dr. Sanders $2,200 for your son's therapy, and he's stopping all sessions until it's paid. Your wife's exact words were, 'Don't make me come down there.'"

He shivers. "Don't worry, I won't. That woman is going to be the death of me yet!"

"That woman is raising your son alone, and that is no easy task." I speak to him like my mother always preached at me. "He is your son, and if I were you, I'd get that bill paid today, or I'm going to arrange for you to take him to Hawaii this summer. Which I think you should do anyway. Boys need their fathers in a special way."

"Call my credit card into the guy and get it paid today."

"Have I mentioned that I like your ex-wife and that she is phenomenal with Jack?"

"You, and all the shopkeepers on Rodeo, love her."

I shrug. "Lonely people shop. They're bored, and they're looking for something to fill the hole. She could be three hundred pounds, but instead, she shops. You probably never went home, and she used shopping as a Band-Aid. That's what I did."

"I'm your boss, Haley, and I do not need a shrink."

"Well, that's debatable."

"You women blame everything on us men, and you don't have the first sign of guilt over it. You shop too much, and, somehow, you manage to make it our fault. It's because we're out earning the money to keep you in that lifestyle. And is anyone grateful? No, you say you're lonely. I tell you, we can't win."

I roll my eyes. Like Mrs. Seligman is winning anything, raising that troubled boy all by herself. *Give me a break.* The phone rings, so I keep my opinions to myself. But really, if all he's going to contribute is money, why should she maintain a home for him?

Ack! Sounding bitter again. "Bud Seligman's office."

"Haley, it's Lily. Can you meet me in the cafeteria? I have to talk to you."

"Can you give me ten, so I can get Bud off to his first meeting?"

"No, I can't. I'll be right up. We'll use Bud's office. Usher him out as soon as possible."

"How am I supposed to do that?"

"Be creative." She hangs up on me, and Bud comes out of his office, perusing some notes.

"That was your meeting. It's been moved up a few minutes." I stand up fast, so fast that I fall over onto the desk. "Balance isn't what it used to be." I laugh, pointing to my wrapped foot.

"Haley, what is the matter with you today? You didn't get a brain injury with that fall, did you?"

"No, that happened long before today." I pick up the files he'll need for his meeting and tuck them in his arms. "Better get going. The best donuts will be gone if you're not there on time. You'll be left with a tofu twisty or an apple soy muffin."

"They'll wait for me, Haley. I'm the boss."

"All the more reason why you should set a good example." I grab his jacket. "You'll want to look professional, too. Tells everyone what they should do to get in your position."

"Haley, what on earth? Are you sneaking a man in here?" He points at me, wagging his finger. "I know. You met the underwear model."

"Bud, give me a little credit, would you?"

"He's a good-looking guy."

"He poses in his *chones* for a living. I do have some aspirations in life, and it's not to have my man plastered across Times Square in his skivvies. Call me ambitious—"

"You're fresh off a divorce, you're ready for a tryst, you know, to get the confidence back again. Where is he?" He opens the coat closet. "He's not here yet, huh?"

"We are not having this conversation. You know, you are text-book sexual harassment. I should get one of those programs set up and force the whole staff to attend."

"Sure, hon."

"Go to your meeting. And if I'm going for one of your clients? I'm holding out for Hugh Jackman, not some second-rate male model." I laugh lightheartedly. The truth: If I wanted a good-looking man with the absence of love, I'd try to get my husband back.

Lily walks in and sees Bud standing there, then looks at me and frowns. "Oh, Bud, you're still here. I think they may have started without you downstairs," she says, as calm as you please. "Isn't that your meeting?"

"I start the meetings!" He rushes out the door, tossing his sport-coat at me. "They wear a jacket for me, not the other way around. Got it?"

I salute again, and he jogs out the office. "Hold that elevator!" I hear him yell.

Lily shuts the door and leans against it. "Hi," she says breathlessly. "I thought he'd never leave."

"Lily, what could be so important?"

She takes in a deep breath and walks toward the window. "I know you told me that you didn't want to know who fathered Rachel's baby."

"And nothing has changed. It's just like getting caught up in a soap opera, what's next? I find out she's really a man?"

"She just thinks like one."

"I still don't want to know, Lily, so if you came up here to gossip . . ."

She shakes her head. "When have I ever gossiped? This relates to you directly, or I'd mind my own business. I thought she might settle in with Jay and that would be the end of it and you need never know."

I can't help but wonder if Rachel tried to pass this baby off as Jay's, or if he told her straight out about the vasectomy. "How could it relate to me? I'm done with Jay, and more importantly, he's done with me. I got the last of the money from Hamilton. You told me yourself I should dare to dream. Well, I'm not dreaming about either of them, let me tell you."

"What did you do to your foot?" She focuses on my wrap.

"I fell."

"Again?"

"I think I got a date out of it, though, so it may have been worth it." I meet her gaze. "Soccer players don't make any money, do they?"

"David Beckham does. Haley, stop changing the subject, I have to tell you this before it's plastered on *Entertainment Tonight*."

She has my attention. "You say this relates to me?" *Gosh, I hope whoever he is, he makes Kevin Federline look like a slice of heaven.* "How could this relate to me?"

"Let me rephrase. It relates to your settlement."

"I got all of my settlement. I just have to cash the check. For some reason Hamilton sent me the balance."

"Go. Cash it now. Don't pass Go. Do not pause to look in any shop windows. Get it cashed and in some sort of CD where no one but you can touch it."

"Lily, what on earth? It's my money, it's all laid out in the agreement."

"The baby's father . . ." She looks to make sure the door is shut and my stomach tightens. I close my eyes and wait for it, praying it's not Jay's. I know what he said, but I can't help my prayer, it's guttural. ". . . is Craig Lynchow!"

My body relaxes. "No, Lily, he's Jay's business partner. His name is just on all of Rachel's contracts because of the business. I'm sure someone read something and got confused."

"No, Haley, he's the father of the child, and more importantly, he now wants to be the father. He and Rachel claimed that they tried to refrain from one another, but the baby was the cement. They're in love."

I have to find myself a seat. "Anna's husband?" I think back to all her cackling laughter about how it would cost him too much to leave. Apparently the price came down. I can't help but see Anna's reaction to the news play out in my head. There will be no laughter, no callous treatment of the divorce. Her life will be torn apart, and the fact is, she was always more comfortable in her role as a trophy wife than I was. This will devastate her. "How could one woman cause all this havoc? What's her point, Lily? First my marriage, now Anna's . . ."

"To tell you the truth, I think originally it was a business move. She thought Jay was the controlling partner in the production company when she first got involved with him, but apparently doing the more artistic film cost Jay quite a bit privately. There's not nearly as much in an art house film as there is in a good on-screen belch."

"So let me understand this. Jay took the hit for a movie I suggested he make. Rachel, an unlikely choice, gets cast as the star, and she walks off with an award and his business partner?"

"Jay got into some financial trouble to make that movie for Rachel and borrowed pretty heavily from Craig privately to make it work. He couldn't find investors for it, but he believed in the film strongly and wanted to see it made no matter what."

I know this is completely selfish, but the first thing to hit me is that I'm a terrible producer. That was my idea. My film. Maybe Jay will remember that small fact now that it's tanked at the box office.

I don't feel the pain in my foot any longer. How can people be so cruel? How can they think only what they want matters and whoever gets hurt is simply collateral damage? "Does Jay know?"

"Rachel and Craig are telling Jay today. She wanted to make sure she was covered legally, as Craig plans to dissolve the business." She pauses and comes over to stroke my shoulder. "I thought you should know to cash your check immediately in case Craig tried any funny stuff."

I shake my head. "Craig can't do this, Lily. That business is everything to Jay. It's his life's work!"

"Apparently, this agreement has been in the works for some time. Jay thought he'd like to do more artistic work, and so he thought it best. Craig and Rachel have made Jay believe this is his idea."

"Jay never thought any such thing until Rachel won that award and he got suckered into thinking he'd have more value if Hollywood didn't laugh at him. Laughing makes money, Lily! What's wrong with making people laugh?"

"Nothing, Haley. But I seem to remember a young woman who didn't believe in herself too strongly, and it wasn't all that long ago."

"You girls believed in me, and I found my worth. Maybe, despite the way he's treated me, I need Jay to find his. Lily, what can I do?"

"You can brace for impact and cash that check before it isn't any good."

"But I can't just do that. So . . . so is Craig's marriage over, too?"

"Unless his wife wants to share him with Rachel. I think so."

"Why would she have led Jay to end his marriage? *My marriage*? If she really wanted Craig?" I drop my head to my desk. "This makes no sense, Lily. No woman could care that little for her fellow woman."

"That's what you might think, but you're a strangely naïve woman for all you've been through. Listen"—Lily lowers her voice—"I shouldn't have told you a word of this, but as your sister, I need you to protect yourself. There might be nothing left of that business when Craig is through with it and I don't think Jay understands that."

I shake my head. Protecting myself is not remotely on my mind. "I'm fine. *My* worst fears already came to fruition. I'm better for it, Lily, but Jay's ego has never had a blow like this. He's not a strong person. He only *acts* cold-hearted and callous, but he's like a little boy who has been hurt so many times, he has stopped feeling altogether. This business is all he has. I honestly believe he won't feel anything with the betrayal of Rachel. He probably expected it, but thought they'd make the next great Hepburn and Tracy films together."

Lily pulls her long ponytail around to her chest and fiddles with it like a child. "It's time he handled things for himself. He won't ever change if he's not forced to. How can you possibly worry about him now?"

"Because I know where his business is on his life scale. This will utterly devastate him, and he was my husband. I loved him as best I could, and I don't want to watch him be destroyed. Just last night, I read a proverb about a beautiful woman. It said that beauty was fleeting and charm was deceiving, but a woman who loves the Lord shall be praised. I want to be that woman, not someone who happens to be tall and blond. There's no real value in that."

"The Bible also says to be as shrewd as serpents and as gentle as doves. Don't allow yourself to become ensnared in this trap again."

"She took my marriage down, Lily. I'm not letting her take my husband there too."

"Ex-husband. I've got to get back to the office. The board should be discussing plans for the clients working with Cutler & Lynchow as we speak." Lily brushes her hair back. "I can't believe I told you all this. I could get sacked if it ever comes out. I've never broken a work confidence like this, but I can't watch you get hurt anymore. God forgive me, but cash the check for me, will you?"

"I'm going to find Jay." I hobble up onto my feet and pull my handbag from the drawer.

Lily stands in front of the door. "I can't let you do that, Haley. I told you this in confidence. If it gets out that I leaked it, our business could be devastated, and we'd both lose our jobs."

"Get out of the way, Lily. I'll do what I can to protect the information."

She presses her palms to the door. "You're not going anywhere but to cash that check."

I pull the check out of my purse and crumple it up in a ball before stuffing it back in the outside pocket.

"Haley, don't be crazy!" I run out the door, as quick as my lamed foot will carry me.

I press the elevator button, but with all the bigwigs in the meeting downstairs, it's not coming. Lily follows me out of Bud's office.

"Lily, you girls taught me about sacrifice. You showed me why I have to leave room for God, and now that's real for me." I'm convicted by my very own words. "I don't want Jay to hurt like I did. I don't want anyone to feel that way if I can do something to stop it."

Lily smiles. "Now you've come a long way, baby. But you can't stop this, and I could lose my job and you could lose $20,000. As wise as a serpent, Haley."

"I won't say anything to harm CMG, but I've got to go to him."

She nods. "God be with you, Haley. You'll need Him."

"He is," I say. "He absolutely is."

"Haley, hi." I turn around to see the dancing stalker with a large bouquet of flowers.

I point at him. "Singing stalker boy."

"Right," he says enthusiastically. "Actually, the name is Jim Lewiston."

"I can't stop now, Jim!" I tell him. "Urgent business." As I hobble onto the elevator, the door closes on my shoulder and knocks me inside the doors.

"These are for you," he calls out as he jumps in the elevator with me. "Your advice worked."

"How did you get up here?" I ask.

"I took the stairs. Your elevators are ridiculously slow."

"No, I mean past security."

"I signed with the agency this morning. Your advice worked. I'm a dancer. More importantly, I'm about to be a paid dancer. I got work in the new production of Hollywood's latest musical, so I wanted to thank you." He thrusts the pink tulips and spring mix at me again.

"Fabulous news. I knew you could use that stalker intuition for good." As the elevator moves, I lose my balance and fall into him. "So I suppose dancing really helps you with balance, yes?"

"Yes."

"I'm sort of in need of someone with balance at the moment. Are you free? And more importantly, do you have a car here?"

"Yeah, why?"

I put my arms around his shoulder and maneuver him out of the elevator past the meditating wannabes in the lobby. "Jim, I do believe that you may have something to teach me in regard to stalking prey."

Chapter 18

My friendly stalker and I arrive at Cutler & Lynchow at precisely 10:28 A.M. and I look to him. "Should we synchronize our watches?"

"I don't have a watch," Jim says. "But I do believe I'll come with you. I never did trust producers, and, besides, perhaps my presence will help them be on their best behavior."

I've become quite the praying sort. Maybe it's because I'm alone all the time, but I find myself praying for every little thing throughout the day. I tell God that I cannot go into detail at this very moment, but He knows what I need and would He please supply it. Whatever that might be.

As I go to pull the office door, it's locked, and I struggle with it a few more times before it registers. I begin to pound on the metal frame. "I know you're in there, Craig! Let me in!" I pound some more until Craig and Rachel appear in the doorway, and they look at each other with all the telltale signs of guilt. Good. At least they still have some.

How could you, I say to them with my eyes, and they both avert their gazes, so I know it's true. I know I've given my life to God now, but I can barely stand the amount of hatred I feel for the two of them. It reminds me how very human I still am and will always be. *Money.* How could money ever be worth ruining people's lives for? As it is, the two of them could do anything they wanted in this lifetime. And instead of vacationing in Tahiti, they choose to destroy lives and steal what belongs to others. Power and greed are two truly heinous desires.

"Open this door!" I shout at them.

"Jay isn't here," cowardly Craig calls toward me.

"Open this door or I will call Anna straightaway and tell her where you are and why you're really here!" As angry as I am, they need to just try me. Craig comes to the door, his boyish haircut looking remarkably blond for its only being June.

"Haley," Craig says, like we've seen each other recently at the golf club. "You're looking fabulous, as usual. We're presently having a business meeting, and I'm sure you're just looking for Jay, is that so?"

Rachel stands behind him, and only her eyes appear above his broad shoulders.

"Come out from behind him. You can't hide there forever, you know."

"Haley, listen, I'm sure whatever you have to say can wait. We have urgent business this morning," he says through the glass door.

"You are not . . . I repeat not stealing this business from Jay Cutler. You would be nothing without that man! Either one of you!"

"We have creative differences, Haley. That's all. These things happen. We're not stealing anyone's business. Where did you get such an idea?"

I try to think of an idea of how I know anything when I see the most shocking thing of all.

Hamilton Lowe appears in the doorway. "Hamilton?" *Not you too, Hamilton.*

"Haley."

"What do you want, Haley?" Craig asks me, and with everyone staring at me, and Hamilton here too, I lose my train of thought, and all the cutting words I practiced on the way over go bumbling through my head like a box of loose jigsaw pieces.

Jim, my stalker friend, stands beside me, and though slight, he is truly an actor because I watch him puff himself up. "We're here on business. It's come to our understanding that the business arrangement you have with Haley's husband—"

"Ex-husband," Hamilton corrects, and I meet his gaze.

"Haley's ex-husband has come under some recent consideration. Haley, having a prior stake in the business, would like to know what Jay owes you, Craig."

Wow, you remembered all that? I nod to let him know I am thoroughly impressed. See, a guy who is classically trained in Shakespeare is exactly what you want for this kind of work. *They remember everything.*

I may have found the man for Helena.

"He owes me $2.5 million, Haley," Craig answers.

Five minutes ago, I thought I had some power with my twenty-thousand-dollar check. I will never learn. "He'll pay—you back, if you give him the opportunity, Craig. You know that."

"I do know that, but I have projects I want to get behind, and I can't be furnishing cash for every art film he thinks is a contender."

I step forward and look directly at the suddenly mousy Rachel. "Who told him they were contenders, Rachel? Because if you two are working this out together, I do believe that has collusion of the worst kind written all over it, and there will be legal ramifications. Hamilton, what say you?"

"This is a legal matter that doesn't concern you, Haley."

"It does concern me, Hamilton, and if you had any love for the law at all, it would concern you too."

His mouth twitches, but he's silent like good little lawyers always are when there's trouble and they're on the wrong side of it.

I hear the jangling of keys and look behind me to see Jay entering the building. He blinks at the sight in front of him, and I'm about to warn him off when I see a tall blonde behind him. She looks . . . she looks like me, quite frankly.

"Jay," I sputter. "Who's your friend?"

"Haley Cutler, meet Nancy Fabro."

The blonde stretches out her hand, and I note her dark brown eyes. Adult blondes do not have brown eyes, it's a genetic impossibility. Sort of like women with boy hips having breasts the size of cantaloupes. I don't reach out my hand to the fake blonde standing beside my husband. I do, however, look to Rachel to see what the heck is going on with her.

"Yeah. Rachel dropped me for Craig. I thought you would have heard by now," Jay says. "I've got to make some phone calls, baby," he says to his new squeeze. "Sit down, and we'll get lunch at the Ivy when I'm done here. Haley, what brings you around? You sniffing around for more money now that the tabloid story died?"

"You could just go back to work like this? With these two?" I wave my hand in front of Rachel and Craig.

"It's business, Haley. It's just business."

"I was here to do you a favor, Jay."

"What's that, sweetheart?"

"Can I talk with you outside, Jay?" I look to Craig, Rachel, and Hamilton. "Please?"

"Sure, Princess."

The fake blonde pouts when he calls me this, but she, like any good Labrador-in-training sits and waits, pulling out a copy of *Us* magazine from her Louis Vuitton. Which reminds me of another skill I have acquired.

"That bag shouts fake from a mile away. Here's a tip, if you're going to have a Sugar Daddy, you should make him put forth some real effort. Know what I'm saying? And try Sarah at Yoshi's. She'll get that color to look natural and not so brassy."

I follow Jay outside, and he does what he normally does, looks at everything and everyone but me. "What do ya need, Haley?" He snaps his fingers. "Just hurry up, I got things to do."

Once again, I start to bumble, looking for my words. His lack of patience always did fluster me to the point where I forgot what I had to say, or said it so poorly that he would criticize my communication skills. I lean against the wall, sticking out my bad foot, which is now throbbing from being on it for so long.

"You broke up our marriage for Rachel Barlin and now you're not with her any longer?"

"Is that what you wanted to talk to me about?"

I refocus. "No. Jay, do you owe Craig money?"

"It's nothing. We always share money back and forth. Right now, he's just holding the cards. The tides will turn, they always do."

"Not this time, Jay. This time, I think Craig plans to sell you out."

Jay actually looks me in the eye. Dang, he's handsome. I am truly cursed by his presence because I still feel a certain loyalty to him even though he does have the fake me waiting just inside the door for him. "Where did you hear that?" he asks quietly, pulling me away from the door.

"It doesn't matter where I heard it, does it? I'm probably full of crap, like you always say I am, but I want you to be warned. This business is your life, and I don't want you to lose it. Not over *her*." I look down at my bandaged foot. "Why are men so incredibly blind to a beautiful woman? She's heartless, Jay."

He looks at the office doors. "Beautiful women command respect. It's just a fact, really."

"From who?"

"Everyone," he says plainly. "A man sees you walk in with a woman like Rachel Barlin, and you hold the cards, know what I'm saying?"

"Jay, that is a total lie! Do you know what people say about a man who is twenty years older than a beautiful woman? They says she's only with him for his money and that he's basically paid for her."

"Ah, but you see, Haley. He *can* pay for her, and that only proves my point about commanding respect."

"Sell the house if you have to, Jay, but don't lose the business to them."

"Haley, do you really think—" He grabs my hand. "Never you mind your pretty little head about the business. I do appreciate your trying to rescue me though. What a gem you turned out to be. I was right about you. You would stand by me through everything."

"I thought you fired Hamilton Lowe."

"I did. Craig hired him immediately. Seems the Lynchow divorce isn't going to be quite as clean as ours."

"You have an odd definition of that word."

"Haley, are you by any chance dating Hamilton?"

"Your lawyer?"

"Ex-lawyer."

"No! Why on earth would you ask me that?"

"Just always thought he had a thing for you. Always pushing for more for you. I gave him money to buy you one of them new Nissan mini-SUVs and he comes back with a Porsche. I should have fired him then. " Jay laughs. "Just thought he would have made his move by now." He pats me on the shoulder, like an old high school buddy. "Take care of yourself. And Haley?"

"Yeah?"

"Cash that last check, will you?" He walks into the office, and I'm left standing on the street alone, yet again. Until my favorite stalker comes out.

"You ready?"

"Can you take me by the bank?"

"Washington National, right?"

"How?"

"You stopped by after work that day I followed you."

"I have someone for you to meet, Jim."

"For you, Haley. Anything."

My cell phone trills as Jim gets into the car, "Hi, Lindsay."

"Haley, your mom is looking for you. Will you give her your new cell phone number so that I can have mine back?"

"I'm sure she has great advice for daily living, Lindsay. Wouldn't you miss that?"

"No, I wouldn't. Call her. Oh, and did you give my number to some guy you met on the beach?"

"Oh . . . maybe I did. I thought I gave him my new number."

"Well, I hope you got his number because Ron answered, and let's just say, he was not kind when he said he'd met the beautiful blonde running on the beach. My marriage was on the rocks until he explained how she fell, then Ron knew."

"I resent that."

"Whatever. Anyway, I don't think the guy is calling back, so I do hope you got his number."

"I didn't. He was totally my new lab rat. Does Ron have any idea what he's doing to my sense of self-worth?"

"I think he can deal. Call your mother!"

We hang up, and I brace myself for a long-winded mantra on the positive aspects of crafting within one's life. "Go ahead, call her," Jim says from the driver's seat. "The bank can wait."

I exhale deeply and dial. "Hi, Mom, it's Haley. Did you get my Mother's Day gift?"

"Haley," she cries, in full blubbering mode. "Oh I've been trying to call you for days."

"Sorry, I haven't checked the messages at home, I guess. Why didn't you call me at work?"

"Oh, Haley, you're going to be so disappointed. I didn't want you upset at work."

"I am?"

"Gavin's getting married, darling!" She wails this. "He's invited you to the wedding in the fall and I didn't know how to reach you and I knew you'd be devastated. You never got another chance, Haley! It's so unfair. You weren't ready to date the last time you met! Why does God punish me like this?"

Right back atcha, God. "Mom, I have to go. I'll come home for the wedding."

She sniffles some more. "All right, dear. I'll buy a present from the family, I know that would be too difficult for you right now."

"Thanks, Mom. I really appreciate that." I snap the phone shut. "Well, what do you know, Jim. I've been dumped by three different men all in the span of an hour. I'm good. I really like soccer too. It's a pity, really."

"Haley!" Hamilton runs out of the building and though the logical thinking Haley wants to run, the emotional, pitiful Haley stays with her feet planted solidly on the ground.

"Let me get this out," Hamilton says. "Don't stop me or I will not say what I came to say and I need to say it."

I nod, encouraging him to go on.

"Haley, I'm not an emotional man."

"No, you're not."

"But when I'm around you, it's like my body completely betrays me. I have to fight to stay away from you, to act appropriately and lawyerlike, when in fact, you make me feel like an actor. All emotion and no sense."

"Is that a compliment? Or are you saying –"

"Don't!" He holds up a palm. "Don't confuse my words, Haley. I would never say anything, do anything to hurt you. I carried out my job according to the oath I gave as a member of the Bar Association, but I'm done with that now. Jay fired me. Craig hired me. I had no idea what his intentions were at the time, or I never would have signed on. He told me he needed legal documents drawn up because he was going to be a father. Do you think it would have occurred to me that he was having a baby with someone other than his wife?" He whacks his head. "Never. I never get it! I quit the next day, and Jay had a proposition for me, but I can't discuss that."

"That makes two of us. My faith in Jesus isn't perfect, but I know enough to see the heart of man is not pretty."

He pulls away from me and rubs his forehead vigorously, while he paces up and down the sidewalk. "You're the ideal, Haley. I thought that made me shallow and that God had some perfect, virginal woman out there waiting for me. Man, I'm a putz. The first thing I did when I heard from Jay was plot how I might make you notice me. I thought my faith was so deep, but it all went out the window when I heard you were free. I gave you that flyer, and I prayed that I would get over this infatuation." He stops pacing and meets my gaze. "But now, I think it's more than infatuation."

I start to back up.

"You're freaked out. I knew I would freak you out. See? I'm either in lawyer mode or complete emotional idiot mode. There's no middle ground with you. Now it sounds like I'm blaming you."

"Stop. You changed my life, Hamilton. If it weren't for you, I never would have found the Trophy Wives Club and without them pursuing me relentlessly, I never would have known what I needed. A little compassion goes a long way." I brush my hand on his cheek. "I'm grateful for you, Hamilton. You tried to be decent. I wish I had appreciated that more at the time, but my mind was not really in a place to appreciate you."

"I've dated women, Haley. It's not like I obsessed about you being the gold standard, but—"

"I have to get to the bank, Hamilton." I shake my head. "I'm feeling so many different emotions. I feel this incredible elation at realizing I'm a daughter of God, I feel this great sadness that my marriage never was what I thought, and I don't know where you fit into that picture. Not right now. I can't give you any type of response."

He nods, flattens his lips together, and walks away. He turns and in his best Arnold the Governator voice says, "I'll be back."

I sigh. Wouldn't it be great if God just blew an air horn in your ear and told you exactly what to do? It's that whole free will business. Gets in my way every time. The old Haley would fall into his arms and believe every word.

Chapter 19

There are certain fall days in northern California where the fog rolls over the hills and settles in the valley. This leaves the coast in pure, clear sunlight. You can see for miles along the rugged cliffs of the beach, but since it's overcast where everyone lives, no one thinks to come to the beach on such dreary days. That leaves these days for those of us in on the small secret surrounding the mystical rules of the fog.

These are my favorite days here, because I can look out into the open expanse of blue without a soul around me and realize what a speck of sand I am on this earth. That God gives me any mind at all is a miracle. That He created me in His image is more than I can bear when I see the tumbling surf and know He holds its power in His hands.

I raise my hands to the sky—just like that weirdo does in the lobby at work—and I let the sunlight warm my cheeks. The wind goes right through me, and I bring my arms down and clutch my middle. I close my eyes to listen to the pounding surf. I am soon taken away into my own place of peace and gratitude. I fall to the sand and kick my shoes off. *This is life.* When Jesus said He came to give us life more abundantly, I'm certain He meant for moments like this.

"Haley?"

I open my eyes and shield them from the sun. *It can't be.* I clasp my eyes shut again, but the voice calls out again. "God, is that you? I know I cannot be seeing what I'm seeing."

"Haley, cut it out!"

I open my eyes to see Hamilton Lowe, just as I did the first time. Jumping up, clutching my flip-flops in my hands, I start to jog and sing a hymn to drown out his deep voice behind the waves. I turn to see him still running after me and gaining in ground.

"Get off my beach!" I yell over my shoulder. "Haven't you done enough?"

Hamilton is keeping an easy stride behind me. "Haley!" he calls again.

"Go away! I heard what you did in court. Did you think I wouldn't hear?" I sprint to gain some ground on him, warding off the pain I still feel in my ankle. It never did heal properly. That's what I get for listening to a soccer coach loose on the shores of Los Angeles.

He tries to call out over the waves, but they block his voice, and only his mouth moves, as in a bad Samurai film. I find a certain amount of humor in the situation and start to giggle as I run. If only it were that easy to shut him up all the time. He smiles back at me, and I can tell he thinks I'm being coquettish, which changes my mood immediately.

"What?" I turn and shout at him. "What are you doing here? I already have a stalker in my life!"

"I saw you get baptized a few weeks ago at church."

"And you flew here to tell me that?"

"I wanted to explain what happened with Jay. I couldn't before today, and Lindsay explained you were up here for a wedding. I thought it might be the perfect opportunity to wipe our slate clean."

"That's weird, Hamilton."

"It is weird, Haley. That's what you do to me. You make me not act rationally, you make me a complete victim to my emotions. Do you know how emasculating that is?"

"We barely know each other."

"You know me. Look into my eyes and tell me you don't know me."

I'm lost in his gaze when I do. In Hamilton's eyes I see everything I want for a future and yet, I can't. This is exactly what I felt with Jay. "This is infatuation. Lust, if you will. This isn't real."

"How can I prove otherwise?"

"You can't. There's too much water under our bridges."

"God has taken me through the wringer to show me my sin, how I judged you."

"Your sin?" I laugh. "I didn't think you had any sin. Pure as the driven snow, no dirt under your fingernails."

"What you did for Jay that day at the office."

I laugh. "Yeah, telling him not to get hurt, when he already had someone new lined up. I really showed him, didn't I?"

"You were going to give him the money back." He takes off his sweatshirt and puts it around me. "You thought he needed it. Don't tell me I barely know you, Haley. With the exception of your short-lived attempt to exact revenge, I know you always tried to be a good person. Even before you knew Jesus."

Hamilton has witnessed every possible humiliation in my life. He's watched me figuratively bash my head into the wall countless times. "I want to forget all this. You only remind me of every mistake I ever made in my life." Tears begin to fall from my eyes, and the cold wind leaves a sting on my cheeks. "I should have known they were talking more money than I will ever have in my lifetime. I really am as dumb as all that. You think you can rescue me from that, but it's not true. It's a lie. I am loyal to a fault."

"Haley, Jay was staging a takeover of his own. He has the business outright. He borrowed money from Craig only to weaken Craig's stock with lenders. It was a planned move."

"You helped him do that?"

"Only if he paid you the rest of what he owed you up front."

"That's why he warned me to cash the check."

"Haley." Hamilton puts his hands on my cheeks and my body betrays me.

"You weren't a lab rat."

"Pardon me?" He runs his fingers along my neck, and I close my eyes, relishing his touch.

What am I doing? I will never learn!

"How did you find me?"

"Your mother told me I could find you here mourning the great love of your life."

I laugh. "Yes, Gavin."

"In her defense, she did think twice before telling me how devastated you were."

"I'm crushed!" I put the back of hand to my forehead. "She's really upset because Mrs. Atkinson's pot roast won out over hers. That was the real loss." I take off Hamilton's sweatshirt and hand it back to him. "I'm sorry you felt guilty and wasted a trip, Hamilton. I'm quite content with my life, and I hold no more ill feelings toward you or Jay or anyone. Well, maybe I'm a little bitter that a fake blonde can so easily take my place, but whatever. That's childish."

"No fake blonde could ever take your place, Haley. I know what you've been through, but I'm here to ask if there's a chance for you to take another chance on men. I want to try to be that man to you."

I shake my head. "No, Hamilton. I'm single. Divorced, remember? You will never be the man who can let go of my past."

"You're wrong, Haley. Please try with me. I will do whatever is in my power not to see you hurt ever again. That day in my office with the vasectomy papers about broke my heart for you."

I shake my head. "No, I'll not be rescued by a man. God has deemed me worthy. I'm happy, Hamilton. Can't that be enough for you?"

When I was a small girl, I used to hide in a cliff cave until my dad would come looking for me after a long picnic at the beach. The cave goes on forever, and I see the mouth of it swallowing the waves of the tide just around the bend. It's the kind of cave you could get lost in if you didn't know your way, but I knew it well; explored its every arm, and right now, it offers me solace. I run toward it, ignoring my foot.

"Haley!" Hamilton calls again, as I stand at the mouth of the cave. I jump over the burgeoning waves and enter the cave.

I whirl around to face Hamilton. I am weak around Hamilton. I don't ever want to feel this way again, I never want to be victim to someone else's emotion. It's not a healthy place for me. "Don't follow me. In case you're not familiar with the action of someone physically running from you, this should indicate that I am trying to flee from your presence. It should also imply that I do not wish to spend time with you, that I am avoiding you, and that you should turn around, get in your car, and leave me to my beach. I tell you these things so you might have some good fortune with the ladies instead of being standard woman-repellent at church."

"I didn't come all this way to fight with you. I know you feel what we have, Haley. I know you want to fight it as much as I did, but what if you just gave it a shot? I'm not asking for a lifetime commitment now, Haley. I just want to be the one you give a chance to because I won't hurt you again."

I don't allow myself to soften in the least. "Unbelievable. Now you're going to tell me how I should act when you have interrupted my very private meditation on my childhood beach? If you didn't come to fight with me, then I can tell you that you've wasted your time because all I have to say to you involves all-out warfare. You allowed Jay to lose his business when you knew who Rachel was from the start."

"Jay didn't lose his business. Haley, please listen to me!"

But the waves between us get bigger, and I cannot hear him any longer. He's pointing to the waves, and as the wave pulls out to sea, he yells again. "Tides coming in, it's not safe!"

"The tide takes hours, and it's not your concern." When I used to come here as a girl, I pretended I was a pirate. This is where I hid my booty. The waves lap at the bottom of my hands as I watch Hamilton with his arms crossed. I know the cave is the only sanctuary, where I can be alone with God and away from men and pleasing them.

"Will you hear me out? I came all this way to apologize and explain," Hamilton says as he fights the waves to come into the cave with me.

"You shouldn't have wasted your frequent flyer miles."

"I paid for the ticket right before the flight took off. Coach. Without any luggage. I got a full-body massage from a man who looked like a bouncer for the sleaziest bar on the Strip, and I beeped. Do you have any idea how infuriating it is to have to empty every last thing from your pockets in front of angry, waiting travelers?"

"Woe, the sacrifice! You say you came to apologize? Or tell me how I've made your life so difficult?"

He grasps me by the arm. I feel his gaze to my core. For all this man has done to me, there is a sweetness, an innocence in his soul that I can't help but see in his eyes. Oh, but who am I to think such things? I married Jay Cutler and thought it would be for life. But I know those thoughts aren't who I am now. I am CMG's best assistant and future agent. I am a card-carrying member of the best friends a girl could ever have in the Trophy Wives Club, and, most importantly, I am redeemed. But I'm not necessarily cleared for romantic takeoff either.

"You're not going to make this easy for me, are you?" he asks.

Just like his eyes aren't making it easy for me. I want to abandon everything I know and test his soul. He brings his hand to my shoulder, and I feel my body go limp at his gentle touch. "Don't do this, Hamilton. You'll regret it if you kiss me."

"You told me that I was blind to what I was doing. That I didn't take any responsibility for my actions."

"And you've had some kind of mountaintop experience that brings you all the way up here?" I raise my brows.

"I saw in you what I did to people. Haley, I'm a lawyer, I believe in the pre-nup, just like I believe in Wills and Living Trusts because when money is involved, people get ugly. But it became something more for me. It became about winning at any cost. My client would be known as an astute businessman because he hired Hamilton Lowe as his attorney. I took so much pride in that. Dangerous pride."

"You got your wish. People do indeed fear the name Hamilton Lowe."

I break away from him and tear into the familiar cave of my

childhood. It's dark, damp, and cold. Looking toward the back of the cave, I see only darkness, but the sun illuminates my path from behind.

Forgive him. I could forgive him, I really could if I thought he got it. But he doesn't get it at all. He just keeps doing what he does, terrorizing women and taking away any security they had. He is just like Jay. He finds excuses in all of his behavior because he's only doing what needs to be done. *Heartless.*

Forgive as I forgave you. I keep hearing that verse in my head, but how can I forgive where there is still so much raw pain? How can I forgive when it continues to happen? When women don't have a decent car to drive their children to school, but some bimbo drives a Porsche around with the children's father?

Why can't men be like Boaz in the Bible? Ruth went to him humbled and poverty-stricken, and he found mercy for her. She slept at the foot of his bed, offering herself to him for the price of his care. But he was so much more, wasn't he? He gave her his world. He accepted her. He didn't try to steal the wheat she'd gathered from the threshing floor dregs and say it really belonged to him. He gave her the best he had. He shared his life with her.

It's gotten darker as I've walked, and I take my Minnie Mouse penlight from my key chain and light my way with its measly beam. The cave is as it always was, and I run my hand along its low cold ceiling, reliving a time when I controlled the high seas of the Pacific.

"Aye, matey, the booty you will never find. It is hidden well." I smile to myself. I once had a faith like a child's too. I always thought it was too late to go back to that little girl, fresh as a daisy. But I was wrong.

Even my boss, who Lily herself called human steel, has more mercy than Hamilton. This man, who calls himself a Christian and posts Bible verses on his wall. He actually took the time to be that much of a hypocrite. He took the nails and drove them into the wall with his own hands.

My knees feel the stinging cold of salt water and I look down. The waves have followed me in, and the cave feels much smaller than when I was a girl. Or perhaps I'm just bigger. I have to turn around. On this one thing, Hamilton had to be right. I look behind me, and the hole to the outside is darkening as the ceiling gets lower and the waves come in fast and furious. The tide has swelled and my entrance to the outside of the cave is under four feet or so of harsh, northern California surf. I don't see Hamilton's silhouette in the opening, and I breathe both a sigh of relief and terror at the idea of swimming through the waters against the rocks. The water is frigid. I shiver. Hamilton did the smart thing and got out.

My dad taught me to swim into the tide. Never try and go around it, let the waters lead you in, but of course, the waters will only lead me to the back of the cave. I turn around again and see that the water is too high, and too rough to swim in. There's only one thing to do. Get to the back of the cave and find the crack in the mountain that shed a small sliver of light toward the end of the cavern. Years ago, there was a shelf where I used to lie on and look up at the sky. Of course, that was always when tide was out. My father would never let me come in with any kind of surf. If the cave hasn't changed it, it will be there until the tide goes out. If the water doesn't fill the cave completely now, all these years later.

I use my penlight to light the back of the cave, but it's still not visible. My light gets sucked away by the darkness, and I can only see around my knees. A piece of seaweed tangles around my ankles, and I scream at the slimy chain. I start to run toward the back, but the weight of the water slows me, and more seaweed clutches at my ankles. I pull my feet out of the sand with each step, and it's like wet cement at my feet. I am prayerful that I don't get a mouthful of sandy rock in my next step. *God, if You've ever kept me from a wall, keep me from one now! Let there be enough space to swallow all this water, without swallowing me too.* The light behind me is completely gone, but I'm not scared. I have complete peace. Only I'm lonely. I'm reminded how I've always had to handle crises by myself. First when I learned my mother wasn't able to rescue me, then when I learned Jay wouldn't.

I stand in complete darkness, but I have to keep moving. I can't let the waves take over. Will I be washed out to sea in some romantic gesture to show I am cleansed? I think about the last interaction I had with Hamilton and feel the need to confess.

God, You know I've admitted my sin, but I have to add in what I just did to Hamilton. I don't want that one counted against me. Tell him, too, will You?

Since I'm alone in the cave, I think the sound of my own voice might actually calm me down. "I've given my life to You. This is what You choose to do with it? Just wash me out to sea?" I always thought I'd go in some dramatic accident, like falling down an elevator shaft or getting pushed off the Golden Gate Bridge by some foreigner, who didn't see me, while taking a picture. "Do you need any more ideas? Because this one really stinks, if you don't mind my saying so. The worst part is Hamilton will know my own stupidity killed me. You're going to let him have the last laugh, aren't You? Just because I wouldn't forgive."

"I would never do that."

I jump at the sound of Hamilton's voice. "Hamilton?"

"Yes." His hand clutches for mine, and I take it readily.

"Hamilton," My throat closes at the emotion, as I've never been so happy to feel anyone in my life, even Hamilton Lowe. I shine my penlight behind me, and Hamilton is right there. "We're trapped," I yell over the surf.

"We are," he yells back.

"Why did you come in here? You predicted what would happen."

The wave recedes, and an eerie calm descends. "Because I told you I need to apologize, and that this was an incredibly stupid idea, and you didn't listen to that either. I thought I might be able to knock some sense into you in the cold dark cave. Give me the chance, Haley. I'll make the best choices with you. Not for you."

"You have really good teeth."

"Turn that thing off, we'll need the batteries!"

It's not like I'm cerebral at the moment, so I keep the light on his teeth. I have always loved his mouth. I've always hated what it said, but I loved the way it looked. I'll admit, since seeing him at church, I have thought more than once what it would be like to kiss a man like Hamilton. Would he show any emotion? Or would it be rudimentary and compulsive?

"I don't want your death on my hands," I scream over the next wave. After each rush, there is a relative calm that follows. The water isn't that high, and we both know there's no real sense of danger, but we cling to each other like the next wave might take us down. "Then I have to forgive you all over again!" I can't see his face. I can't see my own hand. All that I can see is the wall on the side of us closing in and getting narrower and that only because I feel it. I don't see a thing, but the sounds are different and the water is rising more quickly as the walls narrow.

"We have to keep walking. Go back."

"There used to be an air crack back here. It's not big enough to climb out of, but I thought if I could get there, I could wait out the tide. Maybe have a nice quiet time where no one could interrupt me."

"When's the last time you saw this air crack?"

"When I was twelve, but it was here throughout my girlhood. Maybe God kept it for me, for this moment. It was my own private knowledge. I even found it on the hill once."

"Maybe He did. Caves don't usually change, Haley."

"It could have!" I scream over a new wave.

"It may have, but it's usually counted in geological ages, not a young woman's life."

"You didn't have to follow me. If you thought it was dangerous, you should have stayed outside and protected yourself." The latter implies that was what he'd always done.

"I wasn't leaving you here."

"I don't need anyone to rescue me."

"I get it, Haley. I always did know you'd make it. The fact that you made it without tabloid money is to your credit." We're both out of breath, as we try to race the waves toward the back of the cave. I keep praying for that sliver of light to come into view, but instead more darkness envelops us, and my penlight's batteries are waning into an amber stubble of light.

"Hamilton, the batteries are dying. How will we know which direction to head?"

"We'll just have to go by Braille and stay with our backs to the waves when they come in."

Before I know what's happening, I'm swung into Hamilton's arms. He smells divine even mixed with the pungent odor of the damp cave air.

"Put me down!" I squeal, but admittedly I cling tightly around his neck.

"God told me to lift you up, and this time I'm listening."

"Hamilton . . ."

"What?"

"We're talking to each other."

"Really more of a screaming thing going on."

"No, the waves are quieter. Hamilton, I think we did it!"

"Did what?

"The cave is shaped like a T. Go to the left."

"Haley, no, we have to keep heading back."

"It can't reach the T all the way, Hamilton. Go left."

"Haley, it goes against my intuitive nature to go left into what might be a wall."

"If you want my forgiveness, you'll listen to me this time."

"That's blackmail."

"Yeah, how does it feel to be on the receiving end of it?"

There's a thunderous roll, and our voices are drowned out again.

"Run!" He puts me down and grabs my hand.

I cling to Hamilton's hand with what strength I have left in my frigid fingers. I point the penlight, but it fizzles again. The last of the battery gives out, and it wanes into complete darkness, but as the water falls to my knees, Hamilton picks me up again. It's getting harder to breathe with the constant pounding pressure of the cold waves. Hamilton must not be able to feel anything in his legs by now.

"We've got to climb, Haley. Find a ledge or something."

"No, we have to get to the sunlight." I jump from his arms and yank him to the left. In a few steps, there is less water. "I think it's there." I point, but, of course, he can't see me. "If you had one wish for your life, Hamilton, what would you have done?"

"I wouldn't have followed you into this cave." He laughs. "I'm kidding. One wish . . ." He breathes hard as he keeps the pace. "One wish. I would have abandoned myself to love someone at least once. I would have risked more, thought less. I wouldn't have waited for the perfect woman to come along and rescue me from my fears."

"Truly?"

"Truly."

"I thought you would have wanted to handle Tom Cruise's divorce settlement or something."

"What about you? What would you have done differently?"

"I would have recognized that my husband never loved me. I would have admitted to myself that I had already failed as a wife. Fear paralyzes you, doesn't it, Hamilton?"

"We've been walking forever. Where's the end?"

"We should have hit it by now. I don't know where we are. I've never walked this far inside the cave. I must have taken a wrong turn." My voice trembles with cold.

"Then this might be my only chance." He lifts me up again, and this time his arms feel different. They are not merely carrying me, they are firm and tight. "I don't want to have any regrets. You owe me that much."

He stops walking, and I can touch the water with my arm dangling. It must be up to his waist by now, though the noise has quieted. The motion of an incoming swell pushes us forward, and he wobbles under the wake.

"Haley Adams, if I had it to do over again, I would have grabbed you in the office nine years ago and told you what that dirty old man was trying to do to your life. I would have told him to take his money and stuff it where the sun don't shine, and I would have tried to rescue you then. When I should have. When you might have rescued me from my ignorance and misunderstanding of women."

"I don't need rescuing. I told you. I made my own stupid choices."

"I needed rescuing, Haley. *I needed it*."

He continues to walk, but I pull myself closer to his chest and snuggle into his luscious-smelling neck. I won't have time to regret this. If I'm going to take my last breaths of oxygen, this is as good a way as any to use them. I feel the warmth of his face close to mine, and I put my hands on his jaw, turning his face toward mine, and our lips find each other in the darkness.

Silence.

There is no noise. No pounding, thunderous surf or rising water. All my fear momentarily evaporates. I kiss him with all the emotion I didn't know was still within me. I thought that part of me was dead already.

"All those years, I thought I was doing everything right. But there is no right when you abandon everyone's feelings, when you deny that what you can do has the power to hurt them. I never cared for anyone. Not really. I told myself I did, and when I saw you come in that day to rescue Jay, even though he didn't deserve a bit of it, I finally knew what you meant."

"I had too many feelings. I never looked at reason, and I took Jay's word that he loved me, though I can't think of an instance where he showed it. Not for my sake."

"You can't let him take that from you, Haley. You always thought of other people, there's no shame in that."

Hamilton pauses. "I never extended anyone grace, I just became locked away in this emotionally retarded state, like all the men I worked for. Now I know, there's nothing more than grace. It's all about grace—because I clearly didn't do anything right. You gave me a real faith, Haley. I wanted to live right by God, but the thing is, you can't do that on your own power."

"I couldn't do it alone either. It was when Bette, Lindsay, Penny, Lily, and Helena came into my life that I realized relationships are a two-way street, and I could count on people."

Hamilton takes three steps forward, and I see it.

"It's the sun!"

"I think you're right."

But in my mind, I'm thinking maybe the coldness has made us numb, maybe we're going toward the light that is our maker. But as he sloshes through the water, it has receded to his knees and the hole really is there. And with it comes a second chance. For both of us.

Acknowledgments

Thanks to Avon Books and Cynthia DiTiberio for their hard work on this manuscript and to Jeana Ledbetter, my agent, who continues to deal with me.

Dear Reader,

My passion for this book doesn't come from something I've experienced myself. It comes from watching terrible destruction happen to already broken individuals. Sometimes as Christians, we often think it's our duty to mete out punishment, and because we are flawed, we can make the situation worse. Divorce is an outward symptom of inner brokenness. What I hoped to show in Haley is not a belief that divorce is the only viable option, but that pat answers aren't enough for those who suffer from its wrath.

Sincerely,

Kristin Billerbeck

People may think all their ways are pure,
but motives are weighed by the Lord.

—PROVERBS 16:2

Discussion Questions

1. Haley is blindsided by the demise of her marriage. Do you think there's more she could have done to be aware of her situation? What were her false expectations of Jay?

2. When Haley meets Hamilton Lowe again, there's a chemistry between them that defies logic. Have you ever felt that way? Did you couple it with reason before diving into a relationship?

3. One of Haley's biggest troubles is that she doesn't fit in with her husband's crowd. Have you ever felt left out in a group where contact couldn't be avoided? How did you handle it?

4. Is there a particular clothing style or food that you like, but don't wear or eat because other people might speak poorly of you? Why?

5. Haley resorts to the comfortable and shuts down when she has no destination in life. Have you ever felt adrift in your lifetime? How did you change it?

6. Jay's ultimate betrayal of Haley are the lies within their marriage. Have you ever known toxic people in your lifetime? Did you ever see them do something that made another feel responsible for their sin?

7. Haley is very unsure of the church after a rocky upbringing with a flaky mother. Do you have friends who might benefit from a little extra warmth in your friendship? How might you go about making this happen?

8. The Trophy Wives Club's members pursue Haley with abandon. Have you ever fought to be someone's friend when they gave you every indication they were fine on their own? Was it a good experience?

9. Haley's church group is a collection of oddballs connected by one terrible incident in their histories. Do you have friends who know your dirty little secrets and help you hold your head high? What have they meant to you?

10. Haley's money woes turn out to not be an issue, and she discovers she's not as covetous as she might have thought. Is there something in your life as an idol that you've had to abandon? If so, how did it turn out?

Kristin Billerbeck

Photo courtesy of Jodie Westfall

KRISTIN BILLERBECK, one of the first Christian chick-lit authors, has been featured in *The New York Times*, *USA Today*, *The Atlanta Journal Constitution*, and *World Magazine* for her work. She also appeared on *The Today* Show for her award-winning book, *What a Girl Wants*. Kristin has been married for fifteen years and has four children. She makes her home in California.